Old Dog

Old Dog

A Traveler's Tale

MARK SEELY

RESOURCE *Publications* · Eugene, Oregon

OLD DOG
A Traveler's Tale

Resource Publications
An Imprint of Wipf and Stock Publishers
199 W. 8th Ave., Suite 3
Eugene, OR 97401

www.wipfandstock.com

PAPERBACK ISBN: 978-1-6667-3692-2
HARDCOVER ISBN: 978-1-6667-9580-6
EBOOK ISBN: 978-1-6667-9581-3

JANUARY 20, 2022 12:53 PM

For Riley

Dogs and philosophers do the greatest good but get the fewest rewards.

—DIOGENES

Contents

Prolog

TENSION. PULLED IN OPPOSING DIRECTIONS. A rubber band stretched between dresser drawer handles. A bowstring at maximum draw.

But not like that.

Power lines high above a treeless strip of forest and adorned with aircraft warning balls like Christmas decorations strung along the valley ridge.

But not like that either.

More like the rainbow skin of a wand-blown soap bubble. Or the tiny impossible surface dents under a water bug's feet as it skates along the rippled edge of a reflected cloud. Or the ripples themselves as they stack upon each other in their not-quite diamond tessellations. A tension that enables and contains. A tension that buoys and braces and sustains—but only for the moment.

The tension just before the bubble pops.

Writing is often like that. But now, especially now, in the churning heat and mounting chaos of late-stage civilization, he can feel the tension approach the bursting point—the bubble's skin is becoming precariously thin.

Theme isn't the issue. He has written about this topic before, and in several different ways. He has approached it through scholarly essay and creative memoir, and even through poetry. But each of these genres has its own fatal limitations. Critical essay, with its systematic presentation and academic appeal to logic, inevitably results in a technologizing of the situation, makes it into just another problem to be solved. Poetry tugs at the brain's emotion centers and has the potential to strike a more authentically human chord, perhaps, but it runs the risk of becoming little more than an aesthetic exercise. On the surface, memoir seems to offer good compromise, but all compromise sacrifices something essential: memoir is too vicarious, too detached, too far removed from the urgency of the present moment—too safe.

Theme isn't the issue, he thought, it's a problem of perspective. A lack of perspective. A too-limited perspective. A distorted perspective. It's a problem of perspective and there is no internal corrective. It's a problem of perspective and there is no external vantage point.

And just then, at exactly that perspective-depleted moment, with the bubble's ephemeral shell tightening to an ethereal density, he glanced down at the dog curled up at his feet.

Symbolic Worlds

1

H E appeared to be just an ordinary dog. Nothing unusual, a confused amalgam of Australian cattle dog and Brittany spaniel, medium sized, a bit on the muscular side, a dull, dusty brindle coat that blended into the background regardless of what happened to be in the background.

Old Dog was, however, not an ordinary dog. He was anything but ordinary. Among domestic dogs, he was a savant and a visionary. Among wild and feral dogs, he was the stuff of legend. If he were human, he would be called a genius and perhaps even a prophet, people the world over would seek his wisdom and solicit his astute advice, and his words would be quoted to the point of cliché.

But he was not human. He was, after all, a dog. And he was no longer living among dogs, domestic or otherwise. He was instead living in a modest house in the suburbs of an even more modest city. At this moment he was in a small room in that house, lying a couple tail-spans from the feet of his caretaker, a man in his early sixties, a writer who spent most days attempting to deserve that title. And with his body tightly curled into a warm patch of late morning sunlight that was slowly stealing its way across the floor, Old Dog was enwrapped in contemplative reverie, reflecting on his past adventures and thinking sagely dog-thoughts that he would never be able to share with his human companion.

2

J UST over a year ago, Old Dog was incarcerated at the local pound, confined inside a narrow chain-link pen with a cold and damp cement floor. The sign on the outside of the building said Valley Animal Shelter, but because the pound still used a low-tech form of carbon monoxide euthanasia, and because the vast majority of animals that came through its doors left as corpses, the word *shelter* was a cruel misnomer.

To inspire a sense of urgency in visitors thinking of adopting a pet, the pound used a primitive system of colored dot stickers to indicate how close each animal was to their scheduled execution day. Newly arrived dogs got a blue sticker on the right margin of the information card affixed to the front of their confinement cell. A couple days later, a yellow sticker was added. One or two days after that, a red sticker. The red sticker was the last one before the animal was taken to the small, concrete-walled room in the back of the building, the room with an industrial fan in the ceiling and a door that sealed tightly and a pipe that ran through the back wall to the outside. One afternoon each week, all of the animals with red stickers were taken into the room—the larger dogs were anesthetized first—and sealed behind the door. Then a thick hose was fitted between the pipe sticking through the wall outside and the tailpipe of an old flatbed pickup parked next to the building. It took only a few minutes for the exhaust to reach lethal density inside. With the exception of holidays, this happened like clockwork every Thursday.

On Tuesday, the day that Old Dog earned his red dot, the writer stopped into the pound on a whim. Well, maybe not entirely whim—his daughter had been pestering him to get a dog ever since she read that dog owners tended to be happier and healthier and to live longer. Something about Old Dog's calm demeanor and intelligent gaze tugged at a primal part of the writer's psyche and wouldn't let go. Old Dog felt the connection too, and, for the first time since his recent capture, a sensation something like hopefulness began to germinate. "If I had room in my life for a dog . . . ," the writer started to say. Then he promptly left, taking Old Dog's unripe hope with him.

Old Dog understood his situation in ways that none of the other animals in the cages around him could. He was, as we have already established, not an ordinary dog. Over the years he had become proficient at reading human-built environments. That was the key to understanding humans. No need to map their subtle psychological landscape or classify the vagaries of their continually shifting temperaments. Humans are not driven from the inside-out, and certainly not in the freewill sense in which they liked to think about themselves. Their behavior is tightly and perpetually molded to the external structures they inhabit, the physical and social structures they have created specifically for themselves. Humans are entirely under the control of their own technologies of containment, and if you want to understand human behavior, all you have to do is learn to see what it is that these technologies are designed to encourage, prevent, restrict, redirect, and contain. Human behavior is a mechanical inevitability, not even rising to the level of an afterthought. If you want to understand humans, simply learn to construe the purposes behind their artificial worlds.

He knew that it wasn't always this way with humans. He knew that humans hadn't always been prisoners of their own technology. There was a time in the not-too distant past when they were not so different from dogs. There was a time in the not-too distant past when human behavior was a seamless response to the living world around them, when daily life was a continuously-emerging expression of their wild human nature. For all but a tiny handful of people, however, that time is forever sealed behind the unyielding door of history. The wild human being that marveled at the potency of the world and participated in its abundance, the wild human being that greeted each sunrise with an irrepressible sense of gratitude and belonging was long ago domesticated into numbness, with any errant expression of residual wildness quickly and effectively suffocated into submission, with each new dawn shining down into an ever-deepening void, a more all-embracing state of estrangement. Much of the living world itself has been forcefully swept aside, its potency unrecognized, its abundance concealed inside the toxic fog discharged from the rusted underbelly of an ever-expanding technological leviathan.

Old Dog had been able to read his situation right down to the colored dots. Although as a dog he was unable to distinguish the color red from a brown-tinged dark gray, he knew what the third sticker on the card outside his cage meant, and he resigned himself to the inevitability of his fate. He always expected he would die this way, the way that uncountable millions die each day at the hands of humans—as a domestic animal, a human-fashioned death was practically a foregone conclusion. He expected the experience would be painful, but that the pain would be brief (fortunately, dogs have no need for belief in an afterlife). He expected that his death would be far less brutal and bloody than that of those pitiable creatures in cattle and hog and chicken factories, where death, as brutal and bloody as it is, comes as merciful relief after a short life of unspeakable suffering.

What he didn't expect was that the writer would return Thursday morning, quite literally at the eleventh hour, and offer him a new home.

3

OLD Dog was not the result of some Dr. Moreau-style mutation or a *Flowers-for-Algernon* scientific experiment. His extraordinary mind was not a product of supernatural intervention or a trans-dimensional alien brain swap. It was a simple statistical anomaly, a random, one-in-ten-billion, extreme-tail-end-of-the-distribution chance occurrence. Despite being an extraordinary dog, he came into the world in a very ordinary-dog way.

He was born into a litter of five, and for what seemed like an eternity everything was warmth and breath and fur and movement and raw, uncontained excitement. There was barely a moment when he was not in physical contact with his mother and at least one of his siblings. There were people there too, with hands that would gather and transport his body through the air, and voices that somehow chirped and chortled and hummed all at the same time.

Then without warning his mother was gone. Next, his brothers and sisters began to disappear one by one until it was only him. The hands were absent as well. And the voices were distant and infrequent. Stillness washed in, with long stretches of hollow silence bathed in cold pinpricks of fear. He spent hours that felt like days and days that felt like years hungry and thirsty and alone in a dry cardboard box in a dark and drafty room that reeked of gasoline and hot plastic. For the young Old Dog, the pain of solitude far outweighed the pangs of hunger. Dogs, like humans, are social animals who feel incomplete in the absence of others. This is particularly true for the very young. Even coyotes, jackals, and dingoes, canids who might spend a large proportion of their time hunting and scavenging on their own as adults, are especially gregarious as pups. As magistrates and prison wardens and interrogation specialists and sadistic spouses have known for ages, isolation is an effective form of torture. As the days that felt like years threatened to collect themselves into centuries, Old Dog collapsed into a slouched half-sitting heap in the corner of the box while the icy pain of loneliness penetrated deep into his bones.

Then, suddenly, people again. Tiny people with sing-song voices that broke into high-pitched squeals unexpectedly, accompanied by sticky-sweet breath and moist hands that were simultaneously playful and soothing. It felt good to be touched. The box was gone, and in its place was a warm floor that connected brightly painted rooms, all of it smelling like the first dusty drops of rain after a long dry spell. Fortune had granted him a home in a house with a fenced back yard and a family fully stocked with happy young children.

The day he learned his name, the day he learned that a particular sing-song pattern of voice referred to him—that a single human utterance draped a symbolic net over the whole of his furry body—was a momentous day for Old Dog. It was, in a real sense, the true opening of his mental life. It was the beginning of what became a life-defining journey of awareness and understanding that would permanently remove him from the world-experience of ordinary dogs. Technically, he didn't learn his own name first. It was the name of the youngest child, Jenny.

There were three children. At eight, Paul was the oldest. Then Kathy, who was five. And little Jenny, who was not yet three. It was Jenny whose voice broke into unexpected squeals. It was Jenny whose moist hands were constantly probing and clumsily pulling Old Dog into her lap. The other two kids would come and go, but Jenny was always there. First thing in the morning, and all throughout the day, her sticky-sweet breath and constantly wriggling body were never too far away. One morning Jenny's mom called out to her from the kitchen. Jenny responded—and with a flash Old Dog made the connection between call and response. That momentary insight was followed by a sudden cascade of comprehension. He had a name too, he realized, and then instantly knew what it was.

Most domestic dogs—and trained mammals of all stripes—have a similar moment of epiphany when they learn that a particular combination of speech sounds applies specifically to them. Most then go on to associate a number of other human vocalizations with actions and objects and places. But Old Dog didn't stop there. His understanding went far deeper than mere association. He didn't stop with his own name and a few other words that were repeatedly directed his way, words that were almost always also commands. He learned to understand human language itself. Not only did he learn to comprehend most of what the people around him were saying, but he came to understand what human language actually was: not just a useful form of communication, but a system of knowledge, a way of organizing the world and framing experience, a way of infusing the world with meaning, a way of creating and navigating worlds that didn't in fact exist.

Language creates symbolic worlds, worlds where things aren't just things, worlds where non-things are given power over people, worlds where things of actual substance may or may not be recognized for what they really are, worlds that are alien and uninhabitable places from an ordinary dog's perspective. Dog's—most dogs, that is—are seldom able to penetrate beyond the symbolic surface. Dogs live in a world of signs and signals, a world of indications, a world of smells and sounds and sights and movement. There is nothing arbitrary about a sign; the relation it shares with the thing that it signifies is direct: a footprint and the foot that created it share an intimate and insoluble bond across time. The aggressive posture of another dog's body is predictive precisely because it is a nonarbitrary external expression of an actual internal state. Not all signs are equally reliable, of course. Some signs are vague indications while others are direct evidence. Still others can be purposely deceptive. Humans long ago evolved the ability to use signs as tools for social manipulation, for example. Facial expressions are perhaps the most obvious case of this. But even in the case of deceptive facial expressions, the signal is nonarbitrary, and linked directly to the manipulative intentions of the signaler and the predictable interpretations of the receiver.

Symbols, in stark contrast to signs, are entirely arbitrary, and can have no bearing on reality at all except by transmutation through a mythical parallel universe, an ersatz universe, an imaginary universe. Symbols can operate only inside a symbolic world, and language frequently leaves humans trapped on the symbolic inside where myth becomes reality and reality languishes unattended in the shadows. Symbols ultimately become barriers to the abundance of the material world. Humans swim in an insulated make-believe linguistic pond, and come to see the whole cosmos as saturated with its rarified waters. And then a strange alchemy occurs in which words, arbitrary symbols, become signs. The arbitrary becomes the determined. And, especially among the civilized, the specific words that

9

are used are treated as if they held more signifying power than *how* they are being expressed. Written language pushes this to the extreme, where the *how* becomes completely invisible, and even the addition of symbols designed to convey the emotional context, special punctuation, emojis, and the like, are unable to compensate for the massive amount of information that is lost in the process. The inside-out topsy-turvy way that civilization reframes reality has made the distinction between symbols and signs sloppy and difficult to untangle. As a result, the symbolic becomes the default, the arbitrary becomes primary. The problem with this should be obvious.

Unfortunately, when it comes to the symbol-enchanted civilized human mind, nothing is obvious.

Most dogs learn to read the relevant signs associated with various acts of human speech that are directed specifically at them. They learn to hear and recognize the acoustic pattern behind their spoken name, but only in terms of what it signals, only as a sign. And even then, most dogs pay far less attention to the words themselves than to how they are being expressed; they pay far less attention to *what* is being said than to *how* the person is saying it. Saying "good dog" in a stern and angry voice causes the dog to cower and tuck its tail, whereas the most heinous threat expressed with a smile and in a friendly voice triggers an excited tail wag, something every child who has spent time with dogs learns and delights in.

But Old Dog was different. He learned to hear *what* was being said and to separate it from the *how*. He quickly made connections between words and everything nameable around him. He started to listen to people with intent. He made a careful study of what they said and could soon understand what they were talking about. Well, most of what they were talking about. There were some words and expressions that eluded Old Dog's grasp. Most words and expressions could be associated, at least remotely, with a conversational consequence or some aspect of the concrete situation; they were either meant as ways of pointing out experienced features of the world, or relationships among those features, or they were references to some kind of activity—all framed in terms of a symbolic context, of course. But there were other words that were different, words that appeared to refer to things that were entirely unreal, things that could never possibly exist, things that were not open to experience and that had no physical substance that could be associated with them at all, words and expressions with meanings that were directed at features of a symbolic world that had no connection to reality whatsoever. Many of these remained a mystery to him for some time.

Long before that fateful day when the writer rescued him from the pound, however, Old Dog had gained mastery over these words as well; and he eventually came to possess a highly refined understanding of the make-believe symbolic worlds in which they operated.

4

I T took several days for the writer to decide on a name. It was perhaps the fourth or fifth name Old Dog had been given, and how the writer chose to refer to him didn't much matter. *Old Dog* was how he thought of himself. It carried a blend of austerity, simplicity, and directness that appealed to his pragmatic canine nature. And with the passing years it had become more and more descriptively accurate as well. It was the name he was given by the one person who came closest to truly understanding him, the one person who recognized the nature of his exceptionality among dogs—the one person who was, more than anyone or anything else, directly responsible for the depth and scope of his knowledge. She was in her own way as unusual for a human as Old Dog was extraordinary for a dog. She was a savant and a visionary and a genius in her own right, although her exceptionality was a burden that carried an awful price. When she conferred on him the ragged title "Old Dog," he wrapped himself inside it like a warm blanket.

But that was several years ago.

Names and naming are unique to humans. No other creature feels the need to apply such an appendage to the multifarious features of the world. Some cultures believe that to name something is to gain a kind of power over it. The most popular religion in the West, in overt acknowledgement of the connection between names and power, begins with a divine act of naming, as an omnipotent deity brings the entire universe into existence with a single word and then bestows upon the first human the honor and responsibility of labeling all of the other creatures—a prescient allegory forecasting modern civilization's obsessive, single-minded drive for complete dominion over every discernable facet of the natural world.

The need to name, the need to individuate and label, Old Dog realized, was not merely a function of the human use of language and the symbolic worlds language generates. It was, at least in part, a side effect of the primate mind more generally, a mind built around opposable thumbs and grasping hands, a mind that organizes the world according to ranges of grasp-ability. The human world is a world populated with things; it is a world brought into being by the need to segregate and isolate, the need to manipulate, the need to *objectify*. Names are the consummate tool of objectification. The human perspective starts with things first, and then, almost as an afterthought, considers the relationships and interactions among those things. The human perspective takes a world of dynamic and interpenetrating interaction, a world in which relationship is primary, and turns it into a world of isolated objects. Modern civilization, of course, pushes this objectifying perspective, amplifies it, and then turns it in on itself: a kind of self-dominion in which living human beings are transformed into mere objects to be manipulated within increasingly-oppressive systems of power and control.

The objectifying framework forced upon the human mind by civilization does something even more insidious than this, however. Not only are people led to think of themselves as isolated and manipulatable objects, civilization also convinces them that their purpose in life is to service the needs of abstract—imaginary—entities. They learn to think of themselves as components of these imaginary entities. There are several ways that this is expressed in everyday language. People talk of the need to make a "contribution to society," for example—as if society is a kind of living being itself, a creature that is capable of collecting their contributions and then acting on them. They talk of having a "role to play" and "doing their part," as if they are actors in a scripted theater production. They live encased within a delusional sense of the transcendent, a sense that as individuals they are small pieces of things much greater than themselves, that they operate as constituent parts of larger meaningful wholes—and further, that their personal lives have meaning primarily in relation to these larger wholes.

Parts and constituents: a machine built from standardized components; an image formed from the patterned arrangement of individual pixels. Civilized humans see their own bodies in this way, as assemblages of systems built from smaller components, organs and other body structures composed of cells, which are themselves composed of molecules, and so on. Moving in the other direction, they see themselves as elemental units embedded in larger social entities, in groups and organizations and communities. Economically, they are fitted into hierarchies of power, leveraged against each other through the competitive pursuit of intentionally restricted resources.

Parts and wholes. There is something that feels right about this. But it feels right for the wrong reasons. It has things backward. Or, perhaps, inside out. The nonhuman world has something of this constituent quality to it, but relationships in nature are neither hierarchical nor mechanical. A forest is not merely a collection of trees in the way that a digital image is an arrangement of pixels, for example. Trees are not autonomous, isolatable individuals. A forest is something far greater than a mere patch of tree-covered land. It is an organism in its own right, a living entity that consists of an enormous number of complex and interacting quasi-constituent systems, with trees sharing nutrients through mycelium, shadow-casting growth instructions to their neighbors, and transmitting information across great distances, coded in wind-delivered chemical and particulate languages—although even this misses the larger point. Old Dog knew this on an intimate level, having spent time living in the forest himself, living among the trees: trees, by themselves, do not make a forest. But more importantly, the transcendent entities that civilized humans see themselves forming component parts of are, unlike forests, entirely fictitious.

Abstraction is a way of simplifying the dizzying complexity of the world, and civilized life reframes the world in ways that lead people to grant more weight to simplistic—and unreal—abstractions than to the actual concrete details of their lived experience. Perhaps the most ubiquitous and pernicious form of this inversion of reality occurs with the use of the first-person plural pronoun, *we*. When someone uses "we," it is assumed that there is an actual collection of people that make up the implicit noun behind the pronoun. Sometimes this is true. However, quite often this is simply not the case. Quite often the collection of people composing the "we" is a phantom, an empty place holder. Quite often there really is no "we" in any kind of coherent or meaningful sense.

There are some trivial examples of this. In school, for instance, American children learn that the US Constitution begins with "We the people," and then they are led to believe—or told outright—that the "we" applies to everyone, not just to the specific "we" who were involved in its original composition. The use of the plural pronoun obscures the fact that the Constitution was meant to apply only to white male property owners. The use of the plural pronoun implies an inclusiveness that simply didn't, and, sadly, never will, exist.

Again, somewhat trivially, *we* is frequently used in ways that are overinclusive to the point of being logically incoherent or demonstrably false. For example, school children might read farther on in their history textbooks that "We ended slavery in the US in December of 1865, with the ratification of the Thirteenth Amendment." But who does this particular "we" refer too? No one alive today was in any way involved. This is the same "we" implied in the sentence, "We elected a racist, misogynist grifter for President in 2016." Really? What of those many people who voted for someone else—or for no one at all? Where are they in this "we?" This is the same empty "we" that lurks implicitly behind all social contract notions of governmental power.

But Old Dog understood that the human problem of *we* is far more malignant than simple overextension. Consider one of the most often-repeated clarion calls of the early twenty-first century: "We need to do something about global climate change before it's too late." Who is this "we" that is supposed to do something? Most sensitive folks would love to do something about global climate change, but there is absolutely nothing that they have any real power to do. Even if a committed individual were to reduce their personal carbon production to the absolute minimum possible while still being able to exhale, doing so would not alter the course of climate change in any way whatsoever. Even more importantly, the "we" who are most to blame for the climate crisis—both as the cause and as the reason that nothing substantive has ever been done about it—are not even human. They are multinational corporations, massive bureaucratic leviathans, abstract legal fictions—creatures without any actual corporeal presence on the planet. It is this latter use of *we* that is the most problematic. The "we" that have caused, and are causing, the climate problem are an entirely different "we" from the "we" who are suffering its effects. And neither of these is a "we" capable of doing anything at all about it.

The climate example is a particularly informative one. The situation with climate change and the hidden deception embedded in the word *we* are not unrelated. They are, in fact, two faces of the same stone. The solution to climate change is extremely obvious. Or it should be. It does not require advanced calculus to plot. Old Dog had it figured out the moment that he first heard global warming explained in simplistic terms on a children's television show. It is the same solution to the problem of overpopulation, and to the problem of pandemic disease, and to the problem of war, and to the problem of poverty, and to the problem of gender and racial inequity. There is one solution to all of these problems. But it is not a solution that could ever possibly be realized because it is buried out of sight behind the illusive word *we*.

That there really is a transcendent entity behind the pronoun *we* is so ingrained in the civilized mind that it is difficult to think about things in any other way. It is a latent perspective that reframes everything in terms of larger entities. The majority of these entities are entirely fictional, but this fact doesn't just go unnoticed, it is virtually inconceivable. It would be like trying to convince a person that she really doesn't have hands, that her hands are actually holographic projections that have no physicality, that everything she has touched was just imagination, just a compelling illusion.

People really have hands, of course; hands actually exist—not as one set of isolated constituent body parts among many in the way that people tend to think of them, but as a feature of the human form. But nations don't exist as either isolatable entities or as identifiable features of physical reality. Neither do political parties or the global economy. Or even *humanity*—a too-frequent catch-all target for the word *we*. These are all abstractions, rhetorical fictions.

It is a strange paradox that people see themselves in both physical and social terms as separate individuals, and at the same time think of themselves as mere appendages, as parts embedded in transcendent abstractions. That is civilization's beguiling spell that traces all the way back to the beginning, back to the very first hierarchical social power arrangements that blossomed during the earliest days of agricultural domestication. In modern civilization, this illusion is used as a tool of control, as a way of keeping people engaged in activity that has nothing to do with their own authentic human needs. In order for civilization to function, people not only need to feel that they are incomplete in themselves, but they need also to believe that the only way they can be complete beings is to act as a part of a larger something else. So, they spend their days engaging with fictional entities and mythical abstractions, experiencing for brief and isolated moments, as they participate in ongoing global genocide, mass extinction, and sweeping planetary destruction, the soothing illusion that their lives have a higher purpose.

Old Dog wished he could tell the writer these things. And he wished he could tell him what his own true name was. But he long ago accepted the communicative chasm between the world of dogs and the world of civilized humans, a chasm that, in evolutionary terms, was carved out only very recently, when small groups of people chose to live in decidedly nonhumans ways and then proceeded to violently impose those ways on everyone else.

The name the writer eventually chose was a stereotypical dog name, plain and somewhat unexpected given the writer's fondness for creative expression—surely, he could have thought of something more unique. Old Dog learned to respond to it in an ordinary-dog fashion, but he never embraced it as his own. He was, and would be for the rest of his life, *Old Dog*.

5

OLD Dog's early years with the family were halcyon days. He grew from a spindly and awkward puppy into a robust and energetic adult dog. All the while, his understanding of humans and their symbolic worlds continued to deepen and expand. He became a meticulous observer of human behavior. He listened and learned from the children, learned vicariously along with the children, learned what they learned. He sprawled across Jenny's lap as she sat on the floor to watch her children's videos and television shows. He sat in on Paul's online math tutorials and watched silly internet videos on the couch with Kathy. And he listened to the conversations between the adults, listened to their phone conversations and to the conversations they had out loud with themselves when no one else was around. There were other people as well, neighbor kids and their parents, the mother's friends from her school days, and the father's work buddies who would occasionally come over to the house to drink beer and watch sports on television in the evening. There were birthday parties and summer barbeques and Fourth of July parades. Old Dog watched, and listened, and studied, and learned. And, most of all, he *noticed*.

One of the first things he noticed was that the children were radically different from the adults. For one thing, they seemed to be alive in ways that most of the adults were not. Or, maybe it was that there was something in the adults that had been allowed to die. Whatever it was, the kids weren't just incompletely formed versions of their parents; the children weren't merely adults who lacked physical size and knowledge about the world. Old Dog saw that the children were fully formed and complete in themselves. They were, like all creatures of all ages, changing along a particular developmental trajectory, but they weren't unfinished people—in the same way that the thin sapling is a completely formed tree despite the dramatic differences between its current form and its future potential. But the children, in their completeness, were strikingly different from the adults in *qualitative* ways.

One difference was that the children and the adults inhabited dissimilar symbolic worlds. The kids spent large portions of their time in imaginary play, deeply embedded in scenarios of their own creative construction. The space between the wall and the couch became a tunnel to the center of the Earth. The swing set in the backyard was also a stage for impromptu plays, and occasionally doubled as a spaceship or a protective fort or a kitchen or a grocery store checkout station. When Paul was around, there was danger lurking everywhere. The oval rug by the front door became quicksand at a moment's notice. And there was no telling when a random patch of ground would become a pool of hot lava or a piranha-infested river. Old Dog himself was frequently transformed into a dragon or a horse or a bloodthirsty wolf—the latter of which bothered him for reasons that he couldn't quite decide at the time.

In spite of their elaborate and engaging make-believe play—or perhaps because of it—the children were in direct contact with material reality in a way the adults were not. The kids lived in the present tense, inside the moment. They occupied time; they were attuned to the present in a way that was immediate, raw, and intimate. They noticed things. Despite the contours of the specific imaginary world they happened to be visiting, they paid attention to their ongoing sensory experience in the real world, responded in the moment as the moment unfolded, and reacted to the emerging situation as it appeared in front of them. They seamlessly incorporated events going on around them into their imaginary worlds: unexpected sounds, a gust of wind or a dust devil, an adult entering the room, an insect on the windowsill, an airplane passing overhead. In short, other than their persistent immersion in worlds built of their own prolific creative imagination, they appeared to experience the real world around them in a very dog-like way. They were especially drawn to natural features of the spaces they occupied, to dirt and rocks and clouds and grass and trees and birds and bugs. On any given summer day, Paul might be found high in the branches of the maple tree in the corner of the backyard as Jenny picked a bouquet of flowering weeds to give to her mother and Kathy searched for colorful additions to her growing butterfly collection.

The adults, however, were not at all dog-like. They were almost always deeply immersed in symbolic worlds that had very little contact with the world of direct experience. They were detached from the present moment and lost somewhere outside of time. They seemed for the most part to be blind and deaf to almost everything happening immediately around them. And, they paid very little attention to local features of the living natural world. They had, Old Dog decided, a tendency toward a kind of tunnel vision. They would lock onto some extremely minor detail—sometimes nothing at all—and drill into it as if nothing else in that moment existed. In the process, they would filter out the most salient and meaningful aspects of the richly furnished world that was forever materializing right in front of them. They did not occupy reality as it existed in the moment. They were always somewhere other than here and sometime other than now. Their attentional focus had a kind of inertia behind it that made them slow to respond to events as they were transpiring, almost as if they had lost the ability to notice. The adults were involved in a kind of imaginary play as well, Old Dog eventually decided. But it was play based on a dark and sparsely furnished fantasy world. What's worse was that the adults seemed to be entirely unaware that it was just a game. The children, however, always seemed to understand that the symbolic worlds they created were only make-believe.

Puppies love to wrestle and scrap with each other, and this play fight-ing helps to prepare them for an adult dog world where they might have to defend themselves from an aggressor. In the same way, children's spontane-ous games are ways of flexing and growing their symbolic abilities in prepa-ration for an adult society in which symbolic thought plays an essential role in community engagement. Old Dog would later learn that there is a sharp mismatch between the requirements for adult community engage-ment in civilization and those that were present in the ancestral societies in which humans evolved. What this means is that when the symbolic play of children transitions into its more sophisticated adult forms, many of the venues for expressing those forms are no longer available. As a result, the adults keep playing, but fail to recognize that it's only play. For them, the game is no longer a game.

The adults Old Dog observed were engaged in a detached sort of play that drained the present moment of its relevance, neutralized it, nullified it, emptied its abundance until it became little more than a hollow stairstep to some imagined future moment, just another stone on the path. It was a desolate sort of play. And, what was worse, they were constantly trying to impose this vision—or lack of vision, as it were—onto the kids, constantly trying to convince the children—sometimes forcefully—that they too needed to learn to ignore the rich pulse of life that constantly surrounded them. They frequently scolded the kids to "pay attention," but what they expected in response was something very close to the exact opposite.

Paul had the most trouble with this. He was having problems at school. He didn't follow instructions well, seemed to be constantly distracted, and was frequently caught staring off into space or drawing pictures of dinosaurs instead of listening to the teacher or working on the assignment. He was given medication that was meant to keep him "focused" and "on-task," but it mostly just made him nervous and agitated and quiet. He started getting headaches and had trouble sleeping. He became moody and depressed. But his teacher reported that things were getting better in the classroom, so the medication continued.

Years later, Old Dog would see a striking parallel between what the adults were doing to the children and the way that civilization has always been forcefully imposed on noncivilized people. The way that adults pressed their worldview onto children looked very much like the process of colonization, the violent historical replacement of natural and organic features of traditional human societies with the structured and standardized social machinery of civilization. The adults in the children's lives were acting as micro-colonizers. Less overt and on a radically different scale, perhaps, but it was the same violent colonial conquest and genocidal eradication of indigenous forms of being. Old Dog would eventually come to understand that this parallel was no coincidence, and that every child's inborn human nature had to be violently reworked in order for them to be able to accommodate the artificial and inhuman mandates of civilization. In order to fit into the civilized machine, their native psychological ore had to be refined and forged and milled into mechanical parts.

During all of his time with the family, Old Dog's increasingly active mental life and his deepening understanding of the symbolic worlds of people remained hidden. He had no way to express his newfound knowledge or to follow-up on his observations by asking clarifying questions. His inquisitiveness, nosiness, and close scrutiny went undetected, always dismissed and interpreted in terms of typical dog behavior. The fact that he never had to be trained to know how to perform all of the basic dog "tricks" went unnoticed as well. He somehow already knew how to sit, stay, beg, and rollover the first time he was commanded to do so, but no one gave it much thought. Neither of the parents had much in the way of previous experience with dogs, and the kids had none whatsoever. So, Old Dog's uniqueness among dogs, including his brilliant mind and his astonishing ability to comprehend human language, remained invisible to the family, due partly to the lack of any real comparison group, but mostly because they simply didn't notice. Everyone saw in him just what they expected to see. To the outside world, then as today, he was just an ordinary dog.

And, in truth, there were many ways in which he *was* just an ordinary dog. He did all of the ordinary dog sorts of things. He sat and stayed and begged and rolled over on command. He ate all of the ordinary dog sorts of foods and he enjoyed all of the ordinary dog sorts of activities. He would retrieve a ball for as long as anyone was willing to keep throwing, and he gleefully participated in spontaneous games of chase around the yard. He crouched silently under the dinner table during meals so the kids could drop him tasty scraps when their parents weren't looking. During the summer he was taken on frequent walks around the neighborhood and to the corner ice cream stand down the street. On cold winter nights he always had a warm place to sleep in Jenny's bed. Life was good during these early years. It was truly a dog's life. Tragically, however, as he was about to find out, it was only one possible version of a dog's life.

The father came home from work early one afternoon and announced that he had been laid off. The company he worked for had "downsized," and although they were calling it a furlough, everyone understood that it was permanent; he was out of a job. Over the next few weeks, his normally cheerful demeanor darkened. His beer drinking increased to the point where he was drunk by midafternoon, and usually passed out on the couch by early evening. He became angry and loud and verbally abusive when he drank, and the children quickly learned to avoid him. Old Dog kept his distance as well.

One day, Jenny accidently knocked his beer off of the coffee table, and the father snapped. He stood up and yelled at her. When she began to cry, he became even more angry. He grabbed her shoulder and started to shake her violently. Old Dog felt a switch flip. There was something inside of him that he had not noticed before, something primal and vicious, something wolfish and wild. Where did this come from? It was right there on the surface. Had it always been there, hiding in plain sight? He felt sudden overwhelming fire in his muscles, and, as if carried upon the tips of the flames, his body exploded with motion. In the very next breath, the father was on his back on the floor. Old Dog was on top of him, growling fiercely, with his teeth embedded deep in the arm that had grabbed Jenny.

What happened next was all in fog. By the time the fog cleared, Old Dog was outside along the side of the porch, roped to the front porch rail. Sometime in the next few days, the rope was replaced with a sturdy wire chain. He would remain like that for almost two years, and would never again see the inside of the house.

Invisible Chains

6

I T is quiet this afternoon. Or maybe it's the relative stillness. There are
sounds here, pervasive and intrusive. A basketball slaps the concrete of
the driveway across the street in irregular but predictable pulses, punctuated by the occasional glancing metallic reverberation of a rusted hoop.
Inside, the refrigerator floats the persistent low-level mechanical drone of
its compressor, accompanied by the liquid pop and crack of its auto-defrost
mechanism, an acoustic mirror image of the basketball.

The two are frequently confused, motion and sound. Maybe because
they frequently cooccur, and even when they don't the missing counterpart is usually filled in. The writer can clearly see the ball recoil off the
rim despite the wall preventing any direct visual contact. And sound and
motion are not separate territories of experience, after all. They are two
poles on a continuum of movement, one inhabiting the microlevel, the level
of molecular oscillation, and the other at the macrolevel, a level that bleeds
into the visual, into the realm of light.

This afternoon's light is a substance in motion, fluid and transient, as
brilliant angular stripes of shadow and sunlight cast themselves through
the narrow-gage window blinds and onto the old wooden toolchest reap-
propriated as a coffee table in the center of the room. The white-gold stripes
vanish, then gradually reemerge, somehow brighter, in response to an itin-
erant cloud.

The dog sleeps on the couch, from the writer's perspective he is
directly behind the toolchest. He is angled into the sunlight, with the entire
front portion of his head suspended in the open air beyond the edge of the
cushions. His forehead also carries the shadow-casted sun-stripes. He is

having an intense dream, and his body shudders and writhes in aborted movement. He whimpers in spasms that, from inside his REM-sleep world, voice full-throated declarations.

7

H is world had become very small. From his place on the side of the porch, he had a narrow view of the street framed within the unkempt branches of a forsythia bush and a small evergreen shrub. It was enough to get a quick glance at people walking past on the sidewalk, and brief flashes of the neighborhood kids on their bikes and skateboards—which provided some degree of interest to an otherwise monotonous visual scene. Behind him was a hedge-bound grassy strip stretching the length of the house and ending at a seldom-used corner gate in the backyard fence. His limited view didn't prevent him from keeping abreast of current neighborhood events, however. Local happenings were readily available through his ears and his nose, organs that, for dogs at least, convey far more useful information than eyes. But even the most sensitive noses and ears have their functional range, and his lack of mobility imposed uncomfortable limitations on his sphere of awareness.

He quickly wore away a chain's-length sweep of the grass along the side of the house. In its place was reddish hard-pack clay that radiated dust and magnified the sun's heat when it was dry, and became cold slick mud when it rained. His chain was just long enough for him to wedge himself sideways under the porch when he needed to get out of the weather. But he spent the better part of most days lying on the bare ground in a slowly deepening dog-sized indentation in the hard clay. The hot days weighed on him like molten iron. And the cold nights brought no real relief. But it was the solitude that hurt most of all. Solitude was a hole, an emptiness, an absence, a psychological ache that burned and throbbed and made his chronic physical discomforts appear minor, even superficial, by comparison.

He was lonely. He missed the kids. He missed the constant excitement. He missed their voices. He missed their roughhousing. He missed being touched. At first, they would stop to talk to him one or two times a day, maybe pat his head or scratch through the dusty scruff of his neck when they brought out his single serving of food each afternoon. Jenny would grab him just below the ears with both hands, pull the skin from his cheeks, and shake his head back and forth while she scolded him to be a good dog. But the kids came to see him less and less often as the months passed. More and more often one of the adults brought his food, usually the mom. Both of the adults ignored him, never spoke to him, rarely even looked his direction—and never made eye contact when they did—as they dumped a scoop of food into his dish, refilled his water pan, or shoveled away his waste. Some days his food never came at all, and those days were happening with gradually increasing frequency. For an entire week during the heat of the summer, his water dish sat empty from evaporation, and he fought off dehydration by licking at the trickle of water that ran down the underside of the garden hose from the leaky spigot on the side of the house.

Loneliness intensified and swelled until it threatened to engulf his whole being. When he closed his eyes, he felt himself once again hunched into the corner of a dry cardboard box in a dark drafty room that smelled of gasoline, mourning the loss of his mother and siblings. He was in pain. But to the family, and to the kids on their bikes and to the people who glanced his way as they walked by on the sidewalk, his pain was entirely invisible. "How could they not know?" he wondered. "Binding a dog in place with a chain—binding any animal this way—is torture. How do the people look at me, see me like this, and then simply walk on past, their expressions absent even the slightest twinge of sympathy?" Not that their sympathy would have made any difference.

Several years in the future he would reflect back on these questions, armed with experience of the world and with knowledge of the ancient emergence of a subspecies of wolf known as *Canis lupus familiaris,* and of the primal symbiotic connection between humans and dogs, and he would have answers. He would know that humans were not always the way they are now. He would understand that humans had not always been so emotionally detached from the living world around them and so insensitive to the suffering of other animals. Humans used to have a deeper understanding of the world, and strong empathy for the pain and suffering experienced by all creatures, and they incorporated this into their rituals and celebrations and traditional hunting practices. Most humans today, however, express very little compassion or empathy. The human capacity to be sensitive to the pain and suffering of other creatures has been muted by thousands of years of animal domestication, and, in modern civilization, by the invisibility of domestication's bloody end results.

Millenia of domestication, thousands of years of selective breeding, have deformed dogs into the docile and apparently stoic animals that they are today, animals that appear, at least on the outside, to be capable of enduring extended periods of monotonous captivity in kennels and cages, or years of their lives bound to a chain staked in front of a small doghouse in the yard, or, as in Old Dog's case, tied to the side of the porch. But selective breeding does not always yield on the inside what it does on the outside. An increase or decrease in an overt behavioral tendency does not necessarily correspond to an equivalent increase or decrease in the internal emotional reactions or the covert subjective experiences involved. You can breed out an animal's tendency to complain openly about a specific type of discomfort or pain without changing the animal's capacity to experience and suffer from that pain.

But domestication works in both directions, and all the while humans were selectively altering the animals in their herds, flocks, and pens, they were also weeding out those human varieties that had difficulty adjusting to domestication-based lifestyles. People who found it hard to ignore their own empathetic and compassionate responses to the animals under their control did not fare so well as shepherds. And so, the capacity for animal cruelty has been gradually bred into the human population as a direct effect of animal domestication, and along with it a congenital blindness to animal suffering.

In the years to come, Old Dog would also learn that it has been only fairly recently in the Western world that animals like dogs have been thought capable of experiencing pain at all. For tens of centuries animals were mere animate objects, psychologically simple creatures who, if they could experience any sort of pain, did so in a way that was not really comparable to human pain. They could register pain, perhaps, but not in a way that was worthy of consideration or accommodation. Animals were not capable of understanding pain in the ways that humans could. Interestingly, this way of thinking about animals was not found—and is still not found—among indigenous people, hunter-gatherers and people living in traditional small-scale horticultural societies. People who live entirely immersed in the natural world can't help but recognize that all creatures drink from a shared experiential well. Even the land itself, the physical ground, and the mountains and the rivers, can feel, and can experience both joy and pain. This is obvious to them. As it should be obvious to anyone. As it is obvious to all young children until the civilizing process takes firm hold over them, until their own wild human nature succumbs to the emotionally numbing effects of domestication.

Domestication brings with it a dumbing-down of the animals involved—both in the minds of the people doing the domesticating and, over the generations, within the animals themselves, as the reflexive expression of their wild nature is selectively bred into the background. Domestication also brings a change in the animals' perceived standing relative to their wild counterparts. In the civilized mind the intrinsic value of any feature of the natural world is overshadowed by its extrinsic economic value as a commodity. As a result, paradoxically, domesticated animals become mere economic property and thus not as worthy of respect and admiration as are their wild counterparts. Their status as a domesticate automatically relegates them to a lower tier in the great chain of being.

But even the pain and suffering experienced by noble wild animals is worthy of only passing consideration in the civilized mind. Some of this might be just a psychological coping strategy, perhaps a response to cognitive dissonance. Something similar can be seen with the acceptance of human pain and suffering and the reduction in the perceived worth of human life during times of war: societies paint their enemies as monsters who are not entirely human and are therefore not entirely worthy of human consideration. This kind of dehumanization can happen with specific individuals too, with friends and family and lovers during periods of falling out. When you treat another poorly, it becomes important to be able to justify your actions to yourself. Only a sadistic monster would treat someone or something poorly if they didn't actually deserve it. So, the enemy becomes something less than a full human being. The wild species that are being driven to extinction, slowly starved, deprived of habitat, or killed outright, are not to be mourned. And animals that are bred as beasts of burden, and livestock raised to be butchered and eaten, become stupid brutish creatures, animal-objects that are immune to true pain and suffering.

Cognitive dissonance likely worked on the children in just this way in the initial days and months after Old Dog was banished from the house. Paul and Kathy, in particular, were at first very disturbed by his situation, checking on him regularly, openly expressing their concern and begging their parents to let him back in the house. But the longer that Old Dog remained tied up outside, the more his confinement became status quo, the less his potential suffering mattered and the more they also came to see him as somehow deserving of his fate. He attacked dad, after all. He obviously had a dangerous evil streak in him and couldn't be trusted inside the house around people. Jenny was still young, however, and she had less in the way of conflicting ideas about the matter, less in the way of incompatible material for cognitive dissonance to work with. For her, there was no conflict: Old Dog was bad, and bad dogs need to get punished. It was black and white. Biting was bad, and the fact that Old Dog may have been protecting her when he bit her father didn't change that simple fact. There was no need for compartmentalization; there were no contradictory beliefs pressing against each other; there was no crack for dissonance to wedge itself into.

Cognitive dissonance provides potent psychological motivation for justifying the status quo in general, making the way that things just happen to *be* seem like the way that they absolutely *should be*. The distinction between pets and food animals can serve as an informative case study of this. Pets are generally granted a higher status when it comes to considerations of humane treatment relative to other animals—simply because they are *already* receiving better treatment. Much of what is considered humane and acceptable treatment for a food animal would be unthinkable if applied to a dog or cat. Dogs and cats are more worthy of moral consideration and respect than food animals such as cows and pigs, not because of any physical or psychological differences with the animals themselves, but simply because, as pets, humans already treat them better and need to justify the existing inequity. There is a province in China that feasts on dog meat once a year during a ten-day summer solstice festival. Thousands of dogs are paraded through the streets in cramped cages and sold, butchered, cooked, and eaten. News accounts of this event in the US are always met with shock and horror and calls to end the grossly inhumane treatment of the animals. This despite the fact that millions of pigs, cattle, and poultry experience equal or worse treatment in slaughterhouses and factory meat farms across the US every single day. The yearly dog feasts are considered horrendous and, to many folks, completely unacceptable, not because of how the dogs are actually being treated, but simply because they are dogs instead of pigs or cattle or poultry.

One of the simplest ways to justify ill treatment of animals is to claim that it doesn't matter to them. There are couple common variations of this approach. The most extreme form is one that was pioneered by René Descartes, arguably one of the most influential thinkers in the Western world. Descartes claimed that animals were simple automatons, machines without conscious experience. This claim allowed him to perform vivisection experiments on live dogs and to dismiss their pained whelps and cries as mere mechanical reflex. A related and perhaps more nuanced justification is to focus on animals' lack of soul. Animals might have a limited kind of awareness, but because they don't have a soul, they do not have reflective conscious experience that is comparable to that of soul-possessing humans. Even if they do experience pain, they aren't really conscious of the experience—or, being soulless, there is nothing really there to register the experience—and they are thus unable to suffer from pain in the way that a fully conscious and soul-infused human can suffer.

Scientific research has failed to support either of these claims, of course. Quite to the contrary, science has demonstrated a strong continuity between humans and the rest of the animal world in virtually every dimension that has been investigated, including both the capacity for reflective awareness and the capacity to suffer. And as for the existence of soul, well, scientists long ago relegated such primitive notions to the metaphysical realm falling far outside of their magisterial purview.

Whether he possessed a soul or not, Old Dog suffered. And he was keenly conscious of his suffering, and his ability to suffer had nothing to do with the fact that he was not an ordinary dog. Any dog in his place would have suffered. And he endured, as any other dog in his place would have endured. But he was not an ordinary dog, and his intellectual abnormalities also provided him with a unique means for coping with his suffering that another dog in his place would not have had access to.

8

To speak of *the world* or *the universe* is to invoke an illusion of coherence and wholeness that is entirely absent from reality as it is actually experienced. Even to call it a *multiverse,* as some have, still leaves an impression of single-thing-ness, an impression that crumbles into a chaotic profusion as soon as it is applied to what is happening right here and right now from the purpose-driven perspectives of living beings.

Consider something as mundane as the paint-sprayed grass along the goal line of a football field. What is the line for a player on the field during a game? What is it for a player on the opposing team? How is it perceived by a referee? By a photographer? By a spectator in the stands? Now compare these closely related but distinct perspectives with that of a small hungry grasshopper on the field trying to sort past the massive irregular clumps and globs of paint spattered on individual blades of grass. Now imagine how the line might appear from 30,000 feet up. Or what it might look like from the moon through a high-powered telescope. The paint-sprayed line on the football field is just another aspect of reality expressing itself, but it is at the same time an uncountable number of distinctly different things, participating in an uncountable number of unique reality expressions.

The universe, or multiverse—or whatever words might be invoked or invented to try to capture *the all* and *the everything*—has no preexisting comprehensible form that might be called its own, but is amenable to an infinite number of manifestations depending on the nature and needs of the entities to which it is manifested. And this is not just a matter of resolution, of taking a larger or smaller perspective, although even doing that can be enough to completely repaint the canvas.

The resolution of Old Dog's world was severely diminished, with a canvas framed by the sweep of his metal chain. Despite this, he was determined to learn all there was to know about everything falling within his limited reach of awareness. His curiosity drove him to probe and ponder and consider and question—at this point, it had become a habit of mind; inquisitive observation had become automatic, reflexive; it was something that he couldn't *not* do. And, bound as he was, confined to a small space on the side of the porch, he began to realize the perspective-driven nature of reality and the pliability of context that that entailed.

And he also began to recognize that the world possessed as much variety and abundance within the immediate and the local as it did in the distant and the remote. This is rather counter-intuitive for a dog, and for any mind that is evolved to navigate terrestrial space. Land animals, he realized, are by necessity oriented toward the linear and the two dimensional. They occupy spaces where length and breadth are the most salient considerations. They live in a three-dimensional physical world, to be sure, but not all coordinate axes are given equal consideration. The x and z axes are primary. Yes, there will be times when it is necessary to contend with the y, the vertical axis, too. Topography varies in slope, and includes crags and crevices and steep hills and sheer cliffs—and dangerous predators can drop out of the sky or from the branches above—but to a nonarboreal land animal, the vertical is mostly just another plane of potential navigation, like the horizontal; even when a crawling insect climbs against gravity up the sheer vertical surface of a window pane, it is still orienting its body to the broadly two-dimensional layout of a surface.

Contrast that with birds, or monkeys, or, perhaps a better juxtaposition, with creatures who live in water, cetaceans such as dolphins, for example. A dolphin's experiential world is genuinely three-dimensional. They at times occupy spaces with no distinct cardinal points of reference. There is an *up* perhaps—life sustaining air is found in one direction only. But there are no limited axes of motion; literally any direction is available. There are also surfaces, of course. But these tend to be interfaces, boundaries: the surface border between water and air is exactly that, a border, a momentarily breach-able limit. Likewise, with the seafloor. Within the voluminous expanses of water between these limiting boundaries, however, there is only a sphere of potential movement, a sphere of omnidirectional potential, a sphere with a center that travels along with the dolphin wherever she moves. What Old Dog recognized was that land animals—himself among them—perceive the world at least partially in terms of surfaces and the opportunities for movement that they represent, and, further, that the default land-animal way of perceiving things is not a privileged perspective, it does not contain within it some kind of overarching, objective standpoint from which to view reality. It in fact adds a potentially powerful bias, and places limits on any attempt to achieve a broader understanding of the world. Not merely a bias, or a slanted framing to the picture, but a concealing shroud draped over large portions of the painting, with unrecognized blind spots obscuring otherwise exposed areas as well. There are things that will remain forever unseen, things that might be seen, but go entirely unnoticed, and things that, even when they are noticed, are reflexively disregarded as trivial or irrelevant, dismissed as insignificant details occupying spaces of marginal importance.

The demands of terrestrial life structure the experience of space and time. The terrestrial surface structuring of experience, in combination with the nomadic tendencies of a hunting and foraging species, leads naturally to an emphasis on the distant and the remote, and to a deemphasis of the immediate and the hyper-local. That which lies at a distance, that which is *away*, becomes the habitual focus of attention—whether *away* is a few feet or several days travel. Food is over *there*. Danger lurks *out there*. There is an asymmetry in the perception of the world in which the distal is given more weight than the immediately proximal. At no point, however, can an infinite universe be asymmetric. It is equally infinite in all directions, and there is just as much to learn within a single inch of dusty clay as there is across a thousand miles of open terrain. Despite the fact that evolution has biased the focal spotlight of attention toward larger macro expanses, the micro realms are equally abundant and equally worthy of careful consideration.

Old Dog set about to acquaint himself with the small creatures that lived in the rocks and dirt and grass around him—a microcosm of activity that in surprising ways mirrored the larger world. He was particularly fascinated with ants. There was something about them that reminded him of humans. But this was only on the surface: their purposeful scurrying. What the humans around him were doing, as they scurried off to school and to their jobs, as they carried their backpacks and briefcases and lunch boxes and psychological burdens back home, was something different, something that made what the ants were doing look intelligent. At this point he wasn't quite able to articulate the differences, however.

He looked as well to the trees and bushes and the many small plants that grew along the house and around the porch. He noticed how their leaves twisted and oscillated in the breeze, each moving according to its specific shape. This couldn't be accidental. This wasn't just an aesthetic feature of leaf-bearing plants. There was some larger need of the specific plant that was at work here, some reason they needed to expose more surface area to the atmosphere. Was it to cool themselves? Was it to circulate the air they absorbed? Was it to capture ambient moisture? He was several years from learning the specific details about evolution, but he had already deduced the main drivers of natural selection, and the intimate relationship between form and function. He understood that purpose and meaning were built into the natural world. And he was beginning to understand the scope of the disconnect between all of this and the ways that meaning operated in the fantasy worlds where humans spent most of their time.

His focus on the immediate and the local intensified as his first summer alongside the porch approached a noisy crescendo, with afternoon cicadas providing a resonant backdrop to all other sounds. There was a particular moment of what could only be described paradoxically as a consonant dissonance that happened when the buzzing whir from two cicadas stepped on each other's solos as one was winding down while the other was ramping up—two monks traveling in opposite directions crashing into each other along the path to a mountain shrine.

Sound is not like other sensory energy. It can be ignored, but can never be stopped. He made a point of not ignoring it, and spent long periods drifting in a sonic world, lost in a lavish profusion. He immersed himself in the symphony of wind through leaf and branch. He became a devotee of evening cricket chirp, and connoisseur of morning squirrel chatter. He learned to read the calls of the local birds, and discovered that what many of them were doing when they sang out was just trying to keep track of each other. The nesting pair of robins in the tree on the parking strip, for example, would call and respond to each other as they went about their daily food gathering.

"Where are you now?"

"I'm over here."

"And now?"

"I'm here, where are you?"

That was pretty much all they said all day long. It was as if the distance separating their bodies was nullified by the reassuring sound of the other's voice.

Old Dog was lonely, and he was confined, but he discovered that he wasn't isolated. Far from it. He was surrounded by activity, by life expressing itself in its myriad local forms, perpetually bursting forth moment by moment right next to him. He was living a life of solitude, but it was a solitude of abundance.

9

H E pushed his nose firmly into the wind. His ears pressed against his skull like a greyhound pounding the racetrack with paws like fists, chasing a rabbit-shaped mechanical dream in life-draining circles while people in the stands chased paper-thin slices of happiness.

But Old Dog was not a greyhound. His paws were flat and still. He was chasing an organic dream that flowed like a warm river across his face and filled his nostrils with stories. "There's a dead cat in the alley behind the apartment building," the wind said. "The setter two blocks down is in heat." He wanted to explore these things. He wanted to test the wind's claims, to see these things for himself. He wanted to run. He wanted to feel his lungs burn with exhaustion the way they did after a long game of chase with the kids in the yard, the backyard that was locked away on the other side of the gate behind him, the backyard he hadn't seen in almost two years, the kids who no longer seemed to notice him.

He sat back and considered his chain, the one hundred thirty-two twists of rusty wire that kept him bound in place. Suddenly it occurred to him that in all the time he had been tied up he never once thought of attempting to escape. The chain was hooked with a rusty clip to his weatherworn collar, which had grown steadily loose on his neck. He could, he reasoned, if he wanted, simply slip his head out backward. The other end of the chain was wrapped in a single loop around the corner post and attached to itself with a spring clip that, rust wise, was in even worse shape than the one attached to his collar. It would be easy enough to snap it apart with a couple well-placed slaps from his front paw. There were individual links in the chain itself that were of suspect integrity. He could easily free himself.

He could leave any time he wanted. Why didn't he? If the chain wasn't keeping him bound to the side of the porch, then what was? Why had he accepted his lack of freedom at face value? Why had he accepted it at all?

This perplexed him for some time. Despite the superficial trappings of involuntary captivity, the leather of his collar and the metal of his chain, his lack of freedom was not something being forced on him from the outside. It wasn't entirely involuntary. He was somehow complicit in his own daily imprisonment, held in place by a personal commitment to his own helplessness.

He was in some ways like the dogs in the experiments he would later learn about, the dogs who were bound in slings while their feet were forced onto an electrified floor. Later on, the slings were removed and the dogs were provided with a way to escape the electric shocks, but they never attempted to get away. Instead, they curled up in the corner of the cage and suffered through the pain. The psychologists who performed these heinous experiments called it learned helplessness. The dogs had originally and accurately learned that there was nothing that they could do about their situation, but then transferred this learning to situations where they were not, in fact, helpless. But Old Dog's situation was somewhat different than that. He was not entirely helpless when it came to his physical circumstances, and he knew that. He was free to leave whenever he decided to do so. There was something else involved. Perhaps it had to do with the idea of freedom itself; there seemed to be a haziness, an elemental ambiguity, a logical frailty embedded within the very notion of freedom.

He had heard the words *free* and *freedom* several times before, and in several contexts, and thought that he understood the core idea. But his previous understanding of these words quickly dissolved when he tried to apply them to his present situation. On the surface, and unlike so many other human notions, the idea of freedom was not an entirely alien concept from a dog's perspective. What made it strange to him now was its obliqueness, its indirectness, the fact that the words *free* and *freedom* make reference to the exact opposite of the actual issue at hand. There's an inside-out, chicken-egg circularity involved here. Freedom as a concept only makes sense in juxtaposition to its own potential nonexistence—the meaning of the word freedom points in the opposite direction of the concrete facts of any situation to which the word could be applied as an example. Freedom, like so many other abstractions, is commonly treated as if it is a thing in itself; freedom is considered to be a positive state of being, a feature of experience, an actual something. But it is not an actual something. It is an absence of something, specifically the absence of a particular kind of negative state—and there is something almost nonsensical about the way freedom can only be defined in terms of its own absence.

There are other human words like this, words that make reference to something obliquely by indicating its absence or its inverse, words that attempt to define an undetectable not-thing in terms of its distinction from an actual thing, and then treat the not-thing as if it, rather than the actual thing itself, is what really matters. Freedom, like several other of those curious abstract words that Old Dog still struggled with, only makes sense when considered in terms of its opposite. Restraint—the actual thing that gives freedom its meaning—is the lack of freedom, but if freedom is simply the lack of restraint, then freedom can only exist in situations where restraint is possible, and it has no real referent once the restraint has been removed. Freedom is only really relevant when you are not, in fact, free. What sense does it make to point out that you are not now restrained? Why point out a negative? There are an infinite number of things that are not happening right now; why have words to talk about any of them? The word *hungry* makes sense. Hunger is a salient feature of the situation—it is a sign that incorporates physical symptoms. Likewise with *afraid* and *tired* and *angry* and any number of descriptions of actual states of being. But free? Why single out the lack of restraint when lack of restraint is—or should be—the default condition?

Or maybe he was overthinking things. Maybe it was much simpler than he was making it out to be. Maybe, for civilized humans, freedom was not at all a default condition. Civilized life is life spent generally bound and contained and restrained—by obligations and expectations and rules and procedures and protocols and directives and laws and, in some circumstances, direct physical force. The idea of freedom might be analogous to the idea of relief, a state experienced immediately after the removal of something causing discomfort or pain, a positive feeling that results because the discomfort was so persistent or so intense that its sudden absence is briefly experienced as an actual, tangible state of being in itself. Perhaps freedom was like that, and life under the weight of continual civilized restraint makes freedom into an actual thing by giving shape and form to the fleeting dreams of restraint's absence. If so, a Paleolithic hunter-gatherer would have no need for such a word as freedom. Escape, maybe, but not freedom.

Old Dog realized right from the beginning that, for civilized humans at least, language is not expected to reflect features of an actual, tangible reality. It is, rather, a way of altering how people think about reality, a way of creating fictional alternatives to the present situation. In this, language has potent survival value: the ability to offer up preferred versions of reality to serve as templates or guides for action, and, in a civilized context, as a way to provide potential direction to a life that has come to feel increasingly directionless. Freedom, the word, the idea, is a tool for building preferred realities, a tool that would only be necessary if actual reality was chronically or recurrently aversive. It is especially useful in a society where manipulation, control, restriction and restraint have become the norm.

Obviously, restraint doesn't have to involved direct physical force. And it clearly didn't in Old Dog's case. At least not entirely so—he could pull his head out of his collar whenever he chose to do so. There was something else at work here, some psychological constraint holding him in place. He was bound to the side of the porch by something that was, in many respects, more powerful and more durable than any physical chain made of mere metal. Maybe restraint was not quite the right idea. Maybe there was something lacking or absent, rather than something being added or applied; maybe his acceptance of his bondage was an active attempt to fill an emptiness, an attempt to supply something that was missing. Maybe it was an unconscious attempt to re-inhabit the primal comfort of the womb. When he was still living in the house, he would often push his head deep into the space between the couch cushions, finding comfort and calmness in the feeling of confinement. Maybe his chain offered some miniscule residual trace of that same comfort. Or maybe it was something else entirely. Whatever it was, on some level he accepted his restraint; on some level he apparently *wanted* to be tied up.

With a sudden start, he realized that he was not alone in this. Everyone around him, everyone in the family, all of the people in the neighborhood that he watched leave and return each day in their cars, and all of the children he saw climb in and out of the school bus, they were all chained to a routine that they had no say in and little ability to alter. They could stop anytime. At any point they could choose to do something else, and yet they persisted in a way that was as if they were attached to invisible collars and leashes. And, Old Dog realized, the restraint quality of their invisible collars and leashes was, like that of his own collar and chain, at least partially, their own creation.

It was the same with the people he saw walking down the sidewalk with their heads bent forward into the digital universe in their palms, and the joggers with their ears electronically muted and a look of blank desperation on their faces, and the old man standing in the doorway directly across the street smoking his cigarette, and the father on the couch inside the house cradling his beer in his lap. It was their lack of freedom that was pulling them forward, like a train that travels great distances and yet remains at all times bound to the rails. But unlike the train, there were no obvious physical rails compelling them to stay the course. In every case freedom was sitting right there, waiting, pleading, and easily achieved at any moment, with even the slightest effort or with no actual effort at all. And yet all of their effort seemed to be directed entirely toward fortifying their own invisible rails. In violent contradiction to simple logic, they pursued their unfreedom with gusto. They reveled in it. And they panicked when they became aware of any potential flaw in their restraints, and took immediate steps to remedy the weakness, repair the rails. Maybe the fear of change was what was behind all this. Humans, he had discovered, were particularly averse to change. They would go out of their way to preserve the status quo long after it had become glaringly obvious that things needed to be different.

He was not really all that different from people in this regard, he realized. He was different in a couple of critical ways, however. First, he recognized that he wasn't free, while most people didn't seem to notice the many ways that they were being held captive. Perhaps they couldn't notice; like a continually present smell or sound eventually slips into the background and becomes imperceptible. Also, because everyone else around them was similarly restrained and appeared to be similarly oblivious to it, their unfreedom may have been rendered undetectable by its ubiquity. In order to know what something is, you have to have some way of knowing what it isn't, you need something different to compare it against.

Second, he understood that his own lack of freedom was somehow, at least partially, his own doing, that he was complicit, that he was, in a real sense, his own jailor. He was living in a prison of his own construction. And it was this second difference that made all the difference in the world. It is one thing to think you are free when you are not, or to redefine restraint as a preferred kind of freedom, or to find comfort in restriction, or to simply be blind to your captivity. But it is another thing to know that you are not free and also realize that your lack of freedom is partially—perhaps entirely—your own doing. Such an awareness could shatter through mountains of illusion. This awareness in fact began working a kind of alchemy on Old Dog's physical and emotional state, melding them together into a commitment that eventually became a resolution and finally a decision to act. He was going to leave. He was going to escape his place on the side of the house and—and then what? Where would he go? He had no answer to the *where*. And the *where* didn't much matter. The idea of leaving intruded upon his solitude and occupied more and more of his day until he had made up his mind. The *where* would remain an open question, but he was determined that the question of *when* would be answered very soon.

The *when*, as it turned out, happened before Old Dog's determination could mature into action. Circumstances intervened before he could put his escape plans into effect. His long days of solitude along the side of the porch came to a sudden and unexpected end, and they would be replaced with an epic journey that, in dog terms, would rival that of Odysseus' famous journey home—complete with monsters and the kindly assistance of a goddess.

10

D ESPITE numerous points of potential overlap, the universe can be a dramatically different place for dogs than it is for humans. This is probably so obvious that it needs no further comment. What is probably less obvious is how different the universe can be from one dog's (or human's) perspective as compared with another's. Statisticians refer to this as within group variability, the differences among members of the same group. The between group variability, the differences between the average dog and the average human, for example, tend to stand out. The within group variability is somewhat murkier. And the within group variability can sometimes be much larger than the average differences between groups. The range of intelligence separating the smartest humans from the dumbest humans is larger than the difference in intelligence between the average human and the average dog, for example.

What this means is that there is no single person (or individual dog) who can speak with any real authority for their species, beyond generalities so broad as to be trifling. For one person (or one dog) to claim to have a privileged perspective is ridiculous. Or it should be ridiculous. Reality can only express itself in first-person experience, from a single and unique point of view. All things in experience have a unique locus of experience at their center. The very same event observed by a woman as she steps out of her luxury SUV can look quite different to someone on the other side of the street sitting on the curb holding a hand-drawn cardboard sign that pleads for a donation of money or food, and different still to the raggedy dog lying on the sidewalk next to him—to the point of whether what is being observed counts an event at all, and if it *is* an event, where its specific boundaries lie.

Old Dog understood this. At any given moment, there were an unimaginable number of living beings experiencing the world, each from a unique one-of-a-kind perspective. And none of these perspectives had any special claim on the reality of that moment. Or, conversely, all of these perspectives had a special claim, which comes to the same thing. To be able to understand the world for what it actually is in itself, you would need to stitch all of these unique, individual, momentary perspectives together into a single tapestry, a single viewpoint. And even this composite viewpoint would not yield a comprehensive weave: its very nature as a point of view means that something is being left out.

There is a deep and abiding humility that goes along with this, with the understanding that what is true for you is only true for you, and, even then, it is only true for you now, for the moment. There is humility in knowing that your transient perspective is not part of some universal point of view, and that a grasshopper's experience is as legitimate as your own. This is the larger part of the human problem, Old Dog decided. Their civilized arrogance leaves very little room for humility.

The differences between dogs and humans are, paradoxically, both far greater and far more trivial than most folks realize. The differences between how a dog sees things and how civilization frames things are not just differences in perspective, they reflect entirely incommensurate worlds. Nevertheless, people, especially people in the Western world, are quick to anthropomorphize, quick to see in their pets what they see in themselves, quick to ascribe motives and emotional states that are of dubious relevance to the animals, failing to recognize the many ways that their own motives and emotional states are being structured by the requirements and demands of their civilized lifestyles, requirements and demands that are not at all generalizable to any other species—nor to those few fortunate humans still living outside of civilization's shadow.

Despite rampant anthropomorphizing—or, partially because of it— civilized humans are convinced that they are a species apart, that they are superior to the other animals, that they are somehow the apex of evolution and possess qualities that are unique in the animal kingdom. The most frequently cited of these qualities is intelligence: human intellect is superior to that of other animals by orders of magnitude. There is a basic logical problem with drawing such a conclusion, however, considering that humans are the ones who have set the criteria for intelligence to begin with.

For example, a knee-jerk argument for human intellectual superiority is what could be called *the argument from technological prowess.* Human technology clearly stands out as something far, far beyond what any other creature is capable of. Human technology has cured pandemic diseases and delivered people to and from the moon. Some other animals make and use tools, but nothing any other animal does can come close to the simplest human appliance. A major problem with this argument is that it assumes that the creation and use of advanced technology is evidence of intelligence rather than evidence of its opposite.

A quick survey of the negative consequences that have fallen from a lifestyle based around advanced industrial technology should be enough to show that it is not a very intelligent way to live on the planet. Also, how is it, exactly, that helpless dependence on external devices demonstrates intelligence to begin with? The ability to fashion a crutch does not make you walk better than someone who has two strong legs, and the fact that a crutch is needed is direct evidence that something isn't working right. Other animals are able to figure out how to do things for themselves. Other animals are able to function in the world just fine without external mechanical aids. To offer technology as evidence of human intellectual superiority reflects a narrow human-centric—check that: civilization-centric—definition of intelligence that simply can't be generalized to the rest of the animal kingdom.

It is unlikely that any set of criteria for what counts as intelligence could be applied across species because what counts as intelligence is relative to the opportunities and demands of life as it is experienced. What might count as intelligence for a bee is something altogether different from what might count as intelligence for a dog, for example. The claim that humans are more intelligent than other creatures demonstrates a lack of understanding of other creatures—when it's not simple chauvinism. And it's simple chauvinism almost always.

A further nail in the coffin of the technological prowess argument is the fact that humans themselves have lived technologically "primitive" lifestyles for several hundred thousand years, in conjunction with the fact that there are no meaningful brain differences between modern humans and those who were around fifty thousand years ago, with the exception that human brains were on average a bit larger in the distant past—most likely due to a cooler average global climate and the brain's need to maintain its temperature.

It turns out that there is strong continuity among all vertebrates, and humans are not so distant from other mammals in terms of any major aptitude. Even language, frequently cited as a defining human capacity, does not reflect an entirely qualitative distinction. Other primates demonstrate various characteristics of linguistic communication to one degree or another. And it is likely that the human ancestral tree is speckled throughout with creatures in possession of variations on the language capacities of homo sapiens—perhaps even superior variations. The fact that humans are the last surviving hominid that can talk doesn't make them somehow superior to the ones no longer around; going extinct is an inevitability in a world with dynamic climate and geography, not a sign of general inferiority.

Language and the ability to conjure symbolic worlds has likely been an important part of the human condition from the very start. But there is something about life in civilization that subverts these adaptive human capacities, reappropriates them, and directs them in ways that makes civilized humans think that they are distinctly different from all other forms of life on Earth. Civilized humans operate as if they are set apart from the rest of nature, as if they reside in a realm that is separate from everything else, a realm that is outside, above, and beyond the natural world. This is delusion, of course. And it is a particularly pernicious delusion. It is a delusion that is possible only in a mind that can conjure symbolic worlds. But the ability to conjure symbolic worlds did not create this delusion. Humans have existed as symbolic-world conjurers for a long time before civilization came along.

As a consequence of Old Dog's ability to navigate both the world of dogs and the symbolic worlds of humans, he ended up spending a lot of time in his head, lost in contemplation, reviewing memories, and reflecting on various insights he had about the human condition and about the world more generally—insights that he would never be able to express outwardly.

The writer and Old Dog shared a lot more in common along these lines than either of them could ever know. For example, the writer had been accused of "living in his head"—several times and by several people. And he did spend a lot of time thinking, contemplating, absorbed in reverie. That, and his appreciation of the complex and the intellectual and the subtle and the nuanced had left him for years (decades) convinced that the accusation was justified.

There is something of the pejorative in the "in your head" accusation: the person is a silly dreamer or an idealist who is out of touch with reality. Recently, however, the writer had discovered that when he was "in his head," when he was lost in contemplative thought, it was almost always in response to something he had noticed about the immediate material world around him. The moon tonight is slightly thicker than the sliver of a crescent that sat in the same place last night. The wind is causing the spiderweb on the lamppost to flex and recoil in a peculiar strained rhythm. The silhouette formed by the way the informational sticker has peeled away from the glass on the door looks like a small bird. The smell of barbequed chicken doesn't belong in the cold of a January afternoon. When he was "in his head," deep in contemplation and lost in the moment, he was actually *in* the moment, he was actually in touch with reality in one of the most penetrating ways it is possible for a human to be.

And he was convinced that there are even deeper forms of contact available, perhaps far deeper—complete arrogance to assume humans have any kind of privileged access to the universe, he thought. He glanced down at the dog curled up by his feet and grieved that these deeper ways might lie permanently outside of his limited human grasp, forever out of his reach. The dog beside him, however, was not at that particular instant involved in a deeper form of contact with the present moment. He was instead lost in his own head in a way that most dogs are incapable of and the few who are capable of go out of their way to avoid, deeply immersed in an unfolding memory of one of the most traumatic experiences that it is possible for a domestic dog to have.

11

ALTHOUGH Old Dog wasn't privy to most of the specific details, he could tell that the family's economic situation had continued to deteriorate in the time since he was forced to live chained up outside. The father was still without steady work, and his prospects were looking bleaker by the day. The mother was straddling two parttime retail jobs, but the combination was just barely enough to pay for food. To add insult to injury, the bank had begun foreclosure proceedings on their house. There were loud arguments in the evening that would inevitably lead to a solo drunken rant by the father on the porch—one of which ended with Old Dog being hit in the head with a half-full beer can for no reason other than that he was a convenient momentary target for the father's anger. At some point, a decision was made to move in with the children's grandparents—the mother's parents—who lived almost two thousand miles away in a small city in the Midwest. Old Dog overheard enough to know that he would not be joining the family in their cross-country move.

Despite the fact that the children had not played with him in close to two years, despite the fact that he had not been included in any family activities in the whole of that time, and despite the fact that tending to him had become an onerous burden without any positive payoff, it was hard for the kids to accept that he would be left behind when they moved. He didn't quite know what to make of that. Why did they seem to care about him now? Was it just nostalgia on their part? Or was it guilt at the thought of getting rid of him? If it was guilt, then where was the guilt for maintaining him in his pathetic state for the last two years? Whatever they chose to do with him, he decided, was better than continuing as he was. He would embrace any change, even if it turned out in the end to be a change for the worse. He scrapped his plan to escape, and decided to let the family resolve his fate.

They had a yard sale to lighten their material load prior to the move, and sold most of the furniture. Much of what wouldn't sell ended up in a large pile on the side of the curb to be hauled away with the trash. They then shipped their clothes and various personal items out ahead and packed the family van with what was left. In all of the chaos and preparation, they had completely forgotten about Old Dog until the morning right before they left. Because no one had come up with a plan for what to do about him, they carved out a small space between boxes in the back of the van, and loaded him in at the last minute. He was confused, and didn't really understand what was happening at this point, but it was a welcome change from the monotony of the side of the house. Whatever happened would be an adventure, he thought, and he started to get excited about the possibility that he might have a future with the children after all. His mind raced back to the early days, lying across Jenny's lap on the couch in the morning while she rubbed his belly, playing chase games and games of fetch in the back yard on sunny afternoons.

His excited dreams turned out to be hopeful fantasy, however. Just a few hours into the trip, the adults got into a fierce argument over what to do about the dog. The argument ended suddenly when the father pulled off to the side of the highway, yanked Old Dog out of the van and onto the shoulder, got back into the van, and then abruptly drove off, trailing the muted sound of one of the children screaming, leaving Old Dog standing in the sharp gravel on the side of the road, his paws barely visible beneath a slowly settling layer of dust, bewildered and terrified.

Ecotones

12

THE liminal spaces between are spaces themselves: the bent tidal grasses of an estuary, the thick band of cattails along a lazy lowland river, the bush-adorned alluvium at the base of a rocky cliffside, the fading echo of birdcall, the powdery patchwork of gray that precedes dawn.

Each surface sustains a universe at its margins.

Too often what beckons from the other side of the doorway over-shadows the threshold itself. Too often the transition is dismissed as mere passage. But this surely has things wrong side out. There is no destination without first a path. There is no arrival without first the journey. And the rocky summit is a barren place with little to offer, while the slope that leads to it breathes green with living abundance.

And the impossibly short distance between past and future takes an entire lifetime to traverse.

13

T HE linear nature of civilized consumption provides a stark contrast to the embedded cycles of rebirth, the perpetual repurposing and regeneration, the renewal of life upon death upon life found everywhere else in nature. Cities become one-way resource conveyors, inescapable gravity wells that drain the lifeforce from all that is drawn into their event horizons, fragmenting living communities and sterilizing the land. Humans raised inside civilization's ever-expanding impact zone learn to internalize this extractive orientation to the world. They are called consumers because that is their life, that is the role they practice and prepare for as children, that is the only message they hear from commercial media—the ubiquity of which overwhelms all other possible messages. Social status is arrayed on a continuum of potential to consume. And all consumable things serve their designated temporary functions and are then cast aside, discarded without a second thought.

Humans are consumers by civilized mandate. But they are also proximal thinkers by evolutionary design. They possess a powerful psychological bias to inflate the importance of the local in both space and time. Things that are affecting them right now, or due to arrive soon, things that are close by, in their neighborhood, affecting their family or their close friends, take precedence over things that are distant, happening to strangers, or due to occur in the far-off future. There is nothing inherently wrong with this. From a survival standpoint, it makes sense to be more concerned with the small bear standing right in front of you than with the large one on the other side of the hill.

Humans are consumers by civilized mandate and proximal thinkers by evolutionary design. But they are also mammals, and in possession of a deeply embedded set of mammalian responses to potentially threatening situations, the most generally useful of which is active avoidance. Out of sight, out of mind is among the simplest of avoidance strategies. If an image is causing you fear or distress, simply close your eyes, or turn your head and look away. If there is an object in your life that is causing you some discomfort, simply get rid of it, throw it away, leave it behind and think nothing more about it.

These three things, the mandate to consume, the tendency to emphasize the proximal and deemphasize the distal, and out-of-sight-out-of-mind avoidance, fold into each other seamlessly: flush the toilet, toss it in the garbage to be hauled to some distant invisible landfill, poison the weeds growing on the parking strip, buy a new car, build a taller fence, get a divorce, block the annoying relative from your social media feed.

Leave the unwanted dog on the side of the road and drive away.

The road radiated heat. Old Dog watched the family's van slowly fade into the distance, finally vanishing in a visual analog to an audible pop inside a wavy asphalt mirage. He didn't know what to do. For all of his insight, for all of his unusual intelligence, his dog-genius, he was at a loss—both about why the family had left him there, and what he should do about it. Would they come back for him? Surely, they would come back for him! They wouldn't just leave him to die on the side of the road, in the middle of nowhere.

So, for a while, he simply did nothing. He stood there and waited for something to happen, squinting into the distance with his ears folded forward for any sign of their return. But nothing happened. Finally, a car sped past from behind, blaring its horn as it did. The sound shook Old Dog from his trance. He stepped over to the partial shade of some gray rabbitbrush growing along the shoulder, and curled up in a ball on the sharp, small-grained gravel. It was approaching midday. It was July. There was not a cloud in the sky, very little breeze, and the temperature had already passed ninety degrees.

After a time, he decided that he needed to move. He couldn't stay where he was, and he was getting thirsty. He stood up and looked around. On every side was feral pasture and fallow farmland, flat and brown from a months-long dry spell. There was nothing in any direction that suggested that it would be better than any other, so he started walking toward the spot on the horizon where the family's van had disappeared. Bits of broken glass along the side of the road winked and glittered, a colorful counterpoint to the steady high-pitched static of insects in the fields. The sun's heat made the fur around his leg joints feel like wax melting against his skin, with each step the wick burning closer and closer to the bone. By late afternoon, the highway crossed a shallow river. He limped down the bank and waded in until he was shoulder-deep. The water had a slightly sour taste, but he drank until he could hold no more. Then, back up to the highway.

His fur was dry before he made it to the other side of the bridge. Once there, he could see clusters of houses off in the distance, their windows reflecting the sun that was angling behind him. In all the time he had been walking, only a half-dozen cars had passed, but now there was actual traffic. Large trucks kicked up dust and gravel that forced him to duck his head sideways. By early evening he had made his way to the center of a small town. As the streetlights overhead flickered and hummed into luminescence, he slipped down the alley between two darkly stained brick buildings, crawled behind a small dumpster, and slept until late morning the next day.

He was awakened by the crash of a heavy bag of garbage landing in the dumpster just above his head. He peered out of his hiding spot and met the eyes of a short, thin man in a food-spattered apron. The man stepped back, startled, and then relaxed as Old Dog shuffled out into the daylight.

"Hey, pup," the man offered gently, leaning steeply forward with his hands against his knees. "Looks like you've had a rough time of things lately. You look like warmed-over shit. Wait right there, I'll get something for you. Stay. I'll be right back."

The man disappeared through an unframed rust-stained metal door in the wall of the building across the alley, and reappeared a few moments later carrying a small pile of cooked ground meat in a Styrofoam bowl in one hand, and another bowl filled with water in the other. He set the two bowls along the side of the dumpster, stepped back, and said, "that should help." Then he disappeared back through the door.

Old Dog approached the food cautiously. In all of the recent trauma, he hadn't noticed how hungry he was. He ate the meat in one large bite and washed it down with water, continuing to lick the bottom of the water bowl long after it was empty.

What did he say about how I look? Old Dog thought. He twisted his neck back and inspected his side. His ribs were clearly visible. He hadn't noticed how much he had changed physically since the early days with the family. His hips were sharp. His muscles were atrophied but obvious—he pushed his snout up against the muscles in his thigh, and they rolled and twitched while he tried to hold his contorted position.

Old Dog felt gratitude toward the man. What would lead a stranger to be so kind to an animal that he had no connection with? He had seen this before with humans, an empathetic response that seemed completely out of context. Dogs are more tit-for-tat in their dealings with strangers— especially on first meeting them. Any sign of friendliness or playfulness is immediately reciprocated, as is any sign of aggression. Dogs, in both their wild and domestic form, coyotes and wolves and jackals and poodles, are willing to fight and risk injury or even death for friends and family; but none would lift a paw to help a stranger. The needs of a strange dog are of little or no concern. Humans, likewise, are preferential to their friends and family. But they can also be callous and even purposely hurtful to friends and family, allowing those close to them to suffer while they tend to the needs of complete strangers. He had a lot to learn about the contours of the human empathy response, he decided. But he would let those thoughts rest for now. He was a dog, and he could feel his instinctual drive for reciprocity tugging at him. Or maybe it wasn't instinct, exactly, but something to do with the compulsion to bond with humans that had been bred into his kind. He thought momentarily of waiting by the door for the man's return, but something told him that he needed to keep moving. By noon, he was once again making his way down the shoulder of the highway, with the small town shrinking smaller behind him.

The traffic became heavier the farther he went. And there was more variety. Trucks and cars and pickups and delivery vans and motorcycles, all in an increasingly frenetic stream, and a bus tossing diesel exhaust over him in a thick, unbreathable, ephemeral blanket that burned his eyes and left a bitter taste in his throat. Intersections occurred at more frequent intervals. He stuck to the far edge of the shoulder when he could, but there were places where he had to skirt out into the road, onto the hot asphalt, pushing himself along rusty metal guardrails and concrete barriers to avoid being hit. Many of the cars honked at him as they passed. By evening, the traffic had reached a crescendo, and the land ahead gave way to a large sprawling valley that twinkled with lights of every size and color, like the sunlit glass on the side of the road but burning with an internal fire. He had reached the edge of the city.

14

I T's called *transverse orientation,* navigation at night by keeping a fixed angle of orientation to a distant light source. In the natural world, prominent nighttime light sources are invariably celestial and indeed distant, the moon, Venus or Jupiter, the waxing or waning glow on the horizon that precedes and follows the sun. The trigonometry changes dramatically with light from a nearby terrestrial source, a streetlamp, a porchlight, a campfire, and the resulting path of travel becomes an inescapable circular vortex, a nocturnal Charybdis. Moths aren't attracted to light from the window, they are just unable to fly away from it because all plottable courses lead them right back to where they started.

Transverse orientation. People aren't drawn to the city so much as they become trapped by their own navigational trigonometry, caught in a vortex created by the city's consumptive commotion, failing to recognize its source of luminescence is the spark of life being violently extinguished; its siren's song, a fading scream; its beguiling pulse, a death rattle. All plottable courses lead them right back to where they started.

Old Dog stood along the highway, at a point just before it started its three-mile-long downward trajectory into the valley below, into the heart of the city. He was mesmerized by the lights. Many of them were in motion: headlights of vehicles. But even the stationary ones seemed to bob and weave, disappearing briefly behind a wind-stirred tree branch, or shimmering in the asphalt's heat-mirage. He had been paying very little attention to the kaleidoscope of scents arrayed along the side of the road, and at this point, his sense of smell was more-or-less off-line, overwhelmed by traffic exhaust. But the lights. And the sounds as well, a complex and persistent drone riding the warm breeze rising up from the valley, filling in the punctate gaps between the passing cars. Not entirely mechanical. The raspy irregular breathing of an impossibly massive beast, a metal and flesh hybrid. He could feel it vibrating his bones.

But the lights. He had never seen a city like this. He had never seen a city at all. The small town where the family lived had buildings and street-lights and rush-hour traffic, all the accoutrements of a city. But nothing like this. The city followed the somewhat jagged contours of a mid-sized river, and sprawled lazily across the valley floor like a bloated jewel-scaled serpent. As Old Dog began his descent toward the lights, and as the city's not-entirely-mechanical drone passed into his marrow, he could feel himself crossing a liminal space of transition, an incorporeal boundary. He was not sure exactly where, but at some point, he had emerged on the other side of an unnatural, invisible border—he was now *inside* the city.

To be civilized is to be contained, to inhabit spaces defined by exter-nal borders—many of which are intangible fictions. The civilized live inside walled houses and apartments and work inside sealed buildings and commute inside weather-insulated vehicles. These things have solid enough edges. But they also reside inside towns, cities, counties, and states or provinces encased within nations. The borders of each of these artifi-cial, arbitrary, imaginary regions serve as vessels of aggregation, sheaths of containment, and, above all, tools of separation: that which is on the far side of the border is *external, outside, other.*

This is a wholly unnatural thing. Externally-defined boundaries are inventions of civilization. They are technologies of control that have no true counterpart in the natural world. Nature simply will not abide a bound-ary. In nature, what looks to civilized eyes as a distinct border shows the very opposite of a boundary with only a slight increase in resolution: the wavering interface in the spaces along the shore of a body of water, or the biologically rich and expansive ecotone that joins a forest to a grassland prairie—even skin has this quality, and it is only by the human habit of self-objectification that they think of their own skin as a solid vessel of contain-ment rather than as a permeable membrane of attachment.

Other animals are often said to inhabit *territories.* And some will fight to the death defending what appear to humans to be arbitrary patches of terrain. From within the civilized mindscape, such fights can only be seen as a kind of border dispute. Humans are quick to project a civilized interpretation, quick to see parallels to civilized notions of property. But property is not a characteristic of the natural world. Property is a reified construct, a convenient fiction, a tool of power. Property is the spatial analog to clock-time. Terrestrial property does not exist in nature any more than do hours or weeks or Thursdays or the eighth of October. Neither do regions or territories. And especially not nations, provinces, states—or city limits. These are all tools of power, technologies of containment and control. And the boundaries associated with these things are defined in terms of the limits of control rather than, necessarily, by the structures or substances or people contained within.

Dogs and other animals don't recognize boundaries quite the way civilized humans do. Animals—and noncivilized humans—define boundaries by the center. If there is anything that actually corresponds to civilized notions of property or territory, it is something that travels with them, a zone that moves, a zone that expands and contracts around them according to naturally occurring limitations on the capacity to act in the moment. A mountain range, a body of water, an extended stretch of desert, a tree marked with the scent of a member of a neighboring pack, a sacred ancestral site, these things place restrictions on potential movement—no, perhaps not restrictions so much as *conditions*. But these quasi-boundaries change, they bleed into each other and dissipate with movement and travel, and with changes in the traveler's purpose and intentions, because they are defined from the center, from the locus of action itself.

Old Dog was not civilized, and his physical world was one defined by the center, one defined by his own body as a locus of shifting awareness and movement. But his ability to understand human language had nonetheless given him penetrating insight into a variety of human illusions and delusions. If he put his mind to it, he could almost feel the world in ways that humans did. He was beginning to understand how abstract boundaries and limits and interfaces functioned to corral human behavior—and *corral* was a very good word for it. Civilized humans—and civilization itself—are the result of successful self-domestication. The nonexistent borders and boundaries that are seen as solid and obvious by the civilized are the walls of containers, the borders of literal corrals that keep people from escaping into the wildness that beckons them from the other side.

Old Dog's perspective was also that of a domesticate, of an animal that had been altered from its wild form in order to serve human purposes. But dogs are different than other domesticated animals. First, they are the oldest of the domesticated animals, and have lived with humans for an extremely long time, far longer than have the likes of cattle or sheep. When humans and dogs began their relationship, humans were still living authentically human—non-domestication-based—lifestyles. Humans were not domesticators when dogs entered the picture. And the early dog-human relationship was more symbiosis than domestication proper. Once humans became bound to sedentary domesticated ways, however, all of that changed, and *dog* became just another beast to be tamed and broken and twisted for human purposes. Old Dog's ancestry included animals who had been made to live in cages and collared with ropes and leashes for thousands of years. What was once a symbiotic relationship, one that was mutually enhancing and empowering, became a one-sided dominance relationship underwritten by the ever-present threat of lethal force.

All domestic dogs are sensitive and responsive to what, from their perspective, are purely arbitrary and capricious human desires and demands. But Old Dog, as has been noted several times before, was not an ordinary dog. He understood that human desires and demands were neither capricious nor arbitrary, but were instead predictable responses to the imaginary worlds that they inhabited, worlds that they could not see as imaginary, fictional worlds that, drawing power from self-fulfilling prophecy, became absolutely real in their effects after all.

As he made his way down and into the city, he could feel the air around him change, become more electric. He became uneasy, and started to sense the presence of real danger for the first time since he was pulled out of the van and left on the side of the highway. He was not safe where he was. He did not know what the specific threats to his safety were, precisely. There were too many sounds, too many scents. He had yet to learn about the city and all of the unseen hazards and potential perils it harbored. For now, they were just a vague but strong background presence, an instinctually-driven gut feeling. Night and the accompanying pockets of shadow and darkness intensified this feeling, and he decided to remain on the outskirts of the city until daylight, when he could better assess his situation. He found a cozy hollow in a hedgerow growing along a side road just off the highway, and slept until dawn.

15

H E woke up hungry, and the smell of food was everywhere. He started off in the direction of the strongest source and followed his nose back to the highway, and to a cluster of fast-food restaurants. He made his way to the back side of the first one he came to and found the crust-dominant remains of a hamburger in a paper bag resting against a concrete parking stop. He kept to the shade of a line of trees along the far end of the parking lot, then quickly over an exposed grassy berm to a pair of dumpsters where a crow had pulled a veritable five-course feast out onto the ground. He muscled his way into the crow's breakfast, as the bird flapped itself off to the side and complained loudly.

He continued over the top of another grassy berm and into the open sunshine of a third parking lot. Sidling around the corner of the building, he spotted a man with an unkept gray beard and dressed in brown coveralls. Old Dog remained at the edge of the building and watched as the man rummaged delicately through the waste can next to a small outdoor eating area and dropped unopened hot sauce packets into a side pocket of a heavily stained over-stuffed backpack. After stuffing the contents of a napkin container sitting on the table closest to the parking lot into a pocket in his coveralls, the man hoisted the pack over his thin shoulders. He started to walk away, but stopped when he saw Old Dog watching him. The man set his pack back down and returned to the trashcan, where he pulled out a partially eaten burrito and tossed it Old Dog's direction. Without pause, he then re-hoisted his pack as if drawing a bucket from a deep well, and headed out in the direction of the highway. Old Dog approached the burrito and gave it a perfunctory sniff before inhaling it. When he looked up again, the man was gone.

After he had his fill of fast-food scraps, he made his way back to the highway and resumed his path from last night. But the highway was not what it was before. It had become a broad flat street, and the gravel shoulder was replaced with a white concrete sidewalk that became increasingly crowded with people walking and jogging and riding on bicycles and other wheeled devices. A leashed dog barked angrily and lunged his direction with bared teeth as he slipped past. He became frightened and increased his pace to a trot until he came to a side street where he could slip away from the crowd. He continued to move, at a more leisurely pace, in a generally easterly direction, through a network of alleys and side streets.

The sun was almost directly overhead when it finally occurred to him that he had no idea where he was going. He took a left turn and headed down one street at random, stopped, turned around and retraced his steps until he was back where he started, and then stood in a state of indecision. On the highway, it was easy to keep his bearings; although he didn't have an actual destination, he at least had a clearly marked path—one direction, one out of only two real options, a binary choice. He had chosen to follow the family, perhaps unconsciously hoping that he would eventually catch up with them—and then what? Would they take him back? Would he want to be with them again if they did? Would he end up just as he was before, only tied to a different porch rail? He hadn't taken the time to think that part through. He chose to follow them simply because the only other choice was to go in the opposite direction. The van somewhere in the unseen distance was a feather that tipped an otherwise perfectly balanced scale of options. But now he had too many options and no way to weigh them. There were too many streets that went to too many places he knew nothing at all about.

So, he decided he needed to regroup. He needed some kind of a plan, or a dog's version of a plan. Dogs don't organize their lives according to short- and long-term goals quite the way that humans do. Other creatures plot specific paths to desired goals—migrating birds and spawning fish, for example. Insects such as ants and bees compose and follow highly complex and elaborate instructions for navigating to specifically chosen destinations. But humans, or, rather, civilized humans, have been known to map out their entire lives. Their goals are established and pursued *strategically.* They mechanize their goal pursuit. And this makes sense to them because they think of themselves in largely technological terms. Their bodies and minds are machines and their lives are arrayed on a great assembly line.

The downside to the civilized approach, one downside among so many others, is that it imposes severe limits on the ability to respond in the unfolding moment; it restricts the ability to adapt to subtle changes in context and to be able to take advantage of new information as it surfaces in sometimes very unexpected ways. And even when it becomes clear that a chosen goal was a mistake, or that it no longer makes sense to pursue, or that the original destination was the wrong one, it can be exceedingly difficult to change course. And this difficulty only increases the longer the goal has been pursued, as if each step along the path has added an incremental degree of momentum.

The mechanizing of goal pursuit reduces moment-by-moment quality of life as well. A narrow focus on the pursuit of a specific goal bleeds the present moment of much of its experiential potential. The present moment, a rich and unique one-of-a-kind happening, is transformed into a mere means to an end, just another tedious step along the path to something else. The problem with this—and this is obvious to the noncivilized—is that life is not just a collection of goals achieved. Nor is it a destination. Achieving a goal, reaching a pursued destination, represents the tiniest portion of living experience. In terms of just the raw proportion of time, as a sheer fraction of day-to-day existence, life is composed almost entirely of the path itself. A goal-directed focus empties existence, drains experience of its abundance, and life becomes little more than a series of checkmarks on an otherwise blank page.

Dogs are thankfully immune to this technologizing of life. As a result, they are better able to adjust to unanticipated changes in the context— largely because they never really anticipated anything specific from the start. Their goals, if you can call them that, are short-term and practical and tied to immediate needs, and they are subject to spontaneous change— spontaneous change is actually included as a built-in feature of their plans to begin with. Not really plans. At most, they might be thought of as general orientations, or dynamic overall guiding drive-states, clusters of shifting motivations for attention and movement and activity, and always embedded in a broader unfolding context. But, with the family now completely out of the picture, with no way to know where they went or how far, Old Dog lacked even this. He lacked any specific direction for a guiding drive-state or cluster of shifting motivations to follow—he had no immediate motivations. And there was much about the unfolding context that he was unable to clarify. So, he found a place along the side of a quiet residential alleyway, in the spidery shade of a scraggly crabapple tree, and slept for a while. When he woke up, he would think about his options and decide what he should do next—if anything at all. By then, he was convinced, more of the unfolding context will be exposed, and his options would be more apparent.

It was mid-afternoon when he woke up, and he instantly knew what to do, or at least where he needed to go. Last night while on the highway, at the top of the hill overlooking the city, he saw a river express itself in open patches between the trees and buildings. The city, like many other cities— and towns and villages since the beginning of towns and villages—was originally sited along the banks of a river. In the wild, rivers are places of life and sanctuary. For a forager, a scavenger, they provide a cornucopia of nourishing food choices. There is some safety in the sound of running water as well—although this safety is double-edged, as it can mask the footsteps of a predator. And there is water, of course, water that was much-needed in the mid-July heat that was now bearing down on him. So, he walked toward the river, which he could smell clearly even though it was quite distant from where he had napped. He once again, at least for a short while, had a bearing, a direction of travel, and a momentary objective to pursue.

His instincts told him that he needed to keep a low profile. He avoided people by staying away from open areas and main streets, keeping to the alleys and keeping clear of yards and houses as much as possible. The streets and alleys, at first arrayed in rectangular geometric perfection, began to twist and curve and merge more and more with the increasingly varied topography: gullies and small ravines, large basalt outcroppings and "unimproved" vacant areas with clusters of trees, mostly thin young ponderosa pine, as the river got closer. He could hear the water long before he could see it. There was a strong current with seasonally exposed rapids chiseled sharp by the ongoing dry spell. When he finally came to a place where the river was visible, his path to the bank was blocked by a bent and weathered cyclone fence that extended as far as he could see in both directions. He made his way down along the fence line for several hundred feet before he found a gap at the base big enough to slip beneath. He scrambled down to the water's edge for a long drink.

The river flowed through abrupt twists in a generally northwestern direction. Old Dog decided to follow its course upstream. In most places, the riverbank was steep, moss-covered bistre basalt that looked as if it had been in place for several thousand years. But much of the land beyond the very edge was sealed beneath concrete and asphalt in various stages of disrepair and decomposition. Old brick and metal buildings stood like dystopian castles, in a similar dilapidated state as that of the concrete around them. Most of the buildings had obviously been abandoned for years, and their doorways and windows were boarded up with weather-stained and graffiti-layered plywood. The few structures that were still being used had been repurposed, from whatever their original purpose was, to accommodate small-scale manufacturing and repair shops. A few had been turned into makeshift warehouses. The ones farther upstream and closer to the heart of the city had been converted into restaurants and brightly painted specialty shops.

Old Dog was right to follow his instincts about the river. There was abundance here. The many buildings and outbuildings and abandoned heaps of scrap metal and rusted machine parts made for great shelter, offering shade from the afternoon heat and protected places to hide at night. Closer to downtown, there was food aplenty in and around the dumpsters and garbage cans behind the shops and restaurants. He quickly settled into a crepuscular lifestyle, moving up the river toward the heart of the city in the early morning and evening hours, and back downstream to the abandoned buildings to get out of the midday heat and to harbor in a safe sleeping spot at night.

There were numerous other animals sharing the abandoned structures along the river who had adopted a similar lifestyle, all following an unspoken live-and-let-live social contract—which is the natural default—although the many stray cats eyed him warily and gave him plenty of extra space. There was a surprising absence of dogs. He occasionally caught a scent now and again, but it was almost always from a leashed dog that had accompanied its human caretaker for a walk along the river. Raccoons and opossums and skunks were plentiful. The rocky riverbank was the playground of fat furry marmots. And the crows were everywhere. Old Dog left each of these creatures to their own devices. On several of his evening sorties, he was briefly befriended by people, by children playing in the downtown park, or by people at tables outside one of the eateries. But occasionally he came across people who tried to hurt him. Usually by kicking at him or by throwing rocks or swinging sticks and branches. One kid hit him with a projectile fired from a slingshot and raised a large bloody welt on the top of his head. He quickly learned to predict which people were potentially approachable and which to avoid—and erred on the side of avoid.

In a relatively short time, he had settled into a comfortable routine. This would be his new life, he thought, at least for now. It wasn't an easy life, it was potentially dangerous at times, and unpredictable, but it was much better than being tied up on the side of the porch. He was, he decided, free—or something close to free in the relief-from-confinement way that he understood that word. The world had once again proved itself abundant, and the liminal zone, the ecotone along the edge of the river running through the middle of the city, provided everything he needed.

16

T HE city had a pulse to it, a tidal ebb and flow of sound and motion. There were layers to this, strata. There was the daily surge and recoil of traffic, which generally followed sunrise at a slight lag, and anticipated sunset. But there were also layers that expressed themselves across days. On some evenings the park and the restaurants were bustling with people and activity, and the smell of food twisted itself tightly across Old Dog's nose. These evenings were followed by a series of days where things remained relatively quiet, with fewer people and the smell of food more thinly coiled. The restaurants were easy pickings on the mornings that followed the busiest nights, with scraps spilling from the waste cans and dumpsters in quantities enough to supply all of the local scavengers. Despite this, the quiet days were best in general, easiest to find food without worry of harassment, and Old Dog preferred these days and their relaxed tone, when he could go about his business in a more leisurely fashion.

The city expressed many other layered patterns as well, at both higher and lower levels of stratigraphic resolution. All of these oscillations had an artificial, mechanical feel to them. They expanded and contracted to accommodate changes in the weather, and they sat atop the cycle of day and night, but there was something discordant in the way that the city was wedged into these natural changes and cycles. Rather than allow itself to be entrained by the natural flow of movement and transition, the city pushed against these cycles in ways that were aggressive and abrasive, even violent.

The most obvious and ubiquitous example of this was the city's use and distribution of artificial light. Rather than accept and embrace the day-night cycle with its sequential transitions of light and darkness, light was manufactured and disseminated broadly—and in a starkly nonuniform manner. Sundown was followed by a city-wide explosion of street lights, the accompanying sound of which Old Dog used as a signal that it was time for his evening trip upstream. Lights on street corners and over the entrances to buildings and encircling public outdoor gathering places brought deep brooding shadows and extensive regions of blinding darkness into existence. And the buildings themselves became both beacons of luminescence and conjurors of blackness, with shadow-raising light spraying out of windows and doorways. But there were numerous other, less obvious ways that the city imposed its mechanical forces against the living world as well, ways that were gratuitous and entirely unnecessary—or at least they seemed that way from a dog's point of view.

In the future, Old Dog would come to see reliance on artificial light as a microcosmic specimen of the overriding logic of civilized life in general. Civilized life is life lived as indirectly as possible, with layers of technological mediation inserted between the person and the physical reality of the living moment. Civilized life is enacted within human-controlled environments, inside buildings and outside on ground coated with concrete and asphalt and mechanically-groomed chemically-homogenized sod, environments that are designed to insulate people from the natural expression of the world as much as possible.

Civilized life is vicarious life. That is not to say that the civilized don't experience pain and fear and suffering directly in their own physical person. No, in some ways civilization enhances the potential intensity of personal suffering, acts as a multiplier for pain, and by doing so makes fear into a primary motivator lurking behind almost all civilized activities. That's also not to say that civilized humans don't know joy and pleasure and happiness. Although the human emotional pallet may be severely stunted by civilization, it is still present and available. But the vicarious life people are being forced to live is not an authentically human life according to the expectations laid down by their species' evolution, expectations that still register deep in the human unconscious. And perhaps not so deep as well.

Civilized life is vicarious life because it is life that is not lived directly; it is life that is mediated; it is a life of alienation; it is a life of artificial light and artificial relationships. It is life that starts with a distinction between an inside and an outside, and then builds walls—both physical and symbolic— to make the distinction into a reality. But it is not simply that the civilized have to rely on an artificial infrastructure in order to see at night, or to provide the means for satisfying their needs for food and shelter. It is more than that. Much more than that.

Civilization invents needs that were never there to begin with. It creates needs from scratch. It creates needs and then restricts and controls the means to satisfy them—manufacturing the space for need itself to be felt, and, in the process, creating the conditions for privation. Most of these invented needs have very little directly to do with authentic human needs, with the real needs of living breathing people. Most of these artificial needs are designed so that people will behave in ways that promote and maintain and expand the system itself—the only "needs" that have any real importance are those of the system, the machine of civilization and its various component parts. They are human needs only because the civilized are entirely dependent on the efficient functioning of the machine. What the machine needs, humans are made to need. And the human victims of this need-generation-and-exploitation can't see that this has things completely backward. They can't see that it is their artificial separation from the natural living world around them that has put them in this predicament.

There are the obvious ways this dependency manifests itself. The fact that food—100 percent of it for most folks—has to be purchased, or otherwise obtained through an increasingly globalized food system, for example. Even if a person is fortunate enough to have access to land on which to grow some of their own vegetables, or raise food animals, the land is "property;" it is a feature of a money economy; it is regulated and controlled by the system, has to be obtained and used according the system's rules, and is at all times under the system's power; continued access to the land is never guaranteed, and can be revoked by the state at any time through eminent domain laws, or lost as a result of a personal financial crisis.

And there are some equally obvious things that have to do directly with forced participation in a money economy, specifically an economy based on the profit-generating consumption of goods and services sold at a price higher than the cost of production—the *ostensive* cost of production, which is immeasurably lower than the actual cost of production when you consider that human labor involves coercing people to relinquish the unique and precious and limited hours and days and weeks and months and years and decades of their very lives. How much is an hour of life worth? Really? How can anyone justify giving their time over to anything that is not entirely serving their own purposes? An hour of life, whether it is an hour of a human's or a dog's or a grasshopper's life, is infinitely valuable, and yet civilized humans are made to parlay this infinite value down to a microscopic finite amount through a combination of fear and indoctrination, all the way down to whatever the going wage happens to be—and consider themselves blessed to have job!

But there are also countless not-so obvious things, things that have to do with how children's minds are molded to a civilized template early on, and how ubiquitous corporate marketing keeps everyone in a state of relative need regardless of what they already have. Because they are not living authentically human lives, there is a persistent feeling that something important in their lives is missing. Corporate marketing dangles sparkly consumer goods and services in front of their faces and, through a little applied psychology, convinces them that the answer to their emptiness is just a purchase away. Civilized humans are living vicarious lives, mediated lives of technological bondage that are alien from the perspective of their evolved expectations as nomadic hunter-gatherers. And the unease and discomfort created by the mismatch is being nurtured and cultivated and then turned around on them and used to temper their chains and expand the depth and scope of their dependence.

Old Dog was not living a vicarious life. He was living in the heart of the city, but he was living *with* civilization, not *in* it. He was steering his way through and around the artificial pulses and mechanical palpitations of the machine, but he was not part of the mechanism, and he was not dependent on the machine's output. He could, if he wanted, live off of the many small rodents in and around the scrap heaps and abandoned buildings. He could live as an insectivore for a time if he so chose—as long as he augmented his bug diet with occasional green grass; for some reason, eating too many bugs almost always caused him intestinal distress, something he discovered during his time tied up on the side of the porch. But he preferred the life of a scavenger, living off the overspill and abundant dross of civilized consumption. The foraging lifestyle suited him. It was, after all, close to the kind of lifestyle that had been burned into his genetic expectations over millions of years. Wolves are notorious as hunters, but none of his wolf ancestors would have ever passed over the unattended remains of a mountain lion's kill.

And speaking of his ancestors, one morning, when he was on his way upstream, following a narrow twisting path close to the water's edge, he rounded a bend and came face to face with his ancestral self in the form of one of his distant canine cousins, a rather large coyote. He froze in his tracks and could feel his hackles reflexively raise, but he was careful not to show any postural sign of aggression. The coyote stood still for several seconds as well, before dismissing Old Dog with a sound that was halfway between a bark and a growl, and then continuing on his way into the underbrush closer to the water's edge without ever once glancing back, as if Old Dog simply didn't exist. Old Dog stood still for a long time afterward, and then slowly resumed his own path. There was something primal about the way the coyote looked at him, something that he recognized, something that seemed familiar, but he couldn't quite decide what it was or what it meant.

Dogs are really wolves, of course, with only two-tenths of a percent difference between the two in terms of DNA—a fact that can sometimes be difficult for people to wrap their heads around: that, genetically, barely one-fifth of a percentage point separates an eleven-pound miniature dachshund from a one hundred eighty-pound timber wolf. Although coyotes are more dog-like in many ways—both physically and behaviorally—surprisingly, dogs and coyotes are more distant relatives. DNA evidence places the common ancestor of coyotes and wolves at about eight hundred thousand years ago, whereas the first dogs appeared on the scene quite recently, evolutionarily speaking, somewhere around thirty-five thousand years ago. All of these, coyotes, wolves, and dogs, are to one degree or another, foraging scavengers as well as nomadic hunters. Humans too, of course. Human are evolved for a similar kind of hunting and foraging lifestyle. Civilization allows neither humans nor dogs to live in ways that their evolutionary history has prepared them for, however. Instead, they are forced to warp and bend and twist their evolutionary expectations to accommodate an aggressive and abrasive artificiality, forced to live in a discordant state of disconnect from the natural flow and pulse of the living world around them.

Foraging is not necessarily an easy way of life. But it is a natural way of life; and it is an unmediated way of life, a way of life that that involves living directly, non-vicariously. Old Dog enjoyed his solitary excursions up- and downstream. On some days these excursions were not entirely solitary. Occasionally he would come across people, most of whom offered him a friendly word as he passed. A few would offer their hand and a morsel of food. Many of these people, especially the ones he encountered on the quiet days, seemed to be living a lifestyle that was very much like his own, a human version of the lifestyle he had adopted, living *with* but not entirely *in* civilization. Despite these occasional encounters, he was once again living a solitary life, a life of solitude. But this solitude had a completely different feel than what he felt when he was tied to the side of the porch. This was a voluntary solitude, a solitude that was not forced on him from the outside. There were no external restrictions on what he did or when he did it. He could do what he needed to do anytime he felt the need. Shelter and water were abundant. And he had easy access to food—although sometimes he had to work for it a bit. But it was still, in the end, a solitary life, and there were times when he felt a dog's version of loneliness.

17

THE rush and wash of the river was a constant sonic presence, an ambient liquid backdrop. But it was not a passive background sound. It was not just white noise. It was lyrical and melodic, a densely orchestrated fugue with a score composed from a thousand polyphonic threads tenderly knitted together through a complex throbbing beat—a pattern emerging from non-pattern, shifting, unfolding, then folding in on itself only to return to its original shape.

It was late summer now, and the river answered the cool morning air by casting a thin low fog over its banks and around Old Dog's lower legs as he made his way upstream. It had only been a couple cycles of the moon, but the trauma of his abandonment seemed a distant fading memory, perhaps even something from a past life. This was the river's doing, he decided. There was something about its persistent refrain, its beguiling aural ballet that simultaneously expanded and compressed the passing of time—compressing the experience of duration within days and expanding it between them.

Thinkers and writers are frequently drawn to the river as a useful metaphoric vehicle for expressing the passing of time, an analogical impression that likely traces back to the very first civilizations and their dependence on spring floods to replenish the soil with fresh nutrients to replace the ones extracted with the yearly harvests. Rivers have also been an important mode of transport and travel since the early Paleolithic. Rivers are an embodiment of movement, and, as metaphor, provide a veritable case study for time's enigmatic qualities of flow and persistence.

There are other ways that rivers have been evoked metaphorically, some that take the river as a whole, as a unitary being, the river in its entirety, drawing on the dual nature of rivers, which, like all physical things, exist as entities occupying space as well as time. A river isn't just water. It is a living geographical feature of the land. It has a beginning and an end, an origin, its source, and a terminus, either where it merges with another river or empties itself into a larger body of water, a lake or an ocean. Although the main tributary of the Nile begins in a lake, the source of most rivers is in the mountains, in diffuse streams of meltwater from winter snowpack and mountain glaciers, waxing and waning with the seasonal rains and periodic drought.

A river's personality changes as it travels from its source to its mouth. Of course, this is metaphorical too: rivers don't travel anywhere. They are at all times both at their origin and their mouth as well as occupying all places along their course. The river doesn't go anywhere. It is a watery vein embedded in the land itself. It is the water that can be said to travel. But even the water is not entirely new to the cycle. Every drop of the river, every molecule of water, at every moment along the river's course, has been washing through its own cyclical journey of perpetual return, a journey with neither a beginning nor an end, at least not on a scale that could be understood by living beings.

But the sense that a river's course involves changes in its personality is compelling. At its source, the river is exuberant, with waterfalls cresting mountain cliffs in thin curtains of white misty spray, coursing coolly across smooth colorful stones clearly visible through the wrinkled transparency of its surface. In this form, the river is a child, energetic and open and playful. Once out of the mountains, the river becomes a chimera, congregating with numerous other brooks and creeks and streams. It gains power and determination, blasting against boulders, jabbing its way through impossible turns, carving steep banks, all the while gouging the land into forms that accommodate its watery religion, its devout gravity-worship. Here, where the river is still new, still in its self-absorbed youth, it is all-but impervious to the wind (which is involved in its own journey of perpetual return). Then, farther on, the river discards its urgency, and becomes a steadily writhing broad-bellied snake. Its surface is now able to receive the wind, raising scale-like dimples that reflect sunlight in a dancing coruscation of knife-edged sparkles. Still farther along its course, the wind is granted unfettered access, and wind-stirred waves and their echoes pile upon each other in flowing crisscross patterns.

Toward the very end, as the water approaches the great ocean, the great receptacle of all rivers, it broadens and flattens its banks, in some cases so much that it becomes unclear where the river ends and the ocean begins. In reality of course, such a distinction is something that humans add to the scene. The river taken as a whole, as a separate and distinct entity, is a human creation, its characteristics a reflection of human purposes and human biases and contained entirely within the stark limitations of human perception and comprehension, a symbolic overlay cast across infinite variations of landforms and watery expression. No one, after all, with the arguable exception of astronauts, perhaps, has ever seen a river in its entirety all at once. That people are drawn to carve out momentary segments in the water's perpetual cycle of recurrence and return and call this *river*, is entirely arbitrary from the perspective of wild nature. The water in the mountain glacier was once in the ocean, and so, from a more expansive perspective, at a level of temporal resolution that is quite beyond what any single human might live to experience directly, the river is just another feature of the ocean itself, one of the many ways that the ocean splashes itself across time and space. In reality, in a reality that neither humans nor dogs can occupy, there is no river. There is only the intelligence of water.

And yet, a river is more than just water. A river's life cycle is also an expression of the land. A river is given shape and form by the way the land responds, by the way the land both accepts and rejects the river's demands. Rivers start out strong and fast, carving a narrow course that broadens as the banks are made simultaneously wider and deeper. Depending on the slope and material make-up of the land, this might continue until the river broadens and slows, or the land might be eroded into something sharp or something as expansive as the Grand Canyon. Eventually, the river dumps the sediment that it has carried with it from the mountains and becomes broad and shallow. If the land is flat, the river is likely to change course spontaneously, as its banks give way to flood and then reform themselves in a different configuration. A river's course can be altered this way thousands of times during its lifetime. This is how the nutrient-rich soils of the prairies and plains came to exist.

Agriculture began in these broad river valleys. Some of the earliest agricultural societies came to rely on the predictable flooding of their fields, and then suffered immensely during droughts or during years in which the spring rains came either too early or too late for the grain crops they had come to depend on. Irrigation, perhaps the most consequential technological innovation of all time, provided a way of coping with both the unpredictability of rain and with the need to bring the river into places where it wouldn't find its way naturally even in times of flood—this latter need emerging from the ever-expanding population and the insatiable demand for additional land that are endemic features of agriculture.

Not all early farming societies were forced to rely on irrigation. There were those that cultivated land far away from river valleys, on steppes and hills that were rain-soaked by water squeezed out of the sky by a local mountain range. The historical descendants of most of these societies are no longer with us however, except perhaps in story and myth. Civilization as it appears today emerged from the river cultures, the irrigation cultures, the "hydraulic" cultures. The people of the steppes and hills disappeared or were absorbed into the expanding fold of the river people, conquered, eradicated, or assimilated as a consequence of the river people's potent technologies of social control, social technologies that acted as conduits for the power needed to run machines—whose physical components consisted of living people—to redirect river water, power that served to underwrite the structuring of authority needed to apportion an inequitable distribution of grain following the harvest. Power that very quickly took on a martial visage and ushered in a bloody future of perpetual war and genocidal conquests.

The river people became civilization.

The River People's Legacy

18

T HE writer looked up from his computer screen, through the rain-spattered window, and into the street beyond the front yard, searching
for an analogy. He was trying to describe the skyscraper-studded midtown
topography of a large city such as New York or Chicago. He had chosen the
word *canyon* in an attempt to capture the particular way that the massive
buildings carve up the sky and splinter the sunlight into narrow shards.
But there was something about this choice that didn't feel right. It was an
obvious cliché, for sure, but there was something more than its colloquial
overuse that bothered him. It had something to do with the suitability of
using *canyon* as metaphor to begin with. There was something problematic
in the comparison itself, something important that was being left out. Or
something being added that didn't belong. Maybe the problem was much
deeper than that, he thought. Maybe there was a problem with relying on
metaphor to begin with. Instead of embracing things for what they are in
themselves, we seem determined to make them into something else, something that they aren't.

Metaphor is a powerful thing, of course. It is extremely useful to be
able to use what we already know, what we are familiar with, as a way of
understanding something that we don't quite have a handle on—either
because it is too complex or because we don't have much actual experience with it. But the conceptual window metaphor provides can restrict
and distort and bias our view, and lead us to ignore things that are important or essential and grant undue weight to things that are trivial, or even
entirely irrelevant. Perhaps even worse, the use of metaphor and analogy

can mislead us into thinking that we understand things that we have little real ability to comprehend.

Comparing the claustrophobic, street-filled, traffic-clogged strips of shadow that wend their way through angular rows of looming buildings, comparing this to a canyon, reframes a cold and dead manufactured space in terms of a breathing world of river and rock and life—a canyon could not be more antithetical to everything that a city is. There is little life in the heart of megalopolis. There is only the machine and the stain and residue and noxious discharge left in the wake of the mechanical. A building is not a rockface, and a street is not a riverbed, and the cacophony rising from throngs of motor vehicles piloted by human desperation is nothing like the resonant stone echoes of cold mountain rain slamming into glacier meltwater on its way back to the sea; the discordant clamor of horn and siren are nothing like the driving splash of rapids or the joyful peals of cliff-dwelling birds.

The wind is one of the few things that these two places, city and canyon, share in common. Even in the heart of the city the wind finds its way through and over and around the many obstacles placed along its path—for wind, there is really no such thing as obstacle. But the wind is not the same after being strained through the maze of buildings and facades, it is not the same wind it was before, it loses much of the life and hope that it once carried over the land, the spoors and seeds of plants and trees. The wind is first and foremost a transporting medium, an agent of communication, a vehicle for olfactory messages, for pheromones, and scents, and for the particulate matter of life itself. In the city, the wind is battered and squeezed and wrung empty of these messages. In their place is the fibrous residue of fire, the poisonous byproducts of mechanical combustion, the barren waste products of disintegration and destruction, and messages of death.

Light works differently in these two places as well. The momentary slivers of sunlight that do manage to find their way to the street, as building shadows track their course through the day, fall on sterile ground, on asphalt and concrete and metal and plastic and artificial earthen forms that are insensitive to its life-giving potential, uncaring and unresponsive to its yellow warmth. There is no analogy here to the delight the small reptile along the riverbank takes in its diurnal afternoon sunbath. Nor is there anything that can compare with the water plant, with its roots that have firmly anchored it in the shallows in an eddy among the rapids, and its leaves that greet the few moments of sunlight with a flurry of metabolic activity. Or with the tree clinging to the cliffside, whose whole being is raised slightly higher each day as a result of its few precious moments of exposure to the golden rays pinching through the canyon walls.

There are animals and birds and plants and trees in the city too, the writer thought, even in the very heart of megalopolis—and there it is again, the frame of a metaphor, the notion that a city can have a heart is an example of a dangerously deceptive metaphor, one that treats a machine as a living organism. The city that is an entirely mechanical artifact, built from corpses harvested from a living forest and gouged from the Earth and powered with poison—the very antithesis of life—is cloaked in the metaphorical disguise of a sentient being. Cities have no heart. And the feverish activity that emerges from within them reflects the very opposite of sentience. Cities are colossal cemeteries boasting audacious headstones and mass graves that extend for miles and miles beyond their borders. The life that manages to cling to the cracks here does so in spite of the city, in rebellion against the city's false authority. The few wild seeds that find their way into moist places between layers of concrete, cracks in sidewalks, or the buildup of sludge in the overspill zone behind reeking dumpsters, raise their meager flag of life in revolt, as brave martyrs hoping to pry the city open, even ever-so slightly, so that others may follow, and more after them, in a tireless battle that will take centuries, perhaps, but a battle that will be won nonetheless. Time and persistence are always on the side of life.

Time and persistence have no part in the mechanical. Time is the ultimate enemy of efficiency—efficiency: the prime directive of the mechanical. And persistence is irrelevant in a consumer world where obsolescence means increased market potential. And this is the city's weakness (although, once again, to saddle the mechanical with living qualities such as strength or weakness is to disguise the truth), this is why the city will eventually fail. Time is a corrosive in the human-constructed world. Artificial constructions, social as well as physical, are unable to sustain in the face of time's perpetual passage. Persistence requires patience, and patience is not productive, patience is not conducive of efficiency. Patience is anathema to a system that runs on increasingly rapid modes of consumption. If forced to be patient, the city would wither and die in very short order. Cities simply cannot stand still. They require perpetual movement and persistent external input. It has been estimated that grocery store shelves would be empty in less than three days if supply routes into a major city were blocked. Three days is all it takes before the city's inhabitants start to starve. Without a steady input of material support from the outside, a city quickly becomes a hollow exoskeleton.

This fact is clear evidence that cities are not part of the natural order of things, the writer suddenly realized. Civilization is a wholly unnatural thing at its core, and the evidence for this is that it requires a perpetual—and perpetually accelerating—influx of artificially-generated power in order to continue to exist. Without a steady infusion of resources, civilization would very quickly fail, and this fact is evidence that civilization was not meant to exist in the first place. There is nothing else in nature that exists only through an accelerating drive to prevent its nonexistence. Natural forms of life work in the opposite fashion; the energy they generate leads to an expansion of life and of living, leads to more life. Even nonbiological forms in nature follow this general life-enhancing pattern. Granite mountains wear down into foothills, and as they do they become increasingly abundant with living things. The trajectory of physical forms is naturally life-inducing—at a bare minimum, a biological analog to the conservation of energy: the life-energy consumed results in the growth of additional life. Life can only lead to more life. When a living thing dies, its physical being does not disappear into the jungle like a Mayan temple or become desert ruins to be buried by the windswept sand. Instead, it's decaying body become a nurturing source for new growth and new life for others.

Cities run counter to this principle. Cities exist by destroying life, by making the land in and around them progressively more lifeless. Civilization exists only by leveraging death. In a sense, cities are continuously on life support. They need constant input of life-draining energy. If this energy were suddenly withdrawn, city spaces would very quickly revert back to natural patterns. In a short time, buildings and streets would crumble and be replaced by life-supporting forms. Eventually the land would recover its original nature. Eventually the land *will* recover its original nature.

The writer sat forward in his chair and deleted the word *canyon* from the sentence he had written. He looked over at the dog sprawled out on his side on the floor in the middle of the room, and smiled. "At least one of us is unencumbered by metaphor," he said. "At least one of us lives in a literal world." Old Dog smiled on the inside, because he knew that the literal world, the world as it is in itself without any symbolic embellishments, is abundant beyond measure, quite beyond what even a thousand perfect metaphors would be able to apprehend.

19

C IVILIZATION is a container. And its walls of containment are psychological as well as physical. Civilization keeps people contained largely by removing alternative ways of living, or, perhaps more accurately, by removing the choice to consider alternative ways of living.

There is no one right way for humans to live on the Earth. That's not to say that one way is as good as any other. Far from it. Civilization's extensive record of immiseration and oppression and genocide and ecological obliteration provides conclusive evidence that there is at least one wrong way. Humans are a clever and adaptive species, and have been able to find gratification and fulfillment pursuing a number of Earth-based approaches to living. But modern civilized humans are not pursuing anything close to an Earth-based approach to living. And they are not given any choice in the matter. Civilization employs two overlapping strategies for presenting itself as the only possible option. First, it physically eradicates all other options— and the people pursuing them—with maximum prejudice. Second, it makes the idea that there could be anything else virtually unthinkable for a civilized mind.

Civilization is a container, but it is not yet a big enough container to hold everyone. There are still a small smattering of indigenous foragers living in the shrinking outer penumbra of the civilized world, in desert areas of Tanzania and deep in what still remains of the Amazon rain forest. In addition, natural human variation and individual uniqueness make it difficult for a system that puts a premium on standardization, homogenization, and blind obedience, to permanently ensnare everyone, and there are a few folks who slip through the cracks. But even here, civilization has a strategy to assert its topsy-turvy perspective. It employs a subtle but effective form of gaslighting: if you don't fit into the civilized order, there is obviously something wrong with *you*. The onus is always on the individual if they are finding it hard to adapt to the strictures of a civilized lifestyle; it is up to the person to mold themselves into a suitable form to meet the demands of civilization, never the other way around. Civilization demands, people conform. Civilization does not make concessions for idiosyncrasy. Civilized systems will adjust themselves—where they are able to adjust at all—only in order to achieve more exacting and wide-spread conformity.

Civilization is a container, but it is a leaky container. The problem—for people, not so much for civilization itself—is that there is nowhere for the people who spill out of it to go. A small minority of those who spill out manage to fall back into something approaching an authentically human way of life, a way of life not unlike the one Old Dog was living: a way of life that involves living *with* rather than living *in* civilization. This is, however, much harder for humans than it is for dogs. Civilization has little tolerance for explicit rejection. Rejection by dogs is one thing. Domestic animals are inferior creatures who don't really know what they are doing. And even if they did, their rejection carries no real consequence. But when it comes to humans who push back against the demand that they pursue a civilized lifestyle, things are much different. Rejection by humans runs the risk of exposing civilization's most dangerous secret, its greatest and most closely guarded secret, the secret that civilization can only exist through the persistent, unquestioning, moment-by-moment acquiescence of each of its individual human inhabitants. Rejection by even a single human runs the risk of spreading through the system like a California wildfire unless that rejection is shown to be an error, a severe defect in the person. Anyone who would reject civilization is broken, mentally deficient, suffering from serious psychological disorder. And the evidence for this is in the act of rejection itself: only a mentally defective person would reject civilization because civilization is all there really is. You might as well reject oxygen.

Civilization is a container, and it has an expanding arsenal of weapons to protect its many systems of containment and control from anyone who might try to do them harm. The most effective of these weapons are psychological in nature, and are employed proactively when people are very young to keep them firmly yoked to the machine's drivetrain throughout their lives. But there are structural and institutional weapons as well, and undergirding both the psychological and institutional is the perpetual threat of lethal violence: no one is ever *asked* to conform to the system. Civilization's self-protective systems do have one weakness, however. Civilization is well equipped to protect itself from blatant rejection and direct attack, but it has absolutely no way of protecting itself from simple abandonment. There is nothing to prevent anyone from just getting up and quietly walking away.

Nothing, that is, except that there are fewer and fewer places to get up and walk away to. For many people, there is simply nowhere else they can go, nowhere that is not civilization. But having no place else to go is not a particularly pernicious problem for those few who are willing to put up with the uncertainty and discomfort of living a noncivilized life in the midst of civilization itself, those few who are able to fall back upon their evolved instincts and tap into the latent spirit and temperament of their Paleolithic ancestors. Walking away, after all, is built into the very definition of a nomadic hunter-gatherer. And there are an increasing number of folks who are adopting a way of life—either by choice or by fiat—that involves doing just that, a way of life that involves living *with* rather than living *in* civilization.

These people have been called by a variety of names in the past: vagrants, vagabonds, drifters (descriptive terms that highlight the nomadic character of their lifestyle), hobos, panhandlers, or beggars. Nowadays, they are most commonly referred to as *homeless*. This term, homeless, yet again demonstrates the topsy-turvy, inside out perspective being imposed on the civilized. Past terms tended either to highlight their nomadic lifestyle or to provide a description of how they were making a living (panhandling, begging). But *homeless* presents these folks as defective and deficient in a fundamental way—perhaps even the most fundamental way possible for the civilized: lacking any place to call home. There is no logical reason, for example, for not using a term such as "economically-free," or "burden-limited," or simply "unfettered," terms that put the focus on what has been added to their lives by disconnecting from civilization's drivetrain rather than highlighting what they are subsequently missing. With *homeless*, the focus is on the absence of a single thing, a deficiency of residence, rather than on the positive and negative realities of their situation.

And, taken at face value, *homeless* is not a very good description of anything. *Home* doesn't necessarily refer to a specific structure or physical location. It might be argued that nobody is really homeless. They are always living somewhere. And if that somewhere changes daily, that place no less qualifies as a home. But the term *homeless* caries entailments that go beyond the idea of not having a legitimate quasi-permanent physical residence.

In its noun form, homelessness, it becomes a state of being, one that is frequently considered on par with disease. The link between homelessness and disease is an easy one to make because many of the people "afflicted" with homelessness are also suffering from actual diseases—physical ones, such as kidney disease, liver disease, and substance dependence, and less-obviously physical ones such as PTSD, bipolar disorder, and schizophrenia. In addition, the stressors of civilized life can lead to symptoms of all kinds of anxiety and depressive disorders. Some folks are more susceptible to fall-out from these afflictions than are others, and many of these folks end up living on the street.

In reality, civilization causes homelessness. Civilization creates the very possibility of homelessness. But, from civilization's point of view, the individual is at fault, the homeless person bears the blame for their inability to accommodate the social and economic demands of civilization. And, so, homelessness implies a mental disease. To choose the option of home-lessness, either through mismanagement of your fate or through conscious decision, is clear evidence of your disordered state of being.

Old Dog had come across a number of these folks in his daily excur-sions up and down the riverbank. Most kept to themselves in the unspoken way of the other beings he shared his travels with. A few of them greeted him with soft words and choice morsels from their own limited cache. He felt a strong affinity for these people. Like him, many of them were lone foragers living off the overabundant consumer effluence of civilization. They were all part of the same extended pack, at least in spirit. They were comrades. He watched them closely, and learned from them. They intro-duced him to sources of food and fresh water, and places to shelter from the elements. Because they had to carry everything with them wherever they went, most of them traveled lightly. Instead of stockpiling what they needed for future scarcity, they collected a variety of different methods for obtain-ing what they needed when they needed it. If one method was blocked, they usually had an array of alternative methods to choose from. And they were patient, and only rarely displayed outward signs of desperation (although, as he would eventually learn, there are deep layers to desperation that don't always make their way to the surface). Many of them seemed to understand something that Old Dog was only just discovering: the world is abundant and will always eventually provide.

One day, his food search took him farther upstream than usual, past the restaurants and the city park and to the east where the buildings were newer and more thickly spaced and more heavily occupied, one in particular was active with machines that hissed and screamed, and with people dressed in armored masks holding sticks that threw blue and orange sparks. The noise scared him, and caused him to retreat reflexively to the protection of the rocky river bank. As he scratched his way along the waterline, between scrub brush and the partially-submerged eroding remains of an old building foundation, he stepped into an open area under a tall graffiti-adorned rust-and-water-stained concrete railroad overpass, and into a crowd of people. Maybe not a crowd, exactly, but their unexpected presence magnified their actual numbers, which were perhaps something just under a dozen.

He recognized some of them. He had seen them in the park and on street corners and in front of the restaurants in the evenings. The man with the overstuffed backpack who fed him the burrito on his first day in the city was there, his overstuffed backpack resting under his knee as he leaned against a stack of broken pallets. Most of the others were also men, but there were women too. And a wide range of skin colors. And there was a boy who looked to be only a few years older than Paul. The boy was smoking a cigarette and tending a steaming kettle perched over a blackened metal barrel. He smiled broadly when he saw Old Dog, got the attention of two of the men standing close by on the other side of the barrel, and nodded his head in Old Dog's direction; the men turned and looked Old Dog's way.

He felt a sudden hand on his back, and jumped sideways startled. The man belonging to the hand laughed. "A bit skittish, hey? It's OK, boy. Not gonna hurt you." Old Dog lowered his head in a pose that would have shown submission if he presented it to another dog, and the man responded by giving his forehead a soft touch, followed by several slow stroking pets down the back of his neck. Old Dog folded his hind legs, dropped his butt to the ground, and leaned into the man's rough hand.

After a while, another man joined him and the two started talking about the last dog that they had around here, and how they missed her. They speculated on what might have happened, and decided that she had probably been scooped up by animal control during the last sweep.

Some of the folks were sitting or standing around makeshift shelters, lean-tos made from creative combinations of fabric and plastic and cardboard, perhaps a small piece of plywood or corrugated metal. A few people had actual camping tents, in various stages of disrepair. All of them were nestled out of the prevailing wind toward one end under the broad concrete overpass—which Old Dog could now see was the leadup section of a bridge over the river. One of the women had a shopping cart loaded with sundry items sitting just outside the protective concrete overhang. She had taken a blanket and stretched it from the side of the cart to the ground and anchored the corners with rocks to create a shady retreat from the late-morning sun, which was signaling that it would be another hot day.

Old dog stayed at the homeless camp for the remainder of the morning and into the afternoon, moving from person to person, registering and committing their scent to memory. The mood in the camp was calm and relaxed. The few conversations that sprang up were friendly and punctuated with laughter. No one paid much notice when someone came or went. No one seemed to give Old Dog's presence among them a second thought. It was as if he belonged there as much as anyone else did.

In the weeks to follow, Old Dog made the homeless camp a regular stop on his daily river walk. He didn't make it there every day at first, but on more days than not. He learned the name of the man who approached him from behind when he first stumbled into camp was Carl. Carl always greeted him with a pat on the head and a tidbit of food and a smile. By the time the summer grew to a close, he had abandoned his previous base outside the old buildings downstream, and spent his nights under the overpass. He slept off to the side of the main camp, in a position where he could see the camp in its entirety, and also keep an eye on the two main pathways into it, one from the river and another from the street. Later he would learn that one of the theories for why humans and dogs originally connected— as usual, presented from a human perspective—was that humans started keeping dogs around as sentries to warn them of the approach of animals or potentially dangerous people. Of course, that is a major way that dogs have been employed by humans into the present. Old Dog naturally fell into the role of sentry. He liked these people. He recognized in them a kind of strength and persistence that he had only recently noticed within himself. But he also saw that they were vulnerable. Their vulnerability was clearly on display as he watched them on their daily rounds. He felt that they needed his protection, even if all that he was able to do was to bark a warning.

It felt good to be around people again. In a short time, he began to think of these folks as his family, his pack. He kept to his dawn and dusk foraging schedule, for the most part. And although some days were spent napping in his old shelter areas downstream, his nights were spent with the people in the camp.

20

OLD Dog woke, and the world appeared before him fully formed, down to the smallest detail. This did not surprise him, of course. The same thing happened each time he emerged from a long nap, the entire universe fell into place as if all things were meant to be exactly the way they happened to be at that very moment, every nuance, every subtle shade of scent and sound, every shadow, every leaf and every bent blade of grass resting precisely where it had to be.

But this time, for some reason, that last part was a problem for him, that "things had to be exactly the way they happened to be" part. Why? What was it, exactly, about the way that things were that made them *have* to be that way? Was there something privileged about this particular configuration of the universe as opposed to any one of an infinite number of other possibilities? To say that things just happened to be the way they are doesn't make the present moment anything more or less than it would be if things had happened differently than they did. Maybe the problem had something to do with the idea of *possibility*. On the one hand—or paw, as it were— things can never be even the slightest bit different than they actually end up being. But on the other hand—or another paw—it is exceedingly easy to imagine that things could have ended up differently.

Possibility only applies to things that haven't yet happened. But humans, he noticed, seem to point *possibility* in the reverse direction as well, toward the past. They are frequently absorbed in thoughts of what might have happened differently. So much so that they often undervalue, or completely ignore, what actually *did* happen, they undervalue the way things actually are. They spend much of their time and energy with counterfactuals, contemplating worlds that are counter to the concrete facts of the world they actually occupy, struggling with ideas of what could have been—or what, in their arrogance, they think *should* have been. "If only *this* happened instead of *that* . . . ." "If only she did X instead of Y . . . ." "If only he had chosen left instead of right . . . ." I should have . . . ." I shouldn't have . . . ."

Dogs don't think counterfactually. At least ordinary dogs don't. For dogs, what happens happens—it happens for reasons, mind you, dogs are sensitive to cooccurrence, and, like humans, they have an instinctual bias to see the world in terms of cause and effect. And, like humans, they learn from past experience. But they never replay altered versions of the past in order to imagine different outcomes. As a result, dogs are immune to the common human maladies of regret and recrimination. Dogs never feel guilt or seek forgiveness, because they can't imagine having done anything differently than they in fact did at the time. And for similar reasons, although they quickly learn to treat those who have done them wrong accordingly, they never blame or carry grudges: what's done is done. They also can never be deeply disappointed—at least not in the ways that humans can. When things don't go quite as planned, they shrug it off and work with what is happening now. Goals—to the limited extent that dogs have actual goals— are always moving targets, not destinations carved in stone.

But Old Dog was not an ordinary dog. His entanglement with human abstractions, his frequent immersion in symbolic thought, had left him with an uncomfortable awareness of the shear impossibility of the world as it was. And the creeping sense that things didn't have to be the way they actually were threatened to open a floodgate of unanswerable questions about *why* things had turned out the specific ways that they did.

His canine sensibilities understood that this was silly. The question *why* will forever be unanswerable because it is unaskable. There is no way of formulating the question that doesn't assume a hidden purpose. The universe can never be anything other than it turns out to be, and the fact that it turned out the specific way that it did provides absolute and unassailable proof of that. *What* can have answers. *How* can have answers. *When* and *where* can have answers. But *why* yields only figments, fantasies, and illusions.

And for humans, the formless shadow of *why* frequently twists itself into a labyrinthine passage that leads them deep into a counterfactual past.

There was substantial turnover in the camp, with people leaving and returning, and new people replacing ones that never came back. Some spent only a single night or two before moving on. Old Dog came to know all of the regulars. He eavesdropped on their conversations. He spent time with each one individually, sometimes several days in a row. He kept them company on street corners and traffic medians while they held cardboard signs scribbled with pleas for material assistance. He sprawled on the grass next to Carl while he played his beat-up guitar in the park downtown on the weekends. He found that everyone had a story, a history, a unique personal tale to tell. If asked why they were in the camp and living like they were, most would answer that it was bad decisions, or drugs and alcohol, or a failed marriage, or a lost job, or just plain bad luck—or a combination of these things and perhaps something else. Consider the unique stories of just a few of the folks currently living in the camp:

There is Malcom, the man who had tossed Old Dog a burrito on his first day in the city. Malcom is in his mid-fifties, and spends most afternoons standing at the exit to a grocery store parking lot holding a sign that says "God Bless – Anything Helps." He has been living on the street for several years now as a result of a series of catastrophes, each one probably manageable if it had occurred separately; even then, things wouldn't have been so bad if they hadn't all happened in such rapid succession. First, he lost his job at the auto parts store where he worked for almost twenty years when the company invested in a new computerized inventory system which allowed them to get rid of half of their front-counter customer service employees. His wife left him shortly after that. She had been seeing his best friend for years, and was unable to keep the affair secret once Malcom was no longer spending his days at work. Then, right when his unemployment benefits ran out, he had a series of strokes that left his face partially paralyzed on one side. He was unable to pay either the hospital bills or the rent, and, with no family or friends to turn to, he ended up on the street. His facial paralysis makes him look like he is always angry, and most of the folks in the camp leave him alone as a result. Which is a shame, because he is an exceedingly kind person, as Old Dog had already discovered, and very pleasant company.

Mike knows and appreciates that about Malcom, and is pretty much the only one who talks to Malcom on a regular basis. Mike graduated from college a year and a half ago but was unable to find a job, and bounced from one friend's couch to another until he wore out his welcome and ran out of friends with couches. Unlike most of the other folks in the camp, he has an easy way off the street if he needs it. He has family on the other side of the country who are fairly well-off, and they would help him out in a heartbeat if they knew the truth about his circumstances. But there is some bad blood between him and his stepdad, and Mike, for the time being at least, would rather just ride things out and see what turns up.

Denise is in her mid-thirties, but looks like she is twenty years older. She has struggled with depression for most of her life, and had treated it with alcohol and then more recently with heroin and meth. She was evicted from her apartment a few years ago, and then completely fell apart. She has been arrested several times for drug possession and prostitution since, but has been clean now for seven weeks and counting, and is currently trying to scrounge up enough money for some decent clothes so she can start looking for a job. She spends almost every day leaning against a light pole at the end of a freeway offramp a half-mile walk from the camp, holding a commercially printed metal sign that says "Thank you for your kindness" that she found in an alley behind a craft store.

Carl, not quite fifty, is a vagabond in the fifteenth century sense of the word. He has a low tolerance for boredom, and has never been able to hold a steady job. At some point he simply gave up trying, and has been living on the street off and on for more than a decade. He is pretty good with the guitar, and makes enough money busking on the weekends to keep him fed and provide for his minimum material needs. He stays at his daughter's place during the winter when the weather turns cold.

Jane is in her forties. She lives out of her shopping cart and looks like the stock character street lady from a 1980s television police drama. She was diagnosed with schizoaffective disorder when she was a teenager and has been in and out of psychiatric hospitals most of her life. She talks to herself all day long, repeating the same profanity-laced argument over and over—alternating between both sides and changing voices as she does. It isn't entirely clear from the outside what the argument is about, but it is a heated dispute and neither side has any affection for the other. She lives by a strict routine, with each day almost a precise repeat of the one before. Her shopping cart contains a few useless trinkets, a large plastic container of water, about a week's supply of food, some clothing, and more than a dozen pairs of shoes that are not her size. She keeps mostly to herself, but gives freely from her cart to others who are in need.

Jeff is the kid. He calls Jane "Granny," and tells everyone he's twenty-one years old although he is only fifteen. Nobody really believes he is twenty-one, but nobody really cares. Jeff is a runaway who escaped an extremely abusive family situation and has been hiding out on the street since he was twelve. He spends a lot of time with Juan, who works occasional construction jobs and quickly drinks away his wages at a nearby bar. Juan was living in his van until it broke down and the city put it in an impound lot, where it sits right now because he can't afford to have it fixed. Juan is a recent addition to the camp, and has the nicest tent.

There isn't a common thread weaving through these stories. Each of these people is unique and one of a kind, and yet they all ended up, at least for the moment, in the same place. If they have anything in common at all, it isn't the specific things that brought them to this place, it's that they are each a victim of a system that produces places like this as part of its normal operations. And let's be clear, homelessness is a product of civilization—literally something that civilization creates from scratch. Homelessness is allowed to exist because it serves the needs of civilization. In modern consumer society, the threat of poverty is useful as a negative motivator: one of the sticks hovering menacingly behind corporate marketing's many dangling carrots. The threat of poverty serves as the primary fuel driving the gears of the consumption machine; and homelessness acts as a catalyst for this fuel by endowing the abstract threat of poverty with a concrete, visible face.

The idea of *home* itself is a civilized invention, and the modern concept of *home* is a fairly recent one. Not *home* in its trivial sense, *home* as a place of residence, a person's house or condo or apartment or yurt or trailer or mud hut, the place where someone currently sleeps, but *home* in its deeper sense, *home* as a place of origin, that quasi-mythical place that forms the cornerstone in the foundation of a person's self-concept, the place that emerges as the answer to the question, "Where are you from?"

Places that were of formative value and that carry a sense of personal connection and attachment have probably always been part of the human milieu. But home, as a concept, as a place where you belong (*be long*: a place of long-term occupation) is a product of an agrarian lifestyle, a sedentary lifestyle tied to specific parcels of tended land, to pastures and fields, to villages and permanent dwellings. Home is a product of *domestication*—a word that itself derives from the Latin for home, *domus*. The verb *to domesticate,* to tame, comes from a Medieval Latin word that means literally to make a product of the household. The idea of home is at the very core of domestication as a way of life, and part of what distinguishes the civilized from the noncivilized.

What does home mean to a nomadic forager? If there is anything in such a society that corresponds even remotely to the civilized idea of home, it is either something so expansive that it encompasses entire regions of habitation, or it is something that travels with them, something that involves proximity to specific other people as much or more than it does to a specific physical place, something that moves with the person, a perpetually shifting zone that is determined by the active requirements of the moment, a zone that is defined by the center—quite literally "where the heart is." Modern city-dwellers have become increasingly nomadic in recent years. But this is nomadism of a different kind from that of a hunter-gatherer. It is a punctate nomadism in which the person moves from one temporary "permanent residence" to another. Modern civilized life is, for many people, a series of displacements leading to a perpetual sense of dislocation. Home becomes nostalgia for a permanence of place that in reality rarely exists, a Norman Rockwell painting of a place out of time.

Civilized humans are living in diaspora, scattered and dislocated not only from the geographic origins of their various ancestral cultures, but from their ecological origins as a species. It might seem somewhat paradoxical that this global dislocation has its source in the prehistorical emergence of sedentary ways of life, ways of life based on domestication. But there is no paradox. What would it mean to say that a hunter-gatherer is homeless? How can you be homeless if everywhere you go is equally your home, if the entire living Earth is your home?

Prior to domestication, nomadic and semi-nomadic lifestyles were the norm, with people moving from place to place according to the migration patterns of preferred animal food sources, seasonal changes in weather and the subsequent availability of preferred plant food sources, and long-term changes in climate: drought and the varieties of its opposite. Prior to domestication, the word diaspora would be meaningless. From one angle, just about everyone was living in a place different from where they were born. And from another, the idea of *place* was so expansive, involving such vast regions of geography, that nobody was living in a place other than the one in which they were born.

The largest and most extensive diaspora began when humans were first torn away from their natural ways of living and forced to adopt sedentary domestication-based lifeways. All other forms of dislocation pale in comparison to this first fundamental displacement, a displacement that has been reenacted again and again on every inhabited continent. It begins with contact, with civilization's expanding event horizon pushing into spaces occupied by the noncivilized. This initial phase is followed almost immediately by the next two, colonization and genocide—two words for variations in intensity of the same thing: the forceful dislodging of a people from their traditional ways of being in the world.

The violence of dislocation is frequently diminished by the filter of historical hindsight. History, as hindsight, assumes that the present state of things lies lurking, incipient and inchoate, in the past. The results of the civilizing process, as brutal and bloody as they always are, become, through hindsight, inevitabilities, necessary evils—or, more frequently, the very opposite of evil: positive changes, progress. But historical hindsight focuses on the abstract, it speaks in generalities, whereas the civilizing process, as process, occurs at the micro level, at the level of the individual person, where the process continues even among those who already live within civilization's walls of containment. It occurs in children, where it is easy to see, and moment by moment throughout adult life, where indigenous thoughts and desires are colonized and quashed and redirected to serve institutional "needs."

The homeless camp and the many others like it are clear evidence that there are some serious bugs in this redirection process.

21

A SILENT dawn. The drone of the city was muted behind pink morning fog. The leaves held a thin silver glazing of dew—a not-quite frost clung to the very tips like miniscule tinsel, quietly announcing the first day of fall. Old Dog had recently returned from a brief pre-morning sortie downstream, and was lying on his belly on a small rise by the railroad tracks overlooking the camp. A few of the people below were awake and quietly collecting their bodies into workable upright positions. Someone had thrown a couple pieces of damp pallet wood on the coals from last night's barrel fire, and the resulting black smoke was failing to merge with the fog like a muddy Amazon tributary pushing its own unique species of sediment into the river's main channel.

The morning calm in the camp was dissipating, and in its place was a gradually intensifying buzz, an undercurrent of excitement and anticipation that started low and sporadic, but quickly pressed toward a crescendo and spread to all corners. Old Dog hadn't noticed anything different, hadn't heard or smelled anything unusual. His ears almost always told him when something new was happening that he might need to pay attention to, and his nose was usually able to get confirmation long before anyone in the camp noticed, but this time both his ears and nose were a blank. There was a palpable new energy in the camp, and a repeated name being spoken and breathed: "Maddy." From his perch, he was able to trace the undercurrent of intensity upstream toward its source, to a rust-faded blue Ford pickup truck with an old-style over-the-cab camper shell, parked just off the street on the dusty grass by the far side of the overpass—the blind side, as it was referred to by the folks in the camp. Its driver, a stout middle-aged woman with long graying red hair piled into a frayed top-knot, stepped out with quick stilted movements and greeted everyone with a prolonged double-hand wave. She then reversed and lowered the wave of one hand and motioned two of the men closest to her over. The men followed her around the back of the truck, and returned, each carrying a produce box loaded with full paper shopping bags. After a couple more trips, seven large boxes sat lined up beside each other on the dew-damp ground.

Slowly, in no rush but persistently, excitedly, everyone in the camp got up and gathered around the boxes. "Got this yesterday from Greene's on Third," the woman said with a flourish of her hand. Her voice had the sonorous and ragged bark of a chain smoker, but nonetheless possessed a melodic quality that was not unpleasant. "They're going out of business and had all this neatly stacked 'round back by the loading docks. One of the guys said they were just going to toss it out. He winked at me and said he'd look the other way if I wanted any of it. So, I took the lot. Lots of stuff here, even some of that canned spray cheese!" She pulled out a couple bags and reached into one, returning with a six-pack of off-brand cola, and handed it to Juan, who was one of the men who had helped her with the boxes. "Looks like some old Easter candy. Some clothes too. Hats. And baby blankets! Carl, I think there's that can opener you're always looking for in there somewhere too!"

"Jesus, Christmas in September!" Carl replied, with more than a slight hint of sarcasm and a knowing smile that suggested the can opener was part of a private joke.

"Maddy, you fucking rock," someone else said, matter-of-factly and with no hint of sarcasm whatsoever.

During all of the excitement, Old Dog watched from his spot above the camp, enthralled. He had seen scenes like this on television. In the movies he watched with the kids, scenes like this were always fraught with competition and violence. He recalled news footage showing people trampling each other when the doors of a Walmart were opened on the morning of Black Friday, as people pushed their way into the store to be the first to load their carts up with consumer products that were being offered at an only slightly reduced price. And those were people who already had everything they really needed. The folks in the camp had almost nothing at all. For some of them it was a coinflip each day as to whether they would go to sleep that night hungry. Despite that, they were calm and unhurried; each person seemed to be more concerned that everyone else got what they needed, offering the people around them something before taking it for themselves.

During his time in the camp, Old Dog made several curious observations about the camp's social structure—or lack of structure, as it were. Despite the variety of shelters—some clearly inadequate for the rain and the increasingly cold mornings, and some clear disparities in both the quality and quantity of possessions, the camp lacked any suggestion of an economic status hierarchy. In addition, there didn't seem to be anyone in charge. At times he thought that he could detect a loosely shifting social hierarchy based on age or seniority in the camp, or some combination of these. Each person had their own unique range of social influence, but if there was any status or power hierarchy at all, it was ephemeral and situational, and tended to be based on a person's implicit claim to relevant prior experience. Arguments were not infrequent, but usually very minor and short-lived. There also seemed to be a strong sense of equity among the members of the camp, coupled with a culture of reciprocity. For the most part, those who had more of something shared with others who were in need—and each day the composition of the had-mores and the in-needs changed, so that over the course of time any one person was likely to spend at least some time in both groups.

Maddy's gifts distributed themselves quickly, despite the calm demeanor of the recipients. And even the empty boxes and bags were spoken for and collected by the time Old Dog made his way down the hill and into the camp a short while later. Maddy spent the remainder of the morning making the rounds, telling a story or two and talking about politics and the news of the day. She sat with Jane, next to her blanket-shopping cart shelter, for quite some time, smoking cigarettes and telling stories about "bullshit doctors" and discussing the pros and cons of various psychiatric medications. Jane would occasionally interrupt her own perpetual two-sided monolog to respond in agreement.

Maddy, like the folks in the camp, didn't give Old Dog much thought as he laid down between her and Jane. She eventually looked over at him and casually reached out and scratched him between the ears. "Whose dog?" she asked.

"Nobody's," Jeff said. He was sitting close by, working his way through a boxed fruit drink from the stash of items he had collected from the stuff Maddy brought. "Just showed up one day. He's pretty chill."

"Friendly mutt," Denise agreed. "Comes and goes, but seems to like it here."

"I take him spanging with me at the Safeway sometimes," Malcom said. "Always good for an extra five or ten bucks."

Maddy took a closer look at Old Dog, fumbled with the ratty remains of the collar that still hung around his neck despite the fact that it looked like it might fall off any moment. It was little more than a dust-colored strap. The D-ring and tags had long since disappeared, snagged by a branch or scratched loose against the side of a garbage can. And, in truth, Old Dog could just shake it off if he had wanted to. But he didn't. It had become a nostalgic token of his past, perhaps a reminder of his present freedom.

"What are you about, old boy?" she asked him directly.

He responded by standing up, turning her direction, and then tilting his head forward into her lap. That was the best he could do as an answer. What he wanted to do was tell her everything about how he had come to understand himself and the world, how he thought of the people of the camp as his family, how he was still learning about humans and still in the dark about many things, how he still had so many questions. Why did my first family keep me tied up alongside the porch for so long and then simply toss me away on the side of the road? Why do the boys in the park throw rocks at me sometimes? Why do the people at the tables outside the restaurants have so much food while the people in the camp have to stand in line at the mission or beg for handouts or grub for cold leftovers? Where does the light in the street lamps come from?

All of these thoughts and questions and many more flowed out of his simple head tilt. Maddy sighed heavily, and, as if she had heard every word, said, "Yes, yes, I know, old boy, it's a crazy fucked-up world," as she stroked the back of his neck.

22

Freud's idea of libido, an instinctual force that forms the motivational base of all thought and action, seems ridiculous from a twenty-first century perspective. Even more so if considered in terms of its close relation to medieval vitalism, the idea of an animating spirit, a mystical force inhabiting all living bodies. Something similar among the ancient Greeks as well, perhaps, in the notion of psyche, the source of breath and life. All of these ideas point to something that is simultaneously intangible and fundamental. It seems obvious that there is something that drives people, something that compels them, some principle of movement that manifests itself in their motives and then translates those motives into actions.

Invoking libido or vital spirits or psyche doesn't provide a satisfactory explanation, however. It doesn't explain the different forms in which motive can manifest itself. It doesn't explain a given action's specificity. It doesn't explain the specific direction that action takes. It doesn't explain the action's target. Target and direction come from the outside, from externally-imposed limits, and from opportunities afforded by the world itself, limits and opportunities that arise from the unique contingencies of circumstance. People are tightly wound springs seeking to uncoil themselves. They are packets of potential energy ready to exhaust themselves into the present moment. And the world provides abundant means for rendering this potential energy into a wide variety of kinetic forms. A major part of how civilization controls its inhabitants is by channeling this primordial energy: civilization redirects this energy away from its natural, instinctual expression and toward civilized targets. There is something hopeful, perhaps even empowering, in the knowledge that civilization is not yet entirely successful at this. At the same time, however, there is frequently something painful and tragic in the ways that civilization tries and fails.

It was a gray afternoon, a couple weeks after Maddy's visit. A light rain had just begun to fall when City Hope converged on the camp with police vans, a large city sanitation truck, and a half-dozen baton-wielding cops wearing blue latex gloves. City Hope, a police department team tasked with breaking up homeless camps, was mobilized after the mayor launched a city-wide homeless sweep in preparation for an upcoming political campaign rally headlined by the US vice president. The rationalization for the sweep was the need to bolster downtown security. The real reason, however, was purely one of optics. The city had to put on its best face for when national news media swarmed into town.

The people in the camp were loudly and violently pushed and prodded out of their tents and shelters. A few tried to slip away down the path by the river while others made their way for the blind side, but more cops were waiting to force them to the ground face first, zip-tie their wrists behind their backs, yank them back to their feet, and march them toward the waiting vans.

Old Dog was hiding behind a low pile of concrete and rebar demolition waste at the near edge of the camp and watched as Jane's hands were pried from her shopping cart, and the cart, loaded with everything she had in the world, was tossed into the back of the sanitation truck. He watched as Malcom, his face bleeding from a baton butt, was pushed into a van. He watched as the tents were ripped from their stakes, and the make-shift shelters were kicked over and torn apart. He watched as the camp under the bridge was turned into a wasteland.

"Looks like we got a dog over here," one of the cops said from somewhere close by. Old Dog sprinted across the open area and dove behind the stack of rotting pallets. Two of the cops followed him, one with his gun drawn. Old Dog felt the pain in his leg before he registered the gunshot. The bullet had just missed him as it tore through the corner of a pallet, temporarily embedding a sharp chunk of wood shrapnel in his hind leg just below his hip. He yelped and dashed between the two cops, and was able to make it to the thorny brambles behind the pier closest to the river before they could take another shot. He hid in the brambles until the police had gone and the last of the shelter scraps was loaded into the sanitation truck, and then limped his way upstream, into the increasing rain and a growing darkness.

When dawn broke, he crawled out from a hollow beneath a fallen tree where he had slept out of the rain, and continued his eastward journey toward the outskirts of town. The pain in his leg had subsided somewhat during the night, but his injury had swollen and his leg was stiff, making his movements labored and clumsy. In a short time, he found himself outside the city's acoustic bubble, away from the steady mechanical drone, farther upstream than he had been before. The air felt different here. The composite stench of the city still dominated the olfactory landscape, but there were new smells riding on top of it, fresh-mown grass and sun-rotted fruit. The buildings became few and far between, and then disappeared entirely, replaced by more and more trees. He kept to the river as it swung sharply to the north where the surrounding terrain flattened out into a rocky floodplain.

The change of external topography, the transition from city to something more primal and natural, was accompanied by a change in Old Dog's internal landscape. He could feel the tightness in his leg start to ease. He could also feel a general undefined tension that he hadn't noticed before— and the only reason he noticed it now was because it was starting to subside. The city weighed on his body, and he could feel the weight falling off as he stumbled his way over rocks caked with a semi-dry crust of whitish mud. The rocks were surrounded by life, tiny creatures and clouds of flying midges, and even the mud, as it fragmented into geometric chunks under his feet, gave off a smell of decay that signaled that it too was infused with life. The far side of the river was a mirror image of this one, with two marmots chasing each other around the rocks straight across from him on the other side, completing the sense of reflection.

And then, an event occurred that he would return to again and again in the future to marvel simultaneously at its sheer improbability and at its nodal significance in his life. He was making his way closer to the tree line to get out of the direct late morning sun that had already eliminated most signs of last night's rainstorm, when he came across a rust-faded blue pickup truck with an old-style over-the-cab camper shell on top of it, angled into a narrow gap in a small grove of trees at the edge of a monochrome expanse of boney mud-coated rocks. On a lawn chair next to the truck, reading a book with an age-worn cover, was a middle-aged woman with long graying red hair piled into a frayed knot on top of her head. Maddy.

Human Tools

23

T HE writer leaned back in his chair, rubbed his bristly chin, and began reading the screed he had been working on out loud from the screen in front of him:

"My computer welcomes me by name when I turn it on in the morning. The ATM machine thanks me for withdrawing money from my own bank account. The screen on the pay-pad at the supermarket thanks me for my patience. The sign at the top of the stairway asks me to please watch my step. Doors of public businesses explicitly welcome me as I enter and thank me as I exit. Other doors thank me for shutting them behind me.

"The absurdity of this slides right past us; that a mechanical device could be welcoming or feel thankful for anything is ridiculous on its face; that a wall or door or posted sign could act as some kind of conduit for the expression of polite sentiments is ludicrous. The disembodied words 'welcome' and 'please' and 'thank you' appearing on an electronic screen are utterly empty of content. The warning, 'Watch your step' is meaningful—and, in some cases, meaningful to the point of being life-saving—but the addition of 'please' is entirely gratuitous, beyond superfluous.

"Is all of this simply more evidence of the technological outsourcing of our humanity? Perhaps. But if so, it is the outsourcing of a humanity that was long ago stripped bare of its human authenticity. The very idea of politeness, as a separate category of action, is evidence of the degradation of human authenticity. Wild humans engaged in authentically human interactions have no need for please and thank you. To say please and to beg—to *plead*—come to the same thing. In an authentically human society, an egalitarian society where all have access and all give freely, there is little or no need to ask. In such a society, 'thank you' is a brutal insult: to thank someone is to say that their kindness was unexpected."

Old Dog had been listening carefully as the writer read from the critique he was working on—part of an essay on morality that he had been commissioned to write for an obscure monthly magazine. But it wasn't just politeness that was being outsourced, Old Dog thought. It was virtually every aspect of public life, along with a sizeable and rapidly expanding chunk of personal life as well.

This is an inevitable result of the division of labor that emerged when people adopted sedentary lifestyles based around domestication. Once division of labor, and the culture of specialization and expertise that it spawns, becomes part of the normal functioning of society, people get used to relying—*depending*—on someone else to provision their needs. And once reliance on others is firmly established and incorporated as a normal and expected part of life, there is no reason that the targets of reliance should not also include nonhuman things. In a culture of specialization and dependence, humans are not really acting as humans anyway. That is, you are not really dependent on the person *as a person*; you are dependent on what the person is doing, the role they are playing; you are dependent on the person acting as a mechanism in the process, as a device. And lately, with the rise and proliferation of complex digital technologies, nonhuman things are being designed more and more in ways that purposely blur the distinction between what is human and what is device into complete invisibility. Merely speak your needs aloud, and a pleasantly modulated human-sounding voice responds.

There is an interesting relationship between the prehistorical emergence of division of labor and the evolution of complex technology. Mediation is an essential feature of both. Day-to-day life in a traditional nomadic foraging society is substantially unmediated; each individual person has direct control of what they do and when they do it. No one has to wait for anyone else's approval before they act. And they don't have to rely on anyone else in any significant way for providing any of the materials that they need in order to act. And—this is probably the most important thing—there is nothing standing between the person and the resources the person needs to survive, beyond the physical state of the world itself and the person's own momentary whims and desires.

This is absolutely not true for day-to-day life in sedentary farming society. The complexity and cooperative collectivity of an agricultural lifestyle requires each person to be dependent on the scheduled and scripted input of other people. This quickly leads to specialization, and as specialization increases, each individual becomes more deeply dependent on the work and commitment of an increasing number of other people. If any one of these other people stop doing their job, everyone else suffers the effects.

All technologies, complex or otherwise, are mediational in the same sort of way. They serve as intermediaries between the users of the technology and various features of the world to which the technology is being directed. This is precisely what they are designed to do, and a technology's mediational functions are its whole purpose to begin with. But what is not often recognized is the extent to which technology can distance its users from reality, and lead to increasingly indirect forms of engagement with the world, which leads to yet further reality-distancing. For some things, a simple tool such as an obsidian blade, a trowel for digging tubers, a warm fur hat, or a ceramic cooking pot, for example, the mediational role of the technology directly facilitates adaptation to the natural world, and its distancing function promotes survival. Humans—even those living as nomadic foragers—have always been technology-dependent animals. But the distancing function of many other forms of technology can lead to psychological as well as physical separation from the world, insulating and isolating people, and dramatically limiting the potential richness of their direct lived experience. In modern civilization, this separation from the natural world and the insulation and isolation from direct experience is, paradoxically, considered to be a good thing, and frequently rationalized by reference to an organizing principle of immeasurable and almost mystical value that emerged during the industrial revolution called *efficiency*.

Efficiency is considered to be an unqualified good. It is a defining feature of—and often the primary justification for— "progress." Efficiency involves being able to accomplish a task with the least possible expenditure of time and effort, and has perhaps its best expression in the assembly line approach to industrial manufacture. When Old Dog first started to think about efficiency, it seemed similar in his mind to the law of parsimony. Parsimony is the idea that, all things being equal, it is better to choose a simpler explanation than a more complicated one. It doesn't make sense to add complexity where it isn't needed. The universe is an unimaginably complex place, but at no point is it more complex than it absolutely has to be. But he quickly realized that efficiency is entirely different than parsimony in a couple of major ways. First, parsimony is an idea that applies to the realm of scientific understanding, while efficiency applies to the realm of action and lived experience. Second, parsimony guards against adding unnecessary complexity, whereas efficiency is usually obtained only by making things *more* complex than they were before. And, probably a more important point, just because something is more efficient does not mean that it is better in any unqualified sense. Quite often, an increase in efficiency means a *decrease* in quality.

There are pernicious tradeoffs involved with modern society's obsessive focus on technological efficiency. Gains in efficiency are purchased at the cost of increased distancing from reality. Also, with increased efficiency comes decreased transparency, decreased awareness and knowledge, and decreased participation in the ongoing flow of life itself. Consider the difference between a modern thermostatically controlled furnace that is hidden away in the basement, and an old wood stove standing in the center of the room. With the wood stove, there is no mystery. The source of heat and how it is achieved is transparent and obvious to even a small child. Most people have never seen the inner workings of a furnace, however, and have little idea how one actually works. In addition, the wood stove requires regular trips to the woodpile outside, and the woodpile itself involves health-promoting physical exercise, cutting, spitting, hauling, and stacking wood. The hidden furnace is far more efficient, but this efficiency is purchased at the cost of ignorance, increased dependence, and isolation from the natural world.

Or consider the many tradeoffs involved with what is perhaps the twentieth century's greatest home innovation, the microwave oven. An individualized, prepackaged, factory processed and nutritionally suspect microwaved meal emerges effortlessly and instantly in minutes, in stark contrast with the far less efficient traditional labor-intensive and time-consuming kitchen-prepared meal designed to meet the needs of a whole family, that is likely far more nutritionally sound, and that serves as a venue for communal interaction and familial bonding.

One of the more insidious features of complex technology that Old Dog learned about is *reverse adaptation*. And it is this particular feature of technology that is responsible for some of civilization's most corrosive physical, psychological, and social effects. Reverse adaptation occurs when the goals that a specific technology was designed to address change in order to accommodate the use of the technology itself. Old Dog heard a story about what happened to a traditional community of reindeer herders in the

Scandinavian north after they were introduced to snowmobiles, and subsequently adopted the snowmobile as a replacement for skis and reindeer-drawn sleds. The use of snowmobiles dramatically increased the speed and efficiency of the annual reindeer roundup, allowing it to be completed in a single massive operation. But in a very short time, reverse adaptation to the "needs" of the snowmobile—coupled with a number of unforeseen negative consequences—completely eliminated their traditional way of life and dramatically restructured their entire society.

After abandoning traditional winter herding practices that kept the animals and people in close proximity, the previously tame reindeer became feral, and could only be corralled through stampede running effected by an organized assault of noisy snowmobiles. The physical and psychological stress of these mechanized roundups caused fertility rates to fall, and herd populations dropped precipitously. The loss of reindeer numbers was paralleled by a drop in the number of families who could participate in the reindeer herding lifestyle. Not everyone could afford a snowmobile's cost and upkeep, and because traditional herding practices could not compete with the snowmobile approach, many families had no choice but to sell their remaining animals and find factory jobs in the city.

In addition, because some people were better able to adapt to the new way of doing things—economically as well as in terms of mastering the required skills and techniques for snowmobile herding—their social world was bifurcated into clear winners and losers, and their previously egalitarian society became steeply hierarchical and inegalitarian. Also, because they no longer needed to spend the majority of their time with the reindeer, people began to seek out distractions such as television and alcohol—lots and lots of alcohol. Pickup trucks became essential items. Conveniences such as washing machines and chainsaws also became "necessary." And what was once a peaceful, interdependent, self-sustaining, and largely self-sufficient community, became instead a community of competing individuals, each firmly embedded in the global consumer economy. Unemployment and poverty—conditions that were previously impossible—became commonplace.

Reverse adaptation is an inevitable feature of all complex technologies, Old Dog realized. Technologies start out serving specific human ends or addressing a highly circumscribed set of problems. But once they come into being, they shape human thought and behavior in ways that conform to the structure and organization of the technology itself. The technological solution becomes a way of reframing the original problem, and features of the original problem that do not correspond to the technological solution are ignored or redefined.

Once a new technology becomes incorporated as a regular feature of life, a person's behavior changes to accommodate the needs of the technology. This is true even if the technology was created specifically to help people satisfy their own needs, or to make their life easier or more comfortable. There is probably no greater example of reverse adaptation than the automobile, which led not just to dramatic changes in the pattern of daily life, but changes in the entire physical and economic infrastructure of cities as well. More recently, the cell phone has had a similarly dramatic impact in the social and psychological domains.

Reverse adaptation associated with technologies such as the automobile, the microwave oven, and the cell phone has been accompanied by an increased focus on satisfying individualized wants and needs. This no doubt has been a boon for business: homes used to have one communal television set, now everyone carries a screen in their palm wherever they go. Good for the corporate bottom line, perhaps. But these technologies have such an organizing effect on a person's moment-by-moment activity that it is not hyperbole to suggest that civilized humans are living as slaves to their own machines.

The history of civilization is to a large extent the history of technological innovation. Civilization itself can be viewed as a collection of social and physical technologies designed to direct the actions of individual humans toward collective purposes. The problem with this is that many of those collective purposes—through reverse adaptation or intentional design— run counter to the interests and well-being of any of the individuals who make up the collective. This problem originated nine or ten thousand years ago, with the beginnings of large-scale agriculture, a lifestyle that introduced intrusive and distancing forms of mediation that were not previously part of human society.

The writer stared blankly at the screen for several moments, almost as if he had been listening to Old Dog's internal monolog. He repeated the phrase "technological outsourcing of humanity" multiple times, then said, "Fuck. What am I doing with this?" He deleted what he had written, went into the kitchen, and opened a bottle of wine.

24

MADDY finished her cigarette and opened the book resting in her lap. It was an unusually warm day in early autumn. The moon was visible and in the waning end of its cycle, piercing the blue firmament with a silvery fingernail. She was sitting in a ratty folding chair alongside her camper, parked in the gravel remains of a campsite in a derelict private campground bordering on the state park that claimed almost ten thousand acres along the river and up into the surrounding foothills northeast of the city. Only a handful of people knew about the abandoned campground, and Maddy had been staying at this particular spot for so long that it was starting to feel like home.

She was rereading the collected works of Epictetus, one of her favorite stoic philosophers, whose driving idea came down to a more articulate version of the serenity prayer. According to Epictetus, there are things that are up to us, and things that are not, and we create unnecessary pain and suffering for ourselves when we fail to clearly distinguish between the two. He counsels us to put the energy of our whole being into those precious and few things that are up to us, and not concern ourselves with those many other things that fall outside of our limited scope of influence. This was a philosophy that Maddy had attempted to incorporate into her own life, at least since her college days. Maddy was a philosophy major in college. In the end, she came close to earning a double major in philosophy and history. But she never graduated. She was forced to drop out in the middle of her senior year when it became too difficult to juggle the many stressors of school while simultaneously managing her delusions.

Maddy was schizophrenic. Actually, it would be more accurate to say that she was a person who was at one point in her life diagnosed with schizophrenia. Schizophrenic spectrum disorder is a sticky tar pit of a diagnosis. One sip at the water's edge, and the person is sucked in for life. Even if all the symptoms disappear, the diagnosis still holds them fast—"residual," or "in remission," or "currently asymptomatic" are appended to the label, but the label sticks around and follows them into the future. And even a single symptom is enough to trigger a diagnostic confirmation bias, where the smallest crumb of circumstantial evidence for additional symptoms is granted the power to convict.

And then there's the notion of *spectrum* itself. The spectrum idea for mental disorder is a way of making a category label apply to uniquely different people who all seem to share something in common, even though, when you get right down to it, the only thing that they really share is the label itself. It's not a spectrum in the optical sense that the term was stolen from. It's not a continuum of intensity or a range of disability. The word spectrum in the context of mental disorder is just there to make the label more broadly applicable. It suggests the diagnostic process involves a kind of clean two-dimensionality, when in reality it is more like a three-dimensional sack that can be thrown over the head of anyone whose response to reality in any way deviates from societal expectation. Saying that someone suffers from schizophrenic spectrum disorder sounds better than calling them crazy or psychotic, but the diagnostic nuance is only window dressing.

Maddy's main symptom—in actuality the only symptom that there was ever any valid evidence for—was highly elaborate delusions. They weren't the typical delusions of persecution or grandeur that are most often associated with schizophrenia. She wasn't worried that aliens were trying to read her thoughts. She didn't think she was the reincarnation of Cleopatra. Her delusions were usually rather mundane. Her mind would work itself into a state where she would lock onto a wild idea and then couldn't let it go even when part of her fully understood that the idea was crazy and unwarranted. This happened as far back as she could remember, but it wasn't a real problem for her until she was fifteen, and she became convinced that her bedroom closet was haunted, that the ghost of a little girl who died in the house eighty years previously of polio had set up shop in the closet. Clothing items went missing, and then would mysteriously show up on the closet floor wrinkled and smelling of freshly dug dirt. She heard noises in the closet during the day, and on quiet nights she became convinced that she could hear the girl breathing softly just inside the closet door. This disturbed her mother enough to make an appointment to have Maddy checked out, which led to her diagnosis and to her first antipsychotic prescription.

The ghost disappeared when she took the medication. But other things disappeared as well. She no longer cared about things; nothing excited her anymore. She became jittery and restless. She put on weight and started to walk with a clumsy shuffle. She eventually quit taking the drugs, but didn't tell her mother she had stopped. When the ghost returned, she kept it to herself. She was convinced that the ghost in her closet was real—or, better to say that she was unable to maintain the conviction that it wasn't real for any length of time—but it would be her secret. She denied its existence to anyone who asked about it, and dismissed what she had said in the past, claiming she had just let her imagination get away with her. Of course, there was no ghost in her closet. That was silly. On some level she knew that. But on another level, a level that she could not ignore, the little dead girl in her bedroom closet was just as real as she was. She could clearly hear her breathing just behind the closet door when she was alone in her room and the night was quiet.

The delusions followed her to college. At first, they were manageable, she understood them for what they were: just thoughts that she couldn't shake that didn't fit with the world. But by the middle of her senior year the boundary with reality blurred into nonexistence, and she dropped out a semester before she was scheduled to graduate. She moved back home and sequestered herself in her room. When her mother died, the house was sold to pay down her mother's debts, and she moved in with her sister, Irene. Irene agreed to let her live with her and her boyfriend on the condition that Maddy go back on her medication. It was not a comfortable living situation. She never got along with Irene, even when they were kids. Although Maddy was slightly younger, they were close enough in age to be perpetually in competition for the tiny slivers of affection their mother would occasionally dole out. And the ghost in the closet only served to drive them further apart. Maddy had the smarts. But Irene had a callous manipulative streak that bordered on psychopathic. And both of these characteristics, Maddy's intellect and Irene's self-serving callousness, had gained an increased influence over their respective personalities as adults.

When Irene found out that Maddy had stopped taking her medication again, she kicked her out and told her she was not welcome back. But in the few months that Maddy lived with her sister, and while the drugs kept her delusions in the background, she had taken a job at a grocery store, was quickly promoted to night manager, and saved enough money to buy the truck and camper that she was sitting next to today. Between her camper and a small disability check she got each month, and her penchant for talking people into giving her things for free, she was able to get by, and was more or less satisfied with the simple lifestyle she had settled into. But she was not taking any medication, and delusion was a constant companion—even though she was usually able to recognize her crazy thoughts for what they were.

A sudden and overwhelming sense that she was being watched caused her to glance up from her book and out toward the river, where Old Dog was standing, holding the paw of his injured leg slightly off the ground and wagging his tail.

25

"'T HE problem of evil' is an anchor in quicksand," the writer sighed, as he continued reading from the latest draft of his essay on morality. "Evil, as a concept, only makes sense in the context of 'good,' both are grounded in a specific culture's norms about right and wrong, and neither applies to anything real in the world. Evil might be defined in a generic way as those acts that are motivated, at least partially, by the intention to cause pain or suffering. Evil might also be defined more colloquially as a synonym for 'bad.' But in more objective terms, there can be no real problem of evil because evil is an artificial and abstract thing that has no referent in the concrete.

"Nonetheless, I think that it might be possible to apply the idea of evil to concrete events as a kind of organizing principle. There are certain actions and events that seem to be intentionally directed at causing or increasing suffering. Perhaps the paradigmatic case—definitely the stereotypical case—is the Jewish Holocaust, where more than six million Jews were rounded up and shipped off to concentration camps where they were subsequently put to death. There are plenty of other examples of this kind of thing, more recent genocides in South Africa and the Balkans, and the massive-scale (and on-going) eradications of indigenous people in the Western Hemisphere. But the Jewish Holocaust is the most frequently cited and well known—and accepted—example of evil.

"Quite often the quality of evil is assigned as a characteristic feature of a specific individual or set of events. Hitler and the rise of Nazi Germany comes to mind here. But things get fuzzy quickly when you try to establish the actual locus of evil, when you try to identify its foundational source.

Things are complicated further by the fact that evil is not an easily quantifiable thing, and the magnitude of an evil result does not necessarily reflect the degree of evil intent.

"When you ask the question, 'Where is it that evil resides?' the answer is frequently pinned on an individual, within the heart or mind of a specific person. But this simply cannot be the real answer. The Holocaust was not the act of a single person. A single person is limited in their potential for evil by the limits of their physical body and the distance of their reach. Even a giant of a person intent on causing as much pain to as many others as possible, could not, by themself, be able to cause anything beyond very local suffering. People would learn to avoid this person, and their ability to cause suffering would diminish quickly. Or, perhaps, people would pool their efforts and aggressively limit the person's evil actions—even to the point of murder. My point here is that in the absence of a larger institutional system, there is a severe limit to the range and scope of evil.

"Evil is enhanced by technology. If I want to cause others pain, I could hit them with a stick or throw rocks at them or burn their house down in the night. But with technology, I can shoot hundreds of them from the window of a tall building or fly an airplane into that same building or set off a bomb in a highly populated public area. Or I could have six million Jews transported by rail to compounds for holding until they can be slaughtered en masse in gas chambers or with bullets while standing naked at the edge of the mass grave that they dug themselves. Technology allows me to scale up my evil, and there is no actual limit to the extent to which my evil might be expanded and extended and intensified. Through technology, evil is infinitely scalable.

"This fact was brought to light by the work of Hannah Arendt, with respect to the infamous Adolph Eichmann, the German bureaucrat who arranged and organized the transportation of Jews from around Europe to their slaughter. Eichmann may or may not have been an evil person. He may or may not have had evil intent behind his actions. He denied it. And, although it is not politically correct to say so, he may be right. At the very least his evil is not different in kind from that of countless others who acted in the service of atrocities throughout history but were nonetheless held in high regard. Andrew Jackson is a wonderful case in point. He played a significant role in the genocide of indigenous Americans, and yet his portrait was given a position of honor on the US twenty-dollar bill.

"So back to the question of the locus of evil. I would argue that evil is a function of technology, and specifically social technology. And by social technology, I am referring to the systematic structuring of power. Evil is a function of hierarchically structured power relations. It exists in forms beyond the trivial only through such relations. Eichmann was just part of a system, and even if he believed his actions to be entirely evil, even if he was in fact convinced that all Jews should be made to suffer and die, his beliefs would have fallen impotent and stillborn had it not been for the massive bureaucratic machine of civilization that he had at his disposal—that we all have at our disposal. The locus of evil is civilization itself.

"'The Banality of Evil'" was Arendt's way of saying this. She was impressed with how ordinary Eichmann was, how mediocre he was as a person. She was there to witness his trial in Israel after he had been captured (essentially kidnapped) in South America by Israeli secret service. She was there when he talked about his role in the process. Certainly, he was not entirely responsible for the outcome of his actions. He was just following orders and served as one link in a long chain of similar people just following orders. He helped arrange for the transportation. He helped to get the Jews on the trains, but he played no part in their actual executions; he was not responsible for attempted genocide. He was, by all accounts, just a guy honoring is oath of service to Hitler and to the system itself.

"At the time, this view of Eichmann was not acceptable. The events were too horrendous to be explained by normal people 'just following orders.' The Holocaust was a monstrosity, and it needed monsters to carry the blame. Hitler was obviously a monster. And so, everyone under his evil wing had also to be monsters—lesser monsters, to be sure, but monsters nonetheless. If we allow for someone like Eichmann to be just a normal guy following orders, a mediocre man simply acting as a servomechanism in an amoral machine, then what's to prevent scaling that up to Hitler himself? Hitler, along with all of his evil, was just part of the system, after all. There is a fairly well-known platitude (perhaps not so well known, but since I have heard of it, I assume that it is not entirely obscure) that if you want to lead, you need to follow. Leaders are those who are able to see the direction the people are going, and then jump out in front. Maybe Hitler wasn't evil; maybe he was just the guy who jumped in front of a parade of folks already headed toward a moral cliff. The real problem with the idea behind the banality of evil is that if we allow for it to be true, even partially, then the system itself deserves the lion's share of the blame.

"And once again, we are back to the role of technology—and specifically in this case, bureaucratically organized power. Even if it were possible for someone to be, as a person, truly evil (I am at the moment agnostic about this, although I have met people who clearly appear to qualify), without technology to direct and expand and concentrate and focus their power, their ability to act on their evil intentions would be severely limited. And this is how social life plays out in an egalitarian hunter-gatherer band: any evil person who might happen to come along is in most cases nothing more than a temporary nuisance. Imagine what might happen to someone who was regularly pissing off the very people they need for their own immediate survival. Imagine I was that person and you were one of my neighbors. You might put up with me for a time just to avoid confrontation, but eventually I am going to get a poison arrow in my thigh while I sleep, and no one will complain when my corpse is discovered the next morning in the river. That's the true power of egalitarianism: not necessarily that it brings with it the capacity for maximum personal freedom, but because it serves as a prophylactic against those darker modes of human being.

"If evil truly exists, it is not to be found in people, or in specific persons. It is a function of the larger system. Civilization itself is the ultimate source of evil. And we, you and I, are, right now, this very moment, victims of the operations of an unimaginably evil machine.

"But here is where, from a philosophical perspective, the problem of evil starts to fall apart. If, as I have suggested, evil is a function of intentional action, and at the same time evil is something that is systemic, drawing its energy from the mechanical organization of power relations, then evil has no possible dwelling. If it is not necessarily a trait or quality of the individual people involved—all equally victims of the system—and it is not something that can be produced by an amoral machine, then there is no place for evil to reside.

"Perhaps I should start to consider the 'banality of civilization' as something to flesh out. Perhaps I have made the same mistake that many people made immediately after the war, perhaps I have fallen into the same emotional trap. When I look around and witness how civilization has decimated the natural world, how it has tortured and is presently killing millions of people in an ongoing holocaust of unimaginable proportions, it is hard not to fall prey to the fallacy that the cause has to be some horrendous evil. But where is that? Civilization is itself an abstraction, a reified concept that does not reflect any concrete reality. It is a categorical term that subsumes an entire way of life, a way of life that involves the mechanical structuring of power, and the concomitant consumption of the natural world in order to maintain the mechanical structuring of power.

"And that's the truly scary part. If the bad is not to be found in a person, then how is it to be defeated. If the bad is a monster—or even a collection of monsters—then it can be overcome by simply defeating the monsters. This is part of the mythology of civilization, all civilizations have their monster stories, stories of evil agents and their conquest by heroes. In the West, we can start with the most ancient stories, the stories of Gilgamesh and Beowulf and the many monsters faced by Odysseus. Evil can be thwarted, although it takes courage and strength (and perhaps the help of a god or two) to do it. But it can be overcome. But if evil—those things that we recognize as evil—is not something produced by monsters, but by mediocre people just doing their job, if evil is a function of the system itself, then what are we to do?"

26

"H oot! Look at you!" Maddy shouted, when he got close enough for her to look up and notice. She called him over, and he quickened his pace as much as his leg would allow, stopping in front of her with his tail pulsing in an uncontrollable side-to-side arc. There was something about her that he liked. Really liked. At the camp, he was convinced that she could almost hear his thoughts. But there was something else about her as well, something that he could not quite identify, a hidden positive energy, a restlessness stirring just below the surface, as if at any moment she would explode into a whirlwind of happiness and affection. Whatever it was, it was magnetic, and he felt powerfully drawn to it.

"I heard what happened yesterday. Bastards want to sweep all the broken dishes under the rug before daddy comes to visit." She carefully folded her book across the arm of the chair so as not to lose her place, and leaned forward to pet him. "You were lucky to get out of there. The cops would have shot you dead on sight if they got one look at you. I've seen them do it before. Just shoot a dog standing there minding his own business. Pathetic sadistic cowards." Maddy looked at his leg. His fur was caked with dried blood, but he was no longer bleeding. "Looks like they might have tried. Doesn't look too bad," she said. She gently ran her hand over and around the wound. "Don't think anything is broken." She stood up and went into the camper. She came back with a wet cloth, returned to her chair and tenderly cleaned the dried blood from his leg.

Old Dog listened politely as she returned to her rant about the city and how they "Don't give a rat's ass about people, you know, human beings with human beings' needs." The wrinkles around her glassy blue-gray eyes became puffy as she talked. Her ruddy complexion darkened and a red streak appeared across the middle of her forehead. Her voice had a soothing lilt despite its angry edge. Her cadence had a sing-song quality that reminded him of the way Jenny's mom would sing her favorite nursery rhyme song about three mice without eyes who got their tails hacked off. Maddy was a person he could trust. He set his jaw softly across her thigh as she massaged him behind his ears.

"You're welcome to hang out here, stay with me if you want," she offered.

He responded to her offer by immediately curling up alongside her chair.

She looked at him lying there, and instantly knew that he understood what she had said. She knew abruptly and beyond any doubt that he was no ordinary dog. She immediately tried to push that knowledge out of her head, muttering under her breath "No, no, no, no, that would never do, they'd lock me up and put me right back on the crazy pills." But it was too late. It had already taken hold. The thoughts had already burrowed themselves too deep for her to be able to pull them loose. That was part of the way her mind worked—or didn't work, according to the first doctor that her mother took her to when she was fifteen, the doctor who diagnosed her with schizotypal personality disorder and told her mom that there was not much that could be done, that there was no way to fix her delusions, at least not permanently. Her mother couldn't accept that prognosis, and took her to another doctor who put her on antipsychotic medication that made her feet catch like they were made of shapeless rock and left her with a permanent eyebrow twitch. It was this second doctor who hung the heavy iron anchor of schizophrenia around her neck, a diagnostic collar she could never quite shake no matter how loose she was able to stretch it.

She pinched her forehead between her thumb and forefinger, and looked down again at Old Dog on the ground next to her. She could hear breathing behind a closet door in the past. Thoughts that this was not an ordinary dog bloomed and churned, and she knew that they would not leave until she exorcised them. While in college, she developed strategies for testing her thoughts against empirical reality—basically employing the scientific method—to determine whether she should give them credence. It was nothing any therapist or doctor taught her; it was something that she figured out on her own. Delusions and reality can be difficult to untangle, but only one of them consistently followed the universal laws of nature. If her tests turned out negative, that didn't make the thoughts go away—they were still as powerful and potentially intrusive as ever—but it did allow her to flag them, to mark them and relegate them to the "silly thoughts" category, so that when they rudely intruded she was able to brush them aside or attenuate them enough to go on about her business uninterrupted. Eventually they became slightly distracting background noise, like the whine of an old fluorescent light or the squeaky bearing on a ceiling fan or the laugh track from an old sitcom coming through an open window from a neighbor's television set.

After a few moments, she could no longer resist the temptation to put her hypothesis about the dog to test—just a simple test to see if her thoughts warranted any further scrutiny. She continued to look at Old Dog as he lay beside her for a while, then said, without any physical gesture, "Why don't you come over here to the other side of my chair; it looks like it might be more comfortable for your leg."

Without hesitation, Old Dog stood up, moved to the other side of her chair, and resumed his curled position on the ground.

Maddy was quiet for a long time.

27

COMPLEXITY is the norm, the natural state of the universe. Even simple primates have evolved to master the complex, the densely interwoven, the abundant, the multifarious, the dynamic. Neuroscientists credit the brain's right hemisphere, the holistic hemisphere, with the capacity to pilot through the subtle nuances and intricacies of continually changing circumstances, far, far too many details to ever consider analytically, one at a time—let alone map out the meaningful relationships among these details. Complexity cannot be dealt with in a linear, serial, piecemeal fashion.

Humans have several ways of referring to their own inborn capacities to feel-out the contours of complexity: intuition, instinct, presentiment, hunch. A person enters a room, and right away they know something is not right; there is a "bad vibe" or a palpable tension in the atmosphere. The feeling emerges directly, and long before they are able to identify its source. And oftentimes they never actually locate the source. Or they misidentify the source, indicting a feature of the situation that is salient and easily identifiable but ultimately nonthreatening.

Intuition, that potent and spontaneous prod that can make a person turn their head or suddenly change their pace, is an evolved response to complexity. And it is *feeling* that has the rudder. The right hemisphere is not adept at expressing itself conceptually—human concepts being largely a linguistic, left-hemisphere creation—but has, over the eons, become a maestro of emotion. More can be carried atop a momentary impression, a fleeting feeling, than can be packed into a library's worth of well-chosen words.

One of the many paradoxes of modern civilization is that it involves a radical simplification of complexity. Despite its labyrinthine bureaucracies and its sparkly surface distractions, civilization replaces subtlety with garishness and nuance with coarseness. Hues that bleed into each other in novel and unpredictable tones are forcefully overlaid with granular categories, standardized and homogenized for maximum distribution, with a premium on the lowest common denominator. And so, there are reds and blues and greens and their approved variants, but there are not enough words for the densely shaded chromatic spaces between the dominant stripes of the rainbow. There is a single word for lavender, despite the infinity of colors enfolding a solitary flower.

There is an easy conspiracy theory here. Civilization's simplification of the complex, and its demand that its inhabitants focus on specific details—at least explicitly—leaves the big picture unanalyzed. A restricted subset of details is offered up for consideration, and these privileged details, taken one at a time or collected into a composite assembly, present civilization as beneficial—at most benign. Intuition and instinct may be screaming something completely different, but intuition and instinct are not considered reliable information relative to isolatable details—yet another way that civilization pulls reality inside-out. The focus on the benign particulars allows the malignant whole to expand unabated.

Despite the similarity in structure and the large overlap in function of their respective cortical regions, dog brains and human brains operate somewhat differently when it comes to complexity. Dogs, like humans, can isolate problems and analyze them, break them into more easily solved subproblems, focus on details. But, unlike humans—or, perhaps it is better to say unlike civilized humans—dogs deal with complexity on its own level. The big picture impression is the default. Nuance and subtlety are not things added, but are infused through the entirety of the thing itself.

Old Dog knew who Maddy was without an extensive period of empirical observation or any analysis of background information. Her entire being was wrapped into her voice, into her demeanor, into the way her matted hair lay heaped on the top of her head, corralled by a rolled bandana. Her life's history was folded into the creases around her eyes and the deep parallel furrows between her eyebrows. The details weren't important *as details*. They were all there, every smile and every tear, all part of the composite, all woven into the whole, countless broken and frayed threads knitted tightly into an ever-expanding tapestry, bound together and individually unanalyzable.

Maddy knew him too, as she considered Old Dog lying next to her lawn chair, his head calmly leaning against her scuffed and weather-worn military-style boot, she knew Old Dog, knew that he was somehow different, something out of the ordinary, knew that despite his ragged appearance he was not at all a threat, knew that he had been through betrayals and trials and hardships and pain. But Maddy, being human and a product of civilization, and in possession of a left hemisphere fitted with a symbolic system designed for the analytical demands of language, and further in possession of an overactive internal voice that she could not entirely trust to tell her whether what she knew to be true was entirely real, Maddy could not be satisfied with what her intuition was telling her.

Partly this was because what her intuition was telling her was outlandish. It was impossible. It was, in point of fact, crazy-talk. It was precisely the kind of thing that had gotten her in trouble several times before. Dogs are dogs. They can't be anything else. Her instinct that Old Dog was not just a dog, or that he was an extremely unusual dog, could not be accepted at face value. No matter how powerful the impression churning in her right hemisphere, she needed to convince her analytic mind, she had to find concrete evidence, details that could be collectively assembled into a coherent form, a ledger of specific facts in support, a collection of observable details that any ordinary person would agree summed together as evidential proof. Carl Sagan was famous for saying "extraordinary claims require extraordinary evidence." If this dog was truly as extraordinary as he seemed, she would need something more than a gut feeling and a handful of unlikely coincidences.

She started with simple commands. Basic dog instructions such as sit, rollover, stay, and for each command Old Dog eagerly and effortlessly complied, although rolling over was a bit painful on his injured leg. Then she scaled up gradually. She asked him to circle the camper to the left, and when he did so, she asked him to return to the right the way he came—both times being careful not to offer any gestures that would cue direction. Walk backward. Climb on that rock. Tap your front paw on the ground five times.

She was starting to feel seasick at this point. What would it mean if a dog could understand language beyond just a handful of specific words and commands? What does that mean about dogs in general? What does that mean about other animals? What does that mean about humans? She was afraid to take the next logical step in her assessment. She sat back down on the chair and gently held Old Dog's head in her lap. Several minutes passed before she mustered the courage to think up a way that she could scale her assessment of Old Dog to a higher level.

She thought of using a complex array of foot taps, perhaps something like Morse Code, but then remembered the story of Clever Hans, the horse that supposedly was able to tap out the answer to simple math problems. It turned out that he was actually just watching his trainer's body language and facial expressions, and tapped his foot until his trainer's face told him that was enough. When the trainer was out of sight, Hans suddenly lost all of his math abilities. Her test, she decided, needed to be something simple and direct, simple but not simplistic.

She picked up two fist-sized rocks and spaced them about a foot apart in front of Old Dog. She pointed to the one on the left and said, "This rock means 'yes.'" And then to the one on her right, "This rock means 'no.'" I'm going to ask you yes or no questions, and if the answer is 'yes,' I want you to put your paw on the yes rock, and when the answer is 'no' put your paw on the no rock. Do you understand?"

Old Dog stepped to the side and put a paw on the rock to her left. She took a deep breath.

"Are you a dog?" Yes.

"Am I a horse?" No.

"Is it raining now?" No.

"Was it raining yesterday?" Yes.

"Do you have five legs?" No.

"Can birds fly?" Yes.

"Can you fly?" No.

"Can you swim?" Old Dog didn't move. He didn't know how to answer that one. He didn't know if he could swim or not. He had never actually tried. He assumed that he could, but he wasn't sure. He looked up at her with a quizzical head tilt.

Maddy started to repeat the question, and then changed her mind. "Do you know if you can swim?" No.

She added a third rock between the yes and no rocks. "This rock is the 'no answer' rock, for questions that you can't answer."

"Am I holding up three fingers?" Yes.

"Is there a book on the chair behind me?" Yes.

"Is Aconcagua the tallest mountain in South America?" No answer.

"Is my name Maddy?" Yes.

"Are tires round?" Yes.

"Does E equal M times C squared?" No answer.

"Am I speaking Russian?" No.

"Have you always been able to understand English?" No.

"Can you understand other languages?" No answer.

"Did someone teach you how to understand language?" No.

"Is your ability to understand language the product of a secret government experiment?" No.

"Are you the product of my imagination?" No.

Maddy felt herself slowly slipping outside of her own body. She was talking to a dog—and the dog was talking back! Nobody would ever believe her. They would all say she was crazy, that it was just her delusions acting up again. It was *obviously* just her delusions acting up again, she thought. She had finally gone over the very edge. Maybe none of this was real. Maybe the dog she saw standing in front of her wasn't really there at all. Maybe she was in an institution someplace jacked up on meds and imagining all of this.

She looked into the dog's eyes and said, "What should I do about this, old dog?" No answer.

"Am I crazy?" No answer.

28

THE morning sky was auditioning for a part in a play about a deep glacial lake, where the water is a green-tinged azure and frozen in thin ruffled sheets along the shoreline. Maddy was not looking at the sky. She was instead pulling residual pieces of burnt fan belt out of the belt tensioner pully with her head under the hood of her truck. She had been wrestling for days about Old Dog, about his apparent ability to understand spoken English, about his genius-level mental skills, about what to do about any of it. Even though she had put him through an extensive array of tests, and even though in each case he was able to clearly demonstrate his extraordinary talents, she was still not fully convinced that it wasn't all just part of her craziness, just another one of her elaborate delusions. Old Dog, meanwhile, had happily adopted her, and enthusiastically followed her around everywhere she went. He was at this very moment lying behind her, watching her with keen interest as she worked, and listening to her as she muttered a steady stream of profanity.

With the camper as her permanent residence, she had, by necessity, become somewhat of a skilled auto mechanic. She replaced the alternator just a few weeks previously. She bought a new fan belt at that time, but decided not to replace the old belt until it gave up the ghost—a decision that she regretted as she leaned out of the engine compartment and flipped open the lid of the toolbox wedged between her feet.

The manufacture of sophisticated tools is considered by many to be a defining feature of the *Homo* genus. The oldest fossil primate to be gifted with the title *Homo* was *Homo habilis*, "handy man." *Homo habilis* is also the oldest to show signs of Broca's area, a small swelling on the left side of the brain's prefrontal cortex. Broca's area is traditionally associated with language, and specifically with the capacity for speech—damage to this area of the brain can leave a person literally speechless. More recent studies have found that Broca's area is probably not exclusively a speech center, rather its primary function appears to be to allow for the hierarchical organization of complex sequenced behavior. Spoken language just happens to be an exceedingly complex behavior that involves dense layers of hierarchically organized sequencing, both cognitively and behaviorally: sentences are arranged according to constituent noun phrase and verb phrase components that are composed of ordered sequences of words, which are themselves comprised of morphemes composed of ordered sequences of phonemes whose actual vocal expressions depends on where they fall in the sequence, and change depending on which specific phonemes are expressed before and after. In addition to language, there are several other complex behaviors that require Broca's area's organizational functions. Making finely detailed sharp-edged stone tools, for example.

According to one theory, the brain areas responsible for human language were happy side effects of tool manufacture, and Broca's area in particular, which sits at the edge of the motor cortex, evolved in conjunction with environmental pressure to produce more intricately structured tools. The motor cortex areas controlling the thumb, hands, and fingers, along with corresponding areas of the somatosensory cortex, increased in size as a result of the increase in manual dexterity demanded by more highly detailed tool design. Over time, the change in volume of these areas of the brain forced the more posterior regions of the brain into a slightly different configuration. One of the results of this new configuration was the emergence of a junction of association cortices shared by the parietal, temporal, and occipital lobes. This junction became an area of the brain that was capable of processing input from three separate sensory systems, tactile, visual, and acoustic, but whose own activity remained independent of any one of these. So, in simple terms, you suddenly (suddenly in evolutionary time) have an area of the brain that uses information from three sensory and perceptual modalities, but whose own activity is not itself directly linked with any specific kind of sensory or perceptual experience—information that is gleaned from concrete experience, but that is not concrete itself. This is practically the definition of abstraction, and it is the development of this brain region that is hypothesized to be one of the neurophysiological sources of symbolic thought.

Maddy knew about Broca's area, and it was one of the many things that made it difficult for her not to think of Old Dog's uniqueness as delusion. How could a dog have any human language ability if it doesn't have a human brain? Maybe the brain is not quite what we think it is, she wondered. A future Old Dog, having himself engaged in considerable thought about these issues, would have been able to offer an answer to her question—well, if he could have spoken, that is.

Once you have both a Broca's area and brain tissue supporting symbolic thought, all that is needed for the brain to support language, then, is some way to relate the two, some way to connect Broca's area, with its hierarchical structuring capabilities, and the parietal-occipital-temporal junction, with its capacity for symbolic representation. And, as it turns out, there is just such a connection provided by a bundle of neural tracts called the arcuate fasciculus that runs between these two brain areas. Whether this theory provides an accurate description of the evolution of the brain systems responsible for language is still an open question. However, it seems pretty clear that there was—and is—a very close relationship between tool use and human linguistic abilities. Language itself can be seen as a kind of tool—perhaps the most generally useful tool ever developed. And both of these things, language and the use of tools, are fundamental and inseparable features of evolved human nature.

Humans are not the only animals who use technology. Other primates, various birds, and even cephalopods, have been observed manufacturing and using tools. But humans are dependent on technology in a way that other animals are not. Tools provide humans with the ability to adapt to a wide range of geographic and environmental circumstances, and have in the past allowed them to flourish as a species during periods of dramatic climate change corresponding to the ebb and flow of Ice Age glaciation. Something has changed about human tools over the last few millennia, however. There is something radically different about the human relationship with their tools, something about the nature and quality of human dependence on them. It has something to do with the connection between technology and human needs—or with the specific kinds of needs that the technology is designed to fulfill. The needs served by an obsidian spearpoint or a camel hair paint brush or a ceramic cooking pot or a warm fur hat are clearly human needs. But whose needs are really being served by cell phones? By satellite surveillance systems? By international banking corporations?

Externally, the human problem is technology. Specifically, the problem is with the nature of the human relationship with technology within the context of civilization. The problem is with the specific needs being served by technology and with the complete lack of control over the technological process. And the lack of control is perhaps the most alarming part of the problem: humans are tool-dependent creatures; they cannot survive without technological support, and their dependency leaves them vulnerable as individuals in situations where their access to essential technology is under the control of someone—or something—else.

Maddy started the engine and let it idle while she went around to the front and listened for any indication of belt slippage. Hearing nothing but the usual cacophony of sounds from a Ford 360 V8 with over 200 thousand miles on it, she slammed the hood. Then she bent down and latched the lid of her toolbox with a quick twist of her wrist and flick of her fingers, with the habitual unconscious flourish of a Paleolithic hunter cinching the drawstring on a rabbit skin pouch.

Things of Power

29

T HE writer let his back sink into the overstuffed deck-chair pillow and picked up the page proof for his latest article, a piece about the nature of modern knowledge that he had written for a popular science magazine. He was generally happy with the way it had turned out—and the editor loved it—but there was also something about it that bothered him. He had the nagging sense that there was an important issue that he left unaddressed, something obvious that he had missed. He felt as if he was just scratching at the surface, perhaps, or skirting around something of profound importance that he couldn't quite put his finger on. There was an elephant squatting right in front of him on the page, and he had written right over the top of it.

A lot of his writing felt that way to him lately. He would dive headlong into a topic armed with clear ideas and a clear plan, but then come out the other side with the nagging impression that he had missed the true target, or that he had left out something of critical importance. He drew the last swallow from his wine glass, and then began to read aloud, slowly and carefully, trying to catch any stray typos or grammatical weirdness— that was what was of critical importance at this point. It was too late to go elephant hunting now; the article would be appearing in print in next month's edition. Old Dog settled onto the still rain-damp rug in the center of the deck, and listened intently as the writer began to speak:

"Richard Katz, in the prologue to his book, *Indigenous Healing Psychology*, recounts a conversation he had with a Ju/'hoansi healer, his 'friend and guide,' while doing field research in Botswana in 1968, back when the Ju/'hoansi were still living as nomadic hunter-gatherers. Katz had brought a tape recorder to record their conversation, and was playing his collection of recordings of Ju/'hoansi healing dances for his guide, who was absolutely fascinated, and requested that the sounds be played over and over.

"At some point, the healer remarked that the tape recorder was 'something definitely powerful,' and said that he wished he knew how it works. Katz started to explain how the microphone picks up the sound, but his guide interrupted and said that he understood how the microphone works by collecting the sound and then sending it down the wire to the inside of the box, and then dismissed the microphone as a trivial thing, and said that he suspected that it wasn't really the thing doing the hearing. It is obviously inside the box where the voices are being collected, he said, that's where the real power is. And then he repeated that he wished he knew how it works.

"When Katz started to tell him about energy and sound waves, his guide interrupted again, and said, 'We already know those things. But what I really want to know is, how does it work?' Eventually Katz came to realize that he could not answer the question, because his own understanding was really only a superficial sketch of the process. His guide was disappointed, and said that 'Whenever we're given a thing of power by our ancestors— and surely this thing that captures our voices is powerful—we're always told how it works and how to use it.'

"A major difference between the Ju/'hoansi of the mid twentieth century and the inhabitants of civilization is that the latter have no idea about how anything really works—and even less of an idea about how any of it should be used. I'm looking at the cell phone sitting next to me right now. It is definitely a thing of power. And although I could give an extensive sketch of the basics of cellular networks and digital information processing and touchscreen circuitry, I really have no idea how any of it works or how it should be used, what greater purposes it should be applied to. All things of power in civilization are like this, from cell phones and automobiles to global financial institutions and international trade agreements.

"The phrase 'Knowledge is power' was first penned (in its Latin form, *scientia potentia est*) by Tomas Hobbes in his *Leviathan*, although the phrase is often attributed to Francis Bacon. Bacon, however, offered the slightly different version, 'Knowledge itself is power.' Both of these versions express a kind of truth; and although the distinction between them may appear trivial on the surface, the difference is not a subtle one. The first suggests that knowledge is perhaps a *kind* of power, that knowledge can be put to use, that it can do things for you, that it enhances your capacity to act on the world in some way. Knowing how to operate an automobile, for example, increases your potential speed and range of movement. And in the competitive social world—the most frequent context of the phrase— knowing something that someone else doesn't often puts you in a position to take advantage of their ignorance to your benefit. The Baconian version, however, suggests something more than just this: knowledge *itself*—the very fact of knowing—is the source of power, that the degree to which you possess power is, in a real sense, tied to—and limited by—what it is that you know and understand.

"Here in digitally-enhanced twenty-first century global society, we have easy access to an unimaginable and continually expanding corpus of information. And yet, from a relative standpoint, our own personal knowledge and understanding is becoming increasingly limited. This is the paradox of knowledge in civilization: as the totality of knowledge within society increases, any one individual is personally able to possess an increasingly smaller proportion of the available whole. A mid-twentieth century Ju/'hoansi elder could rightfully claim to be in personal possession of a substantial portion of the total body of important knowledge available within the larger Ju/'hoansi society. Access to knowledge was direct and open to anyone who would seek it. More importantly, because of the conditions and requirements of the Ju/'hoansi lifestyle, knowledge was distributed across a small number of broad domains that were meaningful and personally relevant, new knowledge could be easily incorporated, and the sheer quantity of knowledge available was something that could be reasonably managed by a single committed person. Thus, within the context of Ju/'hoansi culture, each individual was maximally powerful.

"A common conceit of modernity is the notion that the civilized are far superior to those living more 'primitive' lifestyles. *Primitive* is pejorative. *Civilized* is a mark of virtue. Life in civilization is complex and sophisticated. We in the civilized world know far more than any 'backward' hunter-gatherer could possibly imagine. But in terms of the knowledge held by any one person, this simply isn't true. All knowledge is local; all knowledge is personal. And from the perspective of the civilized individual, each of us in our entire lifetime is able to entertain only a trivial, microscopic portion of the knowledge that is potentially available to us—to say nothing of the unimaginable expanding corpus of knowable things that remain forever outside of our reach. Unlike the Ju/'hoansi, who could have at least a working knowledge of most everything of importance that there was to know, we can know almost nothing at all. The sharply partitioned division of labor within civilization incorporates a finely calibrated division of knowledge. Knowledge has been outsourced. Instead of personal knowledge, we rely on external information repositories and groups of certified authorities and individual experts who claim custodianship of tiny slivers of detached and isolated domains of knowledge.

"And our proportional ignorance as individuals is increasing exponentially. When I started school, in the early 1960s, the total amount of knowledge in the civilized world doubled every seven years or so. In the mid-1980s, the rate of doubling was 12 months. Now, it is estimated that this doubling occurs every few hours. What this means is that even the most highly educated adult alive today was in personal possession of a larger proportion of the total available knowledge in society when they were two years old than they do presently—and by orders of magnitude! Each of us is getting progressively more ignorant with every passing second. And, as a consequence, progressively more powerless."

The writer sat the remaining pages on the small table next to him, and put his cell phone on top to keep the late afternoon breeze from tossing them into the yard. This was the point in the article that made him uncomfortable in that hard-to-articulate way. It was something about becoming increasingly powerless, something about how ignorance and powerlessness were connected—the flip-side of "knowledge itself is power," how ignorance is powerlessness, how ignorance leads inevitably to dependence. The metaphor of quicksand came to mind. Knowledge in the civilized world was a kind of quicksand. Quicksand? Something that looks innocent on the surface, but once you sink into it you become trapped? No, there was some other quality of quicksand that was relevant, that made the metaphor work, he thought. He could feel it intuitively, but couldn't quite pull it out into the light. Maybe it had something to do with the mythology of quicksand portrayed in the movies and television shows and cartoons he watched as a kid. In order to escape from quicksand, you needed to embrace quicksand's counterintuitive qualities. The more you struggled to extract yourself the deeper you would sink. In order to escape, you needed to lay yourself sideways so that you could slowly roll yourself to solid ground—intentionally immersing more of your body into the mud in the process.

Modern global civilization requires more and more knowledge to operate, knowledge that is spread more and more thinly across more and more finely partitioned divisions of technical expertise. And the more complex civilization becomes, the more complex it needs to be, in an ever-deepening Rube-Goldberg escalation into maximum complexity that will eventually drown the entire planet unless some path of escape is discovered. The real problem, he thought, is in the increasing proliferation of expertise, the increasing *need* for expertise.

He picked up his empty wine glass and went into the house for a refill.

30

MADDY sat in the cab of her pickup parked across the street from her sister's house. Old Dog was on the seat next to her, leaning against the door with his head hanging out the window on the opposite side. Maddy and her sister had not spoken since her sister kicked her out over five years ago, not since the last time Maddy had gone off her medication and refused to go back on.

Her sister wouldn't be home from work for at least another hour. Maddy ran through all the possible scenarios in her mind. One went like this: she would simply walk up to Irene and tell her straight out that she found an amazing, miraculous dog that can understand everything you say. Of course, that sounds crazy, and Irene would immediately start yelling at her to get back on her meds and refuse to listen to anything else she said. There is really no way to tell her about the dog directly, she decided, without it sounding like crazy talk. It was crazy talk. And she was still not entirely convinced that the dog was real, or, if he was real, that she hadn't fallen into a delusional vortex. Maybe she was straight-up crazy. Maybe the dog was just an ordinary dog and she had selectively misinterpreted his ordinary dog behavior through the lens of an elaborate genius-dog delusion. This certainly didn't feel the same as the ghost in the closet. But that's part of the problem with delusions. The way it feels is completely irrelevant. She didn't *want* to have a ghost in her closet. None of her delusions were about things that she wanted to be true. At least not necessarily so.

A second scenario went something like this: she would choke down her bile and anger and pride, and approach Irene in an apologetic fashion, contrite and humble, and say that she missed her and that she just wanted to see her, and try to convince her that she wanted to make amends for the past. She would lie, and tell her that she had been taking her meds and meeting regularly with her therapist. Then, when Irene dropped her guard, she would start saying things to the dog, telling him to do things using words that no dog could possibly understand, ask him to do things that no dog should know how to do, and have him respond to requests in ways that no other dog would have been able to; she would showcase the dog's enormous vocabulary and intellect in such a way that it would be impossible to ignore. Irene would then come to understand how unusual the dog was on her own, and Maddy could fill her in on the details. Or what few details she had at this point. Truth is, she thought, she really didn't have any details about the scope and limits of the dog's unusual abilities, and she knew absolutely nothing about how he came to possess them. She had managed to learn a little about his past through tedious yes-no question-answer sessions. But when it came right down to it, she didn't really know anything about him other than that he was not an ordinary dog.

There were third and fourth and fifth scenarios as well. But even the ones that ended with Irene recognizing that the dog was special—hell, more than special, truly a kind of miracle—fell flat at the next step. What next? What would her sister do? What was there to do? What do you do with a super-genius dog? "What do I do with a super-genius dog?" Should she start a traveling genius-dog show? Should she even tell anyone about him? "I certainly don't want DARPA getting ahold of him," she thought. "They'd turn him into a dog spy—or worse, strap a bomb to his back like they did to those dolphins." Visions of an army of super-dog assassins flitted through her mind. "Best case scenario, they'd crack his skull open and slice up his brain." She said this out loud, and Old Dog stiffened at the thought.

Maddy kept falling back on an even more immediate question. "Why am I here? What am I hoping will happen? Why do I want Irene to know about the dog?" And the answer kept coming back the same: "I want her to finally see that I am not just a crazy fuck-up. I want her approval." The logical flaw in this was as glaring as the late-afternoon sun that was presently winking into her eyes, reflecting off what little chrome remained on her side mirror mount. "I want her to see that I am not crazy by showing her something that is absolutely crazy. And even if I could get her to believe me about the dog, that would still leave me with the question of what to do about him completely unanswered." She let her chest and shoulders collapse in a long heavy sigh, looked over at Old Dog, and said, "There is nothing here for us, old boy." She started the truck and drove back through town and out to her camping spot—her home—along the river.

When the two of them climbed out of the cab of the truck, she walked over to the yes-no rocks, and said, "Old boy, I think it's time to give you a name, but I have absolutely no idea what to call you. Do you have a preference?" Old Dog hesitated for couple moments, and then decided that it really didn't matter what he was called. He hadn't been called by his previous name in a long time, and that name was associated with a lot of mixed feelings, a lot of nostalgic baggage that included more than a little actual trauma. Besides, he had no way of telling Maddy what it was. He studder-stepped over to the rocks, hesitated again, and finally placed his paw on no. Maddy picked up on his reluctance and said, "What if we just skip the formality of a name and I just call you 'dog.'" Old Dog gave the yes rock a glancing half-hearted swipe with the back of his paw. "Come on, dog, let's get you cleaned up, maybe find a replacement for that ratty collar of yours. Make you look a bit more presentable."

It didn't take long, however, before it became apparent that Maddy would not be able to keep to her choice of just calling him by the nameless name, "dog." For some reason, she always wanted to add the descriptor "old." And in a few days, she made it permanent: "Old Dog," she announced, "I guess I have given you an actual name after all." His tail produced a reflexive wag.

31

"Not all kinds of knowledge are equivalent, however," the writer continued, his dry throat recently lubricated, somewhat ironically, with an extremely dry chardonnay. "And there is a stark apples-to-oranges problem with any comparison between hunter-gatherers and the civilized. In a hunter-gatherer context, most all knowledge is in some way related to personal adaptation and survival—either directly, as in knowing which berries are edible and which are poisonous, or indirectly, in terms of cultural customs and practices that maintain a socially healthy community. This is not the case in a civilized context. Much of civilization's knowledge is specific to the complex bureaucratic and mechanistic operations of civilization itself, and, from a survival or healthy community standpoint, entirely arbitrary. As a thought experiment, start jotting down all of the little things that you need to know in order to navigate a typical day. It will become apparent almost immediately that the overwhelming majority of these things have to do either with how to interact with specific technologies or how to coordinate with the capricious requirements of bureaucratic institutions. Much of our knowledge is entirely irrelevant from the standpoint of adaptation and survival. Think about how much of your own knowledge includes superfluous and useless facts related to commercial entertainment and consumer products: the plot of a movie you saw in 2007, which team won the playoffs last year, the performance characteristics of a 1967 Chevy Impala, the price of the latest must-have tech, how to advance to the next level in a popular video game you played as a child.

"There are notable differences between hunter-gatherers and the civilized in terms of where personal knowledge comes from as well. In a hunter-gatherer context, knowledge comes from only two general sources: personal experience and information shared from the personal experiences of others, much of which has been meticulously passed down from generation to generation. Some of our knowledge comes to us through these sources as well. And, of course, we have official educational systems called schools, bureaucratic institutions tasked with disseminating knowledge required for the efficient operation of consumer industrial society. But the vast majority of what we know about the world around us comes to us through ubiquitous and complex networks of information dissemination collectively referred to as *the media.*

"There is a serious and frequently unrecognized problem with basing our understanding of the world on what comes to us through the media, however. This problem is sometimes called the media paradox. The media paradox is the idea that our understanding of the current state of the world is based largely on what we are exposed to through popular mass media, but mass media sources selectively present things that are nonrepresentative of the current state of the world. This is particularly evident with news media. To make it to the news, an event has to be unusual, weird, extreme, or otherwise out of the ordinary. But we have no real option other than to use our exposure to events in the news to decide how normal or ordinary something is. Unusual becomes normal, and what is truly normal slips away completely under the radar. This leaves us with a perpetually reinforced and continuously updated world view that has very little or nothing at all to do with what is actually happening in the world.

"How does unusual become normal? Psychologically, it happens through the joint and interpenetrating operations of availability and perceptual salience. If you had to guess, which of the following would a person be more likely to die from: a shark attack or being hit by a falling airplane part? If you said shark attack, you are in the majority. It turns out, however, that a person is about thirty times more likely to die from being hit with a falling airplane part. Shark attacks are far more likely to be covered in the media than are falling airplane part deaths, however. And because of that, they are more readily available, or more easily brought to mind. Also, shark attacks are far more perceptually salient. It is easy to form a clear image of a shark attack; you can easily imagine the thrashing about and the blood spreading in the water. And where imagination is lacking, it is likely that you have visual scenes from popular movies lurking in your memory that you could borrow from to form an image. It is much harder to form a clear image of what it looks like to be hit by a falling airplane part. Media coverage makes some causes of death more available and easier to think about than others. But availability is not the same as accuracy, and we end up being afraid of things that from a statistical standpoint we don't really need to fear, and ignoring things that, because of their actual threat potential, should terrify us.

"The tendency to hyperbolize and exaggerate and focus on the weird and unusual gives us a false impression of how the world really is. In addition to playing up perceptual salience through dramatic images and graphic details that stand out, media news coverage typically places an emphasis on the concrete, personal, and emotional content surrounding an event, using anecdotes to enhance vividness and provide a compelling narrative in order to elicit an emotional response. Emotions are given more weight than actual data, and anecdotes are remembered better than the actual reported facts. Add to this the fact that news corporations are not motivated to provide the details of an event in anything approaching an objective fashion. Quite to the contrary, the news media present the world in ways that are good for their own ratings and for the bank accounts of their sponsors. And over 90 percent of all media in the US are owned by a small handful of mega-corporations, which virtually guarantees there will be limited coverage of stories that run counter to the corporate party line.

"One result of all this is that, despite swimming in a sea of easily accessed information, the civilized are starved for meaningful knowledge. Meaning itself has been commercialized, commodified, and drained of any real substance beyond a thin and glossy surface. Civilization's need for distraction plays a big part in this, perhaps. It is best to keep things at a surface level of understanding so that people are prevented from thinking too deeply about the reasons behind what they are doing and the actual purposes to which their daily lives have been directed. Purpose and meaning are simplified, schematized, reduced to easily digestible abstractions, couched in emotionally-charged tropes, symbols that are divorced from any concrete reality."

The writer paused and took another swallow of wine. Old Dog had moved to a spot next to the writer's chair, and the writer reached down and spent a few moments stroking the dog's head before continuing.

"Much of what passes for meaningful knowledge in civilization has been rendered into banalities and trite memes and superficial platitudes that leave us with a kind of pseudo understanding—pseudo-knowledge.

The philosopher Daniel Dennett called these *deepities,* those quips and clichés and truisms that seem to be capturing some profound truth, but, on closer inspection, turn out to be meaningless gibberish. If not simply tautological, they are either logically incoherent, so general as to be informationally vacuous, or, quite frequently, demonstrably false. 'Love is eternal.' 'Happiness is where you least expect it.' 'Beauty is only skin deep.' 'Everything happens for a reason.' 'Time heals all wounds.' 'That which doesn't kill you makes you stronger.' 'Age is just a number,' and 'You are only as old as you feel.' And, yes, even 'Knowledge is power.' Several of these are clearly false. Others are entirely empty of content. 'Love is eternal?' Love is either a meaningless abstraction, or, at best, a transient emotional posture. Either way, there is nothing eternal about it. 'Happiness is where you least expect it?' Happiness is a result, an outcome, not an object occupying space. 'Skin-deep beauty?' The surface appearance of beauty is critically dependent on the bone and tissue structures beneath the skin. 'Things happen for a reason?' Much of what happens is simply random, with no reason behind it whatsoever. 'Time as a healing agent? That which doesn't kill you . . . ?' Wounds can fester and become gangrenous with time, and that which doesn't kill you can leave you quadriplegic. Yes, age is a number—we use the enumeration of years as a way of designating the passage of time—but just a number? Really? Even if it was possible to feel a specific age, a feeling can't change how long you have been in existence. We've already addressed the Hobbesian 'knowledge is power,' and here I might add that Bacon's version seems to have something more substantial going for it, something beyond mere meme value: 'knowledge *itself* is power' is a potentially testable claim.

"These deepities seem harmless on the surface. But in a society where 'surface' is all there is, in a society of distraction where we all suffer chronic information overload, where there is little opportunity to consider the truth-value of the many bits and chunks of information perpetually spattered at us, the unexamined is taken at face value, and our understanding of life becomes a piece of cheap box-store furniture: preformed and predrilled for quick assembly, but likely to collapse if actually used.

"Knowledge functions somewhat differently in a hunter-gatherer context than it does in civilization. In the former case, the addition of something previously unknown can serve to enhance the relationships between the individual and the world around them—including the social world. Knowledge extends the individual's ability to operate in the world, and enhances their personal connection with other people. Some kinds of knowledge can function that way in a civilized context as well. But in civilization, the addition of something previously unknown is far more likely to have no real relevance whatsoever in terms of extending a person's ability to engage with the world around them: trivial facts about features of the world that are either irrelevant or of which the person has no actual contact—the discovery of a new exoplanet, for example. Or the introduction of a new video gaming system. Or the latest change in marital status of a popular celebrity.

"And, in civilization, some kinds of new knowledge can actually make things worse for the individual. Because we are reverse adapted to technology, technological innovations can change the very circumstances they were designed to address, causing an increase in personal dependence and powerlessness, leading to increased reliance on the larger technostructure of civilization. Consider, as a simple case in point, the development of GPS guidance systems and their application to automotive travel. A few decades ago, it was important for people who lived in metropolitan areas to learn 'the lay of the land.' People relied largely on memory and landmarks to get around. And if you got lost, you could always consult a map that was usually stuffed in the glove compartment, or pull into a gas station and ask for directions. In other words, finding your way to your destination was something that was under your power. Now, a disembodied voice guides you through the various lane changes and turns to your destination. Memory is no longer necessary, so it isn't used. Neither are the road signs on the highway. That there is great convenience to this is obvious. However, an increase in convenience always comes at a price. There is invariably a tradeoff, and this tradeoff invariably includes an increase in personal dependence—and thus an increase in personal powerlessness—which, quite often, is not readily apparent.

"When I first started teaching college classes years ago, for example, I entered the classroom armed with written notes and a piece of chalk. Soon, I began converting my chalkboard scribblings to overhead transparencies. The convenience of the overhead projector saved considerable time and effort. But with convenience came a new level of dependency. And occasionally, the lightbulb in the overhead projector would burn out and force me to revert to using the chalkboard. Now, all of my classroom materials are coded into a digital format and stored in 'the cloud.' This is maximally convenient. But it has also put me a position of maximal dependence on the technology for retrieving and presenting the digitally-stored information.

If the school's internet connection is compromised, or the computer in the classroom is not functioning properly, I'm completely stuck. And since my lectures themselves have become reverse-adapted to the presentation technology, I am no longer in a position where I can easily compensate by reverting back to the chalkboard—and, to make matters worse, many of the classrooms are no longer equipped with anything resembling a chalkboard to begin with.

"The differences between a hunter-gatherer context and that of the civilized in terms of knowledge, and the concomitant differences in power, can be traced directly to the fact that access to knowledge in civilization is limited. Knowledge is a resource whose access is restricted by its sheer volume as well as by its commodification. Certain kinds of knowledge are restricted intentionally in order to preserve the power of the powerful; but this represents only a miniscule fraction of what is potentially available. With civilization, our dependency is not a direct consequence of control by a powerful elite. It is a consequence of the complexity of civilized life itself. It is impossible for any one person to have access to even the slightest piece of the total knowledge necessary for them to function in society. Consider cell phones again—there is not a single person on the planet who could assemble one from scratch out of raw materials—let alone construct the component manufacturing plants, computer systems, and massive networks of interacting towers—and yet cell phones have become an essential accoutrement, an entry condition for participation. Compare that to any essential hunter-gatherer tool that can be reproduced by virtually anyone old enough to have acquired the requisite skills. Sure, cell phones can do a whole lot more than an atlatl or a ceramic cooking pot, but virtually all of the needs that can be addressed by using a cell phone are needs that have been created by the requirements of a life in bondage to civilization.

"I suspect that Bacon was on to something when he said that knowledge itself is power. I suspect that's why civilization incorporates so many methods and mechanisms for making real knowledge personally inaccessible. Real knowledge is dangerous for civilization. Real knowledge of what civilization is, real knowledge of what it means for each of us to be complicit in planetary destruction, might lead a person down the wrong path, might make them start to question the underlying meaning and purpose of it all."

Old Dog smiled on the inside, and wondered at the serendipity of his life with the writer. It was as if some larger plan had brought the two of them together. And, in hindsight, his entire life had this serendipitous flow to it. It was as if it had been planned, part of some universal intelligent design. He knew, of course, that any life at all would appear to have this quality to it. That was just how the universe is fashioned. Both intelligence and design are modern creations that have no meaning outside of the fictitious worlds of civilized humans.

32

Late morning, Maddy and Old Dog were sitting on the hardpack at the edge of a ravine. A perfect confluence of forest and city in the soundscape: the stream below, a steady liquid presence; shrill birdcall; slight crackle of leaf-fall; no wind, only a very slight breeze; traffic from the road in the distance, a steady pulse of tires in perpetual doppler ascension and descension; an earth mover, its metal blade grinding heavy against stony ground somewhere over the far rise; a small aircraft flying low, its engine's high-pitched howl ricocheting off the far rockface.

A bright yellow leaf falling in the band of sunshine now directly over the stream. Its course is unusual, slow, at a sight angle from vertical, it falls twenty feet, pauses strangely, then twenty feet more—and then reverses course in a way that is shocking until it turns out not to be a leaf after all.

A butterfly.

Maddy came to this spot frequently when she needed to sort things out. It was along a steep and unpopulated hiking trail in the corner of the state park, to the north of downtown and just over a mile from her camping spot along the river. Today she was determined to sort out Old Dog. She had committed herself to becoming his caretaker, and he had responded with a quick "yes" when she asked what he thought about the idea of living with her on a permanent basis. He appeared to be cut from a similar cloth as she was, and he had already accumulated a wealth of experience—the extent of which she could never really know—about living the life of a vagabond.

She thought of him as a kind of miracle, not in a religious or mystical sense of the term—despite her delusions, she had no patience for the fairy-tales of religion. He was special in the most direct and literal sense, and she

154

felt somehow responsible for preserving and protecting him. But beyond that, she had no clue.

There was no way to tell what the extent of his present knowledge was, but simple logic told her that it was limited to the kinds of things he had been exposed to. Mostly conversations, she thought. What can you get from a conversation? Pretty limited. Especially from the kinds of people he was likely exposed to. Some of the folks in the camp were plenty smart. And she had found herself engaged in some intense political and philosophical conversations with Carl on occasion. Malcom too. But still pretty limited in the grand scheme of things. Maddy considered herself to be reasonably-well educated, and, in truth, her three and a half years of college in combination with her broad and extensive reading in the almost two-dozen years since she dropped out had yielded a well-rounded education, something on par with what a typical liberal studies Master's student would end up with, perhaps. Actually, quite a bit more expansive than that.

Then the answer came to her in exactly the way the falling leaf became a butterfly. It was there all along, and she was just not seeing it from the right angle. Old Dog was extraordinary, but he was not a finished creation. And he had so much potential that was being entirely untapped. What would happen if a dog got a college education? What would he be able to do with the knowledge? "Knowledge for knowledge's sake" was a cheap adage she once abhorred. What good was knowledge unless it could be applied in some way? But Old Dog's existence changed all the rules. And maybe it was time to rethink her opinions on this particular platitude. Maybe, in this unique situation, knowledge for the sake of knowledge was exactly right. Maybe "for the sake of knowledge itself" was all the justification necessary.

Right then Maddy decided that she would become Old Dog's mentor and teacher. She would become his guide through the recorded knowledge of the Western world. Or at least that small portion of it that she had ready access too. Old Dog's purpose in life—if there was such a thing as a purpose in life—wasn't something that was up to her to decide. What he did with his knowledge—or if he did anything with it at all—was not for her to direct or control or cast any sort of judgement on. He was not an ordinary dog, but he was still, after all, a dog. And how he used his knowledge was for him, as a dog, to choose. Her task would be to help him acquire the tools to make his own decisions. *Informed* decisions.

It seemed that the actual mechanics of the endeavor would be fairly simple. She would just read to him, and maybe point out some of the issues or complexities or controversies raised by each of the things she read. It would be like running a college graduate seminar with a single mute and illiterate student—a mute and illiterate student who was at the same time a genius. A mute, illiterate, genius student who was also a dog. OK, so maybe it was nothing like running a graduate seminar.

And I can do this in public, right out in the open at the library or in the park or wherever, she thought. Everyone who knows me already thinks of me as a crazy lady. "I *am* a crazy lady," she conceded out loud, causing Old Dog to turn his head her direction suddenly, yanking his way out of the hypnotic trance he had drifted into, enveloped in the scents of the forest and watching the colorful leaves slowly raining an angled course toward the ravine floor below. "And now I'll be known as that crazy lady who reads out loud to a dog. The crazy dog lady!" She laughed so hard her eyes shined with tears.

The *how* of Old Dog's education would be rather straightforward. Now for the *what*. Where would she start? What would her curriculum be and how should it be organized? Should she start with a complete history of Western civilization? That would take years. Centuries. Maybe just hit the high points? Or maybe start with the present state of the world and work backward? Or should she take a more philosophical focus, a focus on ideas, pulling in history only when it seemed necessary to embed ideas within their historical context? Should she include science or should she take a more liberal arts approach or a little of both? Did she have to arrange things in any kind of order at all? Maybe she could start with the classics from a variety of disciplines. She already had a sizeable cache of books in the camper, mostly literary classics and a handful of Western philosophy standards that she kept around from her college days: Homer, Sophocles, Plato, Hobbes, some Shakespeare, Nietzsche, Thoreau, Mark Twain, Mary Shelley's Frankenstein, Proust, Voltaire, Marx, Foucault. But there were also a few that leaned more scientific: Darwin, Freud, William James, and a number of Steven Gould's collected essays—hardly the makings of a well-rounded education, but maybe a convenient place to start.

Then it occurred to her exactly where she should begin: "Know Thyself." The ancient Delphic maxim about self-knowledge makes it absolutely clear where she should start. She should start with Old Dog himself. The curriculum should begin with him. She should start with the story of his own species. She should begin with a curriculum based around the question of what it means to be a dog.

It took very little time for them to work their way through the few dog-relevant readings she had on hand. By the start of winter, just as the cold of late December began to settle in, it was time to move Old Dog's classroom into the local library, where it would remain for the next two and a half years.

33

A CARNIVAL mirror makes an easy metaphor for the way civilized life distorts reality by minimizing the human element. The bulk of daily experience is made to appear diminutive, shrunken down toward invisibility, dismissed as mundane, while the grinding gears of the consumption machine are stretched to fill all of the available space.

This metaphor, however, falls short in at least two major ways. First, a carnival mirror reflects actual reality. The image may be grotesquely distorted, but it can only have the truth to work with, and all features of the image, regardless of how warped and disproportional, reflect features of something that actually exists. The reality that civilization displays is not at all like this. It is an artificial construction in which the most dominant features have no objective substance at all. The images that civilization presents are not reflections, they are figments, illusions. Maybe better to call them hallucinations.

Second, when a child stares into a carnival mirror, she knows she is seeing a distorted reflection of the truth. Her body collapses into a thin vertical line, and her head expands so that her eyes become two blinking watermelons, but all the while she feels herself to be whole and unchanged. When she learns to see herself in terms of civilized society—through an arduous and alienating indoctrination process called education, perpetrated by the people closest to her, the people she trusts the most, people who have her very best interests at heart, people who would never intentionally lead her astray—she learns to disregard her primal responses, dismiss the concrete facts of her moment-by-moment experience, and entrain her thoughts and actions to an incorporeal world of aspiration and obligation, a world of dependency where acquiescence is redefined as strength of character, a world in which individuality becomes a matter of accessory selection.

There is a well-known classic psychology experiment where children are taken one at a time into a room with toy blocks to play with. After playing with the blocks for a period of time, half of the kids are given verbal praise for their block-playing behavior, and then presented with a reward (candy or ice cream or some-such). The other half of the kids are merely allowed to play with the blocks for the allotted time and not given either verbal praise or a concrete reward. Some days later, each of the kids is again taken one at a time into the room with the blocks. Here is where it gets interesting: the kids who were previously rewarded for their block-playing played with the blocks a substantially shorter period of time than the kids who were not previously rewarded.

The explanation goes something like this. Playing with blocks is an intrinsically rewarding activity for children. But when you pair something that is intrinsically enjoyable with an external—extrinsic—reward, the intrinsic motivation weakens until, eventually, the child will no longer play with the blocks unless there is a promise of an external reward. This is called the overjustification effect. People, even young children, continually monitor their own behavior in a basic "what am I doing and why" kind of way. When the person is doing something that they enjoy, something that is intrinsically rewarding, the answer to "what am I doing and why" is "I'm doing this because I like doing it." But once an external reward is added to the situation there are then two possible answers to the "why" part of the question: "I'm doing this because I like to," and "I'm doing this because I'm getting the reward." The behavior is "overjustified." Only one justification is needed, so the most salient one—the one that stands out or is easiest to think about—sticks, and the one that is less salient fades into the background. That good feeling a person gets when they are doing something that they really like to do is a vague, fuzzy kind of thing, and not nearly as easy to think about as an external, concrete, and in consumer society oftentimes monetary, reward.

This applies far beyond children and their blocks, of course.

It took Maddy several years after she was forced to drop out of college to resurrect her intrinsic desire for knowledge. The pressure of grades—especially in her case, where, without a series of scholarships, she would never have been able to afford the cost of tuition and books—slowly siphoned away her natural drive to learn; her need to pursue knowledge for the sake of knowledge morphed into a need to pursue grades for the sake of being able to continue to attend college. Over the course of the last several years, long before Old Dog came into her life, her love of knowledge had eventually reemerged—and with a vengeance. Reading to Old Dog, and organizing his curriculum, only added fuel to an already hot fire.

Old Dog sat and listened politely at the end of his leash—a vibrant blue flat nylon leash that Maddy would clip to his matching blue collar whenever they had to be in public, just to give a good impression. Maddy told the library staff that he was her official "helper animal." The staff already knew Maddy very well, and they knew about her history of mental illness. They believed her without question, and Old Dog was allowed to accompany her and wander through the stacks as she gathered the day's lesson. Old Dog's gentle charm was impossible to ignore, and before long a jar of dog treats was kept stocked for him at the front desk.

Every day went about the same, with the exception of Sundays, when the library was only open for a few hours. They would collect the day's readings from the shelves, then walk down a flight of concrete steps to the basement level where the stacks were densely spaced and ceilings were low, and the air was stale, with traces of mold—the entire first week they were there, Old Dog could smell a half-eaten bologna sandwich somewhere close by, probably in the waste basket next to the stairs. Sounds were closer in the basement, and Old Dog could hear his own breath come back to him without echo. The light was different too, more yellow and somehow colder. Once in the basement, Maddy would lead him down a long narrow corridor of bookshelves to the far wall, which was lined with small study rooms, each with its own window.

They would usually take the room at the far end of the line, where they would spend the morning engaging with the day's lesson. On afternoons when the weather was bad, they would stay at the library and go up to the main level to contend with current events, reading through the headlines from *The New York Times*, *The Wall Street Journal*, and the local paper. Maddy always went for the hard copy, and never bothered with the computers. She wasn't very comfortable with computers, and she no longer even owned a cell phone. She had an intuitive recognition of their addictive qualities and she detested the way they were used as conduits for commercial advertising. And, given her lifestyle, she had no real need for these things to begin with.

She marveled at Old Dog's patience while she read to him. He would lie next to her in an attentive posture with his ears perked. He would openly sigh at times, or roll his head back and forth, in response to a particularly insightful passage. From Old Dog's end, he was in heaven. His mind was an empty vessel, absorbing everything that he could understand, and putting a pin in what he couldn't understand, a mental bookmark with a note to himself to "get back to this" at a future date. Dogs are not all that susceptible to the overjustification effect, and even if they were, Old Dog's motivation to learn had become such a fundamental part of what he was that no amount of external reward would be able to compete with his inner drive.

34

"Passive aggressive. There is power in subtlety. There can be more, perhaps, in nonaction, so long as you are clear on the goal. If the goal is to change the status quo, then nonaction is frequently just an expression of your impotence; and especially so in a system designed to function with or without you around. On the other end of the resistance spectrum, a head-on attack is almost always a quick path to failure. Or worse—by showing your adversary its regions of vulnerability, you have provided it with useful knowledge, and, in the long run, your actions have only increased its power over you.

"But subtlety and nuance, these things can be nearly impossible to guard against. This is what makes satire such an effective counterpoint to belligerence, why the kings of old were forced to embrace it, to own it, to control it and contain it. In this way the court jester's role was more important than that of the royal guard.

"With the current situation, here in the heart of civilization, at the center of the tragedy, satire has lost any hint of subtlety. In a world maintained through perpetual distraction, through constant breathlessness, through evermore sound and fury, nuance is overwhelmed by noise and sparkle and spectacle. A light touch, a nudge, a casual bump, these are overwhelmed by the relentless driving weight of the machine, by its sheer mass. A whispered word, regardless of its timing and placement, regardless of its relevance, its aptness, its shades of meaning, is overwhelmed by the persistent cacophony of accelerating consumption.

"As denizens of the modern civilized world, we have chosen, unlike the kings of old, not to embrace our own humiliation and thereby garner some power over it. We quickly stuff our heads in the ubiquitous sand of consumable distraction with even the slightest peripheral glimpse of our impotence. And we are content to live as emasculated kings, puppets to be manipulated in a tragic play presented for the entertainment of our corporate court jesters."

The writer slowly folded his laptop shut and took a deep breath. He had turned a dark corner that he didn't know existed. He felt as if he had stepped into a place from which there was no return, but he wasn't sure what to do about it. And, although he had no way of knowing this, the dog at his feet understood exactly where he was standing, because he had found himself in a dog's version of a very similar place not too long ago.

Relics

35

O LD Dog sat on the edge of the deck the way he often did in the evening, with his back legs swung to the side and his front legs straight as the pillars of the Parthenon, gazing into the yard, watching as the shadows softened in the spreading twilight, while the writer reclined in the chair behind him, thinking momentarily about evolution and the relationship between twisted self-replicating strands of nucleotides and the dogs they sometimes fashioned. There is a part-whole relation that the writer wanted to explore, but he didn't know where to start. And he could feel the gravity well of infinite regress lurking at the leading edge of each question-begging beginning.

Molecules have no interest in dogs, of course—dogs are merely an emergent property, on a level of scale too far removed to be of any real molecular consequence. And dogs care absolutely nothing about the ordering of base pairs.

That's the problem with science, with analysis, with abstraction in general, with attempting to disarticulate a world that was never articulated to begin with, with slicing apart a part-less universe. And even to call it a universe is a thousand cuts too many and not nearly enough.

The writer's journal sat in his lap, flipped open to the next blank page. A recent exchange with an engineering professor was chewing at the back of his mind like a parasitic worm. The two of them had somehow fallen into a discussion of the worldview presented by science, a view that the writer considered insular and lifeless, and the engineering professor equated with reality itself: "Science tells us what is true about the world," she said. The writer asked her whether she thought electrons were real things or just theoretical constructs. The question seemed to irritate her, and before she could answer, he asked her if she had ever seen an electron, and then went on to tell her, as if he was trying to put her mind at ease, that he thought electrons were obviously a really useful idea, whether or not they were actual features of the universe. The idea of electrons is an extremely functional tool of thought, a way of framing physical reality that leads to an enormous number of useful and consequential applications. But electrons, and most other creations of modern science, aren't actual features of the universe, necessarily, the writer continued. The engineer's face contorted into an expression that was some combination of incredulity and disgust, and her voice immediately took on a patronizing tone as she dismissed the perspective the writer was trying to express as being "just ridiculous." The writer started to tell her about phlogiston, an element thought to be contained within combustible materials in the days prior to the advent of oxygen, but she ended the conversation rather abruptly.

He unsheathed his pen and attempted to drown the mind worm in a bath of fresh flowing ink:

"Empedocles partitioned the universe into four elements, earth, water, air, and fire, a commonsense taxonomy that mirrors the four physical states of matter, solid, liquid, gas, and plasma. Science long ago disabused us of this backward perspective, and the ancient Greek view is now seen for the simplistic and unenlightened—primitive—view that it is. Atomic theory tells us that there are 118 elements, each capable of assuming multiple physical states according to their energy level at the time their physical state is being assessed. The universe is a far more complex place than Empedocles could have possibly imagined.

"But this doesn't seem quite right. Atomic theory tells me that the air entering my lungs is composed of a multiplicity of elements, mostly nitrogen, an inert gas that is somehow also responsible for the sky's particular shade of blue. Atomic theory has to tell me this, because it is not at all obvious. In fact, the composition of the air entering my lungs is entirely beyond my direct experience. The air of a crowded room breathes differently than the air of a forest trail, but the difference I experience is a difference of the air taken as a whole, as a unitary presence, as a coherent and indivisible entity, a difference in its density, its viscosity, its composite of scents, the way that it folds itself around my exposed skin. And, likewise, with the many solid and liquid substances I come in contact with. Wine flows differently than water, but the molecular components responsible for this difference are quite beyond any experiential grasp.

"A perspective informed by science, while useful for scientific purposes, imposes a conceptual barrier to the world of direct and immediate experience, a world that flows and breathes and binds us inextricably to each other and to all other beings."

He flipped the journal closed, called Old Dog over, and gave him a vigorous scratch between the ears.

36

M ADDY kept true to her plan to use the Delphic maxim as a curriculum guide for Old Dog's formal education, at least to start with. She began with Darwin, and some textbook summaries of the basic processes of biological evolution. She would get into the complexities later, she thought. But to truly "know thyself," to have even an inkling of an understanding of who and what you are, you first need to understand how life itself came to be as it is. You need to understand your intimate connections with all other lifeforms. You need to know that you were not born a blank slate, but came into the world with several million years of genetic impetus behind you. And you need to understand that your physical features, and your social, psychological, and behavioral tendencies did not come about through arbitrary happenstance, and that they are the results of complex interactive processes that unfolded across vast expanses of time, subtle yet insistent processes that put a premium on environmental adaptation and successful reproduction.

Evolution. Darwin didn't invent either the concept or the word; both had been around centuries prior to Darwin's *Origin of Species*—and a core understanding of evolution has probably existed for as long as there have been humans who paid attention to the world around them. Evolution simply means "change across time." But the term is quite often misinterpreted as a synonym for "progress." Change across time says nothing about whether the change is positive or negative, or in one direction or another. Progress, on the other hand, implies a specific direction, a trajectory. Progress means to get better in some way. Progress means that the forms of the past were in some way inferior to those of the present. Biological evolution does not follow a specific trajectory, and is not at all progressive. And current organisms are neither superior nor inferior to their ancestors. They are just different. And the differences are usually very slight, at that.

"Survival of the fittest" is probably the most common phrase associated with Darwinian evolution. And it is typically misinterpreted to mean "survival of the strongest," or worse, "survival of the generally superior," which reinforces the idea of progress, the mistaken belief that evolution leads to general improvement over time, as well as the flip side of that mistaken belief, that previous versions of a species were primitive and thus somehow inferior merely because they were previous versions. But that is not what fitness means in a Darwinian sense. What counts as fitness is entirely open-ended. Fitness is determined by context, and context is a continually moving target.

And the fitness-relevant features of context can be anything at all. What enhances fitness in one context may be a death sentence in another. In one environmental context, being big might offer an advantage. In another it might be being fast, or being thin, or being aggressive, or being friendly, or being hard to see, or being impossible to ignore, or being too dumb to notice. Adaptations that look on the surface to be clearly detrimental might actually offer a survival advantage. Sickle-cell anemia is a deadly congenital condition that results from having two copies of a mutated gene. But having only one of these copies makes you less susceptible to malaria, so having several members of a population carrying one sickle-cell gene is adaptive in the long run if they happen to be living in a malaria-prone region of the world, even though tragedy is all but guaranteed for a quarter of their offspring and another quarter is left vulnerable.

Evolutionary change is not a smooth or even a continuous process. It occurs in fits and spurts. *Punctuated equilibrium* is the term that biologists use to describe this pattern. A species that is well-adapted to its niche can continue in its present form, virtually unchanged, indefinitely. The environment acts like a gravity well or an "attractor" that continually pulls variation toward a central norm. When the environment stays the same, there is still variation among individuals, but there may be very little change in the population overall. But when the environment changes, the species is susceptible to population-wide drift or alteration in its present form; when the rules of survival are altered by the addition or removal of a competitor, or a dramatic turn in climate that restructures the opportunities with respect to food or shelter or migration patterns, a change in the number of conspecifics, or just a change in some minor feature of the local situation, some variations may proliferate while others dwindle and perhaps eventually disappear. This can happen suddenly, abruptly, in response to sudden changes in the environment. So, the fossil record tends to show a pattern in which species remain in equilibrium, with very little change for extended periods of time, punctuated by brief bursts of rapid change in a species' characteristics, perhaps to the point of becoming a distinctly different species.

The appearance of civilization definitely qualifies as a dramatic change in the environment—perhaps the most dramatic change since the asteroid that wiped out the dinosaurs. Some folks claim that humans have evolved to accommodate a civilized lifestyle, and that civilization is a characteristic feature of the human species: humans build cities like termites build mounds. But civilization has simply not been around long enough for that to be the case. It is true that civilization has left its genetic mark on various human subpopulations. Because of a long cultural history of animal milk consumption, people of northern African or European descent maintain production of the enzyme for digesting milk sugar past childhood, for example, whereas most of the people on the planet are lactose intolerant as adults. But to say that humans have evolved to live in civilization is really a kind of racism—actually worse than racism: it is to suggest that people from indigenous cultures who have only recently been exposed to civilization are not fully human.

Darwin is famous for showing how natural selection can lead to different species. However, many of an animal's characteristics are not species-specific, but are shared both up and down the taxonomic ladder. A sizeable portion of human behavior, for instance, is not unique to humans, but is behavior that humans share in a general form with other primates as well. Many features of primate behavior are likewise shared more broadly with other mammals. In general terms, mammal species are far more alike than they are different. Because of this, the individual members of a given species share almost everything in common with each other, save for a few relative minor idiosyncrasies. But—and this is part of Darwin's genius—it is precisely these minor idiosyncrasies that provide the hooks for natural selection to latch onto when the environment changes.

Humans pay a lot of attention to uniqueness, to individual differences among people, not because of some instinctual awareness of the forces that drive natural selection, but because small differences among individuals can be extremely informative for social animals. Tiny dissimilarities among people are overexaggerated, magnified into dramatic disparities because tiny differences can sometimes make a large difference when it comes to how a person responds to the complexities and demands of human social life. Proportionally, and taken objectively and in their totality, the physical and psychological differences that exist among individual people are microscopically superficial. Add the homogenizing effects of consumer civilization to the mix, and humans are almost perfect clones of one another, at least when it comes to their general behavior.

This is true of dogs too, of course. Dogs are, first of all, vertebrates. As such, they share an enormous number of physical features in common with every other vertebrate. The fact that they are also mammals adds a few more specifics: warm blooded, live birth, usually a furry covering. Knowing that they are canines adds all but a few details. Knowing that they are wolves resolves most of these details, with only minor exceptions. Knowing that they are a domesticated variation of wolves, a variation that has been subjected to intentional alterations imposed by civilization, fills in those exceptions, and your knowledge of the species is as complete as it can be. From there you are left with variation among individual dog breeds and surface variation among individual dogs—and even Old Dog's tail-end-of-the-distribution exceptionality comes down to just a minor idiosyncrasy.

Maddy gathered all that she could find in the library about the natural history of canines, and read it to Old Dog. When she got to the wolf-dog distinction, things became a bit more complicated. Dogs are essentially wolves, but there is a whole lot of mystery being packed into the hedge word, "essentially."

How dogs and humans came together is still controversial among the scientists who study this. Humans were not domesticators until just recently. And it could be argued—and sometimes is—humans are not really domesticators at all. Domestication is not a characteristic feature of the human species' makeup. Domestication is a kind of lifestyle variation. In the relatively recent past—evolutionarily speaking, just yesterday—some tiny proportion of humans adopted domestication-based ways of life. These ways of life have since proliferated because they tend to be viral and leave very little room for the more authentically human ways of life they replace. What all this means is that dogs, which are claimed as the first animal that humans domesticated, were not domesticated by people living otherwise domestication-based lifestyles. They were domesticated by hunter-gatherers. And this brings into question whether the first dogs to live alongside humans did so as a function of domestication at all. But if not domestication, then what?

There are some "just-so" stories about how domestic dogs came to exist. Most of these tales follow enough of a logical thread to be at least plausible. But, like all just-so stories, they are not necessarily based on compelling stand-alone evidence—or any evidence at all. One of these stories has prehistoric humans occasionally adopting and raising orphaned wolf pups. No doubt this happened on occasion—it still happens today. But as a theory for the primary way that dogs came about, it has little to offer. The real problem with this theory is that wolf pups grow up to be wolf adults, with all of their untamed wildness intact, and not the kind of creature you would want hanging around the campfire with you at night. Modern-day wolves don't make very good pets for the same reason.

Another story, and one that is perhaps a little more likely, is a story that begins from the dog's perspective rather than the more usual perspective that paints humans as the doers and ultimate determiners of things. This alternative story casts domestic dogs as the descendants of misfit wolves, wolves that were not brave enough or not alpha enough or just too lazy to be a functional part of a pack, or wolves that were exiled from a pack, or some combination of these kinds of wolves. These misfits were drawn to human encampments to feed because the pickings were easy— nomadic hunters leave behind a lot of edible garbage as they move from place to place. As these wimpier and less aggressive wolves followed humans around, they interbred with each other, which eventually lead to a more docile wolf subspecies. The proto-dogs were tolerated by the humans because of their relative lack of aggression. They also served as sentries, warning of the presence of predators or other human groups entering the area. In addition, they were a handy source of food in an emergency. Over time, humans brought these less aggressive wolves into their camps for some combination of their sentry services, their assistance with the hunt, and their convenience as food during sparce times—in much the same way that hunter-gatherers still use dogs today, especially in the arctic and in mountainous regions. If this story is even partially accurate, it suggests that the original dog-human connection began as more of a symbiotic relationship than as domestication proper.

When this happened is also somewhat controversial. The evidence is pretty good, however, that the first dog-human relationships were forged at least 30 thousand years ago, and probably much earlier than that. There is some evidence that it happened as early as 36 thousand years ago. But logic suggests that it may have been happening much, much earlier than even that. The humans alive 250 thousand years ago were not living in substantially different ways than were the humans alive 30 thousand years ago, and wolves have been living their wolfish ways for at least as long, with fossil evidence of the gray wolf dating back 300 thousand years. Some form of fellowship between humankind and dogkind may have existed from the very beginning.

Maddy was careful to connect the dots between the subtle workings of natural selection and the emergence of dogkind. And Old Dog was awed by the timeframe involved. Of course, he had no way of expressing his awe other than continuing to give Maddy his undivided attention as she read to him. There was something noble, or maybe noble is the wrong word, something inspiring, perhaps even empowering, about being able to attach himself to a species with a prehistory that stretched across hundreds of thousands of years.

But modern dogs are not a result of natural selection alone. Their most uniquely dog-like characteristics are the product of artificial selection, and reflect changes that have been purposely forced upon them in just the past few millennia, just since humans immersed themselves in domestication as a way of life. Dogs have a history as well as a prehistory. But as Maddy started to explore the historical story of dogs, starting with the earliest beginnings of civilization, she quickly realized that she would first need to cover the beginnings of civilization more broadly, and then the nature of Western civilization and so on. Dog domestication—actual domestication with all of its distortions and deformations—occurred within the context of the emergence of agriculture and the proliferation of civilized ways of life, so she decided to leave the history of dog domestication in the Western world on the backburner. Before picking up the history of domestic dogs, she would first need to take a look at the early history of Western civilization itself.

37

C HOOSING exactly where to start was difficult. She could start with the very first cites, with the first civilizations of Sumer and ancient Egypt and Babylon. But as ancient as these iconic civilizations were, they were not really the start anything. Sumer, ancient Egypt, and Babylon were end results; they were the outcome of changes that occurred long beforehand. The very first cities were the result of a dramatic and qualitative alteration in natural human society that began with domestication, when groups of people abandoned the largely nomadic and largely egalitarian lifestyles that had allowed humans to adapt and flourish as a species for more than two million years.

The prehistoric transition from nomadic foraging to sedentary farming was a game-changer in the most literal sense, and it can be difficult—perhaps impossible—for someone occupying a modern civilized lifestyle to even begin to fathom what life was like prior to the invention of agriculture, let alone appreciate the subsequent far-reaching effects of the transition to a domestication-based lifestyle. It turns out that a comparably dramatic change occurs today in the course of the psychological development of each individual human during early childhood that might serve as a rough analogy—at least in terms of the qualitative nature of the transformation.

Starting when a child is just a few months old, there is a pivotal change in the ability to think that is so fundamental that, in retrospect from an adult perspective, it is impossible to imagine how the world might have appeared beforehand because imagination itself was not possible beforehand. Psychologists use, as an indication of this change, something called object permanence. Object permanence is the cognitive ability to understand that objects (and people) continue to exist when they are not immediately present to the senses—a fact that is not at all obvious to infants at the outset. For infants, out of sight is truly out of mind, and for a child who has yet to develop object permanence, whenever mom leaves the room, she vanishes entirely from the universe.

This seems like a simple and almost trivial thing, but it is far and away the most profound cognitive change that occurs in a person's entire lifetime. Consider what is required in order for mom to still "be in mind" when she is out of sight. In order to know that mom is still somewhere when she is not physically present to the senses, the child has to have something available in memory that "represents" mom, a placeholder in the mind, a mental artefact, a symbol for mom. Object permanence marks the earliest beginnings of symbolic thought, and everything else that happens from that point on in terms of cognitive development is just a matter of expanding, applying, and fine tuning this basic symbolic capacity. So, there is a fundamental and qualitative change that happens practically at the beginning of life that sets the stage for everything else that comes later.

This change must have happened at some point with Old Dog, Maddy thought. How many other animals are capable of capturing features of the world in this fashion? Object permanence is not something that is limited to humans. Old Dog was evidence of that—and even a normal dog understands that the bone doesn't vanish from the universe after it has been buried.

The prehistoric transition from a nomadic hunting and gathering lifestyle to sedentary pastoral or agricultural one was an event that was as transformative in terms of the social development of human society as object permanence is in the development of the mental life of an individual child. In both cases, everything that occurs afterward is just a matter of applying, extending, intensifying, and fine tuning the core results of the change. The former change occurred a few thousand years prior to the first cities. Before this change occurred, all humans everywhere were hunter-gatherers spending most of their time in small egalitarian social groups and living rich and meaningful lives embedded in the abundance of the natural world. After this change, humans started living increasingly inegalitarian lives in larger and larger groups in which the abundance of the world was systematically reduced and meaning became increasingly detached from living nature.

The analogy between the development of object permanence in an individual child and the transition to a domestication-based agricultural society, like all analogies, breaks down at some point. It isn't perfect. And when she tried to express the analogy to Old Dog, Maddy noticed where the major imperfection was. One of these things is a natural feature of the unfolding development of a living being, and the other was an accidental result of an unlikely confluence of contingent events. To equate them is to suggest that the emergence of civilization was a natural thing, as if the transition to agriculture and then to cites was part of the natural developmental progression of human social life, as if this progression was somehow coded into human DNA, as if it was predestined from the very start, as if civilization was at one end of a cultural development continuum with hunting and gathering at the other, as if civilized life reflects the natural maturation of the human species. This is absolutely not the case, she realized. There is nothing natural about civilization other than the flesh-and-blood humans who are being forced to participate in it.

The appearance of civilization a few thousand years ago had nothing to do with progress. And everything that has happened since suggests the very opposite of progress. How is global warming, overpopulation, species extinction, and the toxification of land, air, and water in any way related to progress? The appearance of civilization was an improbable and unpredictable accident of climate change and geology and evolutionary history and a thousand random chance events that, if any one of them had happened slightly differently, civilization would have never come about. At its heart, civilization is the chance result of a viral lifestyle experiment—and an infectious virus makes a much more appropriate analogy in several respects. The transition to agriculture didn't happen everywhere. It originally happened in only a few places, but it quickly and violently spread elsewhere. In this way, it is entirely unlike the infant's development of object permanence, which *is* coded into human DNA, and which happens without exception— no violent external force required—to every ordinary human child as soon as their brain reaches a sufficient level of maturity.

But that's where Maddy decided to begin, with the transition from nomadic foraging to sedentary farming and then to large-scale domestication. She began with the astonishing move from a two-million-year-long stint of hunting and gathering—with perhaps a little small-scale horticulture thrown in here and there—to an agricultural lifestyle. That is really where civilization starts, the point at which civilization became a possibility, and perhaps even an inevitability.

The conditions and contingencies that led up to this transition emerged slowly, over a long period of time, and deciphering which came first or which deserves more or less causal credit would be a futile chicken-egg exercise. The earliest indications begin with a reduction in nomadism in the wake of the last ice age glacial period. Climate change had produced a region of overabundance just east of the Mediterranean, often referred to as the fertile crescent, in which high protein plant foods such as pistachios and acorns, and easily harvested fish, existed alongside readily accessible herds of antelope and ibex and deer. The food in this region was so diverse and plentiful that there was no longer any need to follow the herds around. As groups of people in this area became more sedentary, their populations started to increase. Again, this happened slowly at first, so that by the time the population began to outstrip the once overabundant local food, sedentary life had already become the established mode. So, rather than revert to nomadism when the population increased and food became harder to get, some of these folks expanded their food choices to include the starchy seeds of grasses that were also plentiful in the area.

It is known now that this grain was a Trojan horse; like modern grain, it contained exogenous opiates, compounds that have mild effects that are similar to opium. Eating the local grain and the foods made from it likely led to low-level addiction. Because the availability of this grain was subject to the unpredictable weather from year to year, and because population numbers continued to increase, people started to plant the grain intentionally to ensure a sufficient harvest for what had by then become a dietary staple. That may have been the moment—right there, the intentional planting of these grain crops—that may have been the change that fundamentally altered things for humans forever afterward, the germination of a society based on dependency, a society based on control and restriction rather than one couched in openness and freedom.

Humans have always been clever problem solvers. In a sense, that is what any specific technology is at its core: a solution to a problem. And when drought threatened their needed crops, people came up with solutions. The first thing they did was site their fields in river valleys that flooded in the spring, and this worked wonderfully until growing population size forced them farther and farther away from the riverside. And what they did to solve this problem was probably critical for the eventual emergence of civilization: they invented irrigation. If you can't have your crops near the water, you can always bring the water to your crops. But irrigation is a Trojan horse of its own. Irrigation requires labor to dig the channels and to run the dams and spill gates. It also requires ditch maintenance and timing and a whole lot of other things that encouraged and increased something that was already in its beginning phases by this point: division of labor.

In a hunter-gatherer society, everyone is by necessity a Jack (or Jill) of all (or most) trades. But in an agricultural society it is necessary to divide up the workload. In addition, the level of organization involved requires a control mechanism in the form of systems of authority. Systems of authority are really a kind of social technology. They are a way of mechanizing human action. And when you layer authority over the social world, you force human relationships into a mechanical template.

"People think that dominance hierarchies are a natural thing," Maddy said, as she pulled a book from the center of the stack sitting on the table next to them. "But that's not the case at all. Humans are anarchists by nature." She thumbed through the book's table of contents, flipped through the pages, and then read aloud about something called the pecking order, and about the early 1920s German researcher, Thorleif Schjelderup-Ebbe, and his work on social dominance relations that occur among chickens in hen houses, and the weird things that happen as a result of the artificial environment of the barnyard that would probably never happen in the wild. Schjelderup-Ebbe observed that if there is no rooster around, one of the henhouse hens will spontaneously stop laying eggs, take on a rooster-like watchdog role, and begin to dominate the other hens. In captive chickens, complex hierarchical patterns of dominance and submission emerge as a result, a literal pecking order. Something very similar happens with humans forced to live in circumstances in which they cannot practice a natural human way of life. It is interesting to note that these kinds of pecking orders, these hierarchical arrangements of social power, are largely absent from nomadic foraging societies. Hunter-gatherers rarely if ever have anything resembling a stable hierarchical ordering of social power. Leadership in natural human communities is transient and highly contextual. Some people are better at some things than are others, and they are recognized as such. But the idea that some people should be in a position of authority over others has no traction.

People often point to the human species' closest cousins in the primate world, chimpanzees, as evidence that humans are naturally prone to form violently enforced power hierarchies. However, observational studies of chimpanzees in their natural habitat have consistently found their social lives to be remarkably peaceful and absent any persistent social dominance relations, closely paralleling that found in traditional human foraging societies. Unfortunately, the vast majority of the scientific data on chimpanzee social behavior comes from observations conducted in unnatural and highly contrived situations. For example, the much-cited "gang violence" behavior found by the famous Jane Goodall and her students was based primarily on studies where large caches of food were set up to attract chimps from multiple groups. Limited access to this desired resource produced competitive and aggressive behavior—very much like what happens with civilized humans. But this kind of violence does not seem to occur under normal free-foraging circumstances. And by inference, it was likely rare to the point of being nonexistent in prehistoric human foraging societies as well.

There could never be an egalitarian civilization. Hierarchical arrangements of social power are necessary for civilization to function. And, as a logical corollary, there can never be a civilization without violence and the threat of violence at its core. You can't enforce a power hierarchy otherwise. Although, it must be admitted that the effects of human self-domestication have reduced the degree to which this violence needs to be applied overtly.

Maddy grabbed another book from the stack, flipped it open to a chapter on the colonization of North America, and continued with the lesson.

38

ALMOST two and a half years went by in just this way, with Maddy and Old Dog nestled in their study carrel in the library basement three or four hours each day on days when the library was open, usually in the morning. Late afternoons and weekends were frequently spent hiking along the many trails in and around the state park, visiting friends on the street, or just enjoying peaceful time among the trees in Maddy's spot along the bank of the river.

By the end of these two and a half years, Old Dog had been exposed to a wide range of Western thinkers and writers, and a fair sampling of Eastern philosophy as well. Maddy read from the classics of Western literature, the Iliad and the Odyssey, Virgil, some Sophocles, Cervantes, a broad sampling of Shakespeare, Milton, Voltaire, Goethe, Tolstoy, Samuel Clemens, as well as from a sizable selection of Western philosophy, Hippocrates, Epictetus, Plato's Meno, Aristotle's Metaphysics, Seneca's speeches, Machiavelli, some Montagne, Bacon, Kant, Hume, Kierkegaard, Nietzsche, Lock, Hobbes, Descartes, Spinoza, Rousseau, Emerson, Thoreau, Whitehead, John Stewart Mill, Marx, Kafka, Sartre, and Foucault. She had also included a broad array of general scientific pieces, covering a variety of topics. In short, Old Dog was provided the scholarly content of a substantial liberal arts education.

And Old Dog wasn't a passive listener. He continuously mulled things over. He compared and contrasted the various readings and authors and ideas. He revisited what he could remember from earlier readings and made connections, and he had unique and penetrating insights—of course, none of which he was able to share. He noticed that the Western perspective involved a linearity and a tendency to compartmentalize. He had noticed this linear tendency previously, the tendency to view events as a series of new isolated things rather than as the perpetual unfolding of a complex, multifaceted, ongoing happening. And the tendency to compartmentalize was somewhat frustrating to him. He suspected that both of these had something to do with language. Speech is linear—and written language only exacerbates this tendency. And the symbolic compartmentalizing of ideas within words, along with the simplification of the world through the application of labels and categories, encourages a simplistic, piecemeal, one-dimensional focus that completely ignores the most obvious and salient facts that the world is multidimensional and irreconcilably relational.

The human perspective wasn't always this way, he figured. There was something about civilization that was to blame. Humans existed for a long time in a state of complete immersion in the natural world, a state that is incompatible with a linear compartmental approach. Civilization involves a technologizing of thought, the imposition of a mechanical template, an assembly-line structuring of experience that discards everything that can't be schematized, organized, bureaucratized, or fitted into a power hierarchy. When the great thinkers of the ancient world, Socrates and Plato and Aristotle and those who preceded and followed them expressed their understanding of the world, they were expressing an understanding that had long before been entrained to this mechanical template. The systems of logic that they devised offered a powerful way of approaching the world, but what is quickly forgotten among those who become dependent on rationality is that the world itself is not logical. The universe is not arrayed according to laws or principles. The cosmos does not bow to reasons. All of these things, logic, reason, analytical assessment, are superadded. All of these things are attempts to pull the universe apart so that it can be reassembled according to abstract categories, so that it can be communicated in terms of labels.

This perspective, once allowed to proliferate, only intensifies with time because it is associated with a transmutative orientation toward the natural world that is based on intentional alteration and purposeful reorganization. Prior to agriculture, humans approached the world in the same way that every other creature still approaches the world today. The world, for noncivilized beings, is approached as it is in the moment. It is taken foundationally, as a given. The world is not something to learn to live in, or something to accommodate. It is simply the state of things as they are. If you are thirsty, water is there for you to drink. If it is not, then you will need to find it somewhere else. If you are hungry, food is there for you to eat.

Sometimes it is there in a way that requires considerable effort on your part, but it is always there and always has been and always will be. The world will always provide.

Actually, that's not exactly true. That phrase expresses a civilized thoughtform. The world doesn't *provide* anything. There is no world that could possibly act in such a way. The world is not a thing that acts. The civilized approach turns the world into just another object. It is analyzable and malleable and changeable and movable and reworkable. It is something to disassemble and alter in order to make it fit the structuring of preferred forms rather than something to be taken as it is in itself. It becomes something that *provides,* and what and how and to whom it provides are things to be altered and adjusted and made more efficient.

Civilized humans have been living a technologized existence for so long that the world around them has become just another machine. All has become mechanism. The relative positions of the planets and the movement of continents and the changing weather are explained in terms of mechanistic principles. And to make this mechanistic framing more palatable to an organic human mind, it is cleverly disguised behind a layer of anthropomorphism: the actions of matter are *governed* by certain forces; quarks *participate* in holding the atomic nucleus together; electrons *behave* like both a particle and a wave; tectonic plates join and separate in a *constant dance*; the river *carries* sediment downstream; each body organ *performs* a specific job; prefrontal brain areas *direct and control* motor activity.

The civilized view, like all human understanding, civilized or otherwise, is story-based. But the stories civilization tells unfold inside symbolic worlds rather than within the concrete material world as it manifests itself in the present moment. This is the topsy-turvy role of abstraction. The civilized world is a world of abstraction built upon layers of abstraction, with each layer further removed from anything real, from anything in direct contact with immediate experience. These two things, the proliferation and prioritization of artificial worlds and the technologizing of thought and action, have lured the civilized mind into a kind of fish trap that seems impossible to escape.

Escape is possible, Old Dog thought, but it requires the near-impossible to accomplish. It requires realizing that not only does the trap offer no physical way out, but that it had originally provided no physical way in as well. It was like a Zen koan in which the only answer to the question is to refuse the very possibility of asking the question to begin with.

39

Viruses can't think. Hell, they aren't actually alive, at least not in the way that being alive is normally envisioned. They exist only through a kind of asymmetrical symbiosis. Outside of a host's cell they are just tiny particles of organized matter armed with a couple enzymes and some otherwise innocuous fragments of genetic material. A virus doesn't have a strategy or plan of attack. It doesn't plot an expanding vector through a population of potential victims. It merely exploits the hosts' gregariousness, piggybacks off of their social proclivities, their patterns of connection and incidental contact. And all without forethought or malice.

A virus is critically dependent on its host in a way that, if it could think, would give it pause. A virus ceases to exist when vulnerable host populations cease to exist. If a virus could think, it would realize its own precarious position, its degree of dependency. It would understand that its own future survival is critically dependent on the continued availability of a host. If a virus could think, it would form congressional subcommittees to craft legislation to ensure a sustainable supply of future hosts. If a virus could think, it would have vocal activists and political action committees and celebrity endorsements and a substantial social media presence.

Civilization is occasionally likened to a planetary virus. And although this is usually meant as simile or metaphor, it is a very thin metaphor, only barely metaphor, metaphor in which the target and vehicle are too close to be mere analogy: civilization in a very real sense *is* viral. The planet is being consumed, its biological and geophysical health is being degraded at break-neck speed by civilized forms and structures that replicate and proliferate in ways that closely resemble the lytic cycle of a virus, forms and structures that exploit vulnerable systems of the host to make deadly copies of themselves, quickly mutating around unprepared defensive systems, penetrating ever-deeper layers of tissue until, eventually, there will be nothing left to consume.

Civilization is un-strategically parasitic. Civilization exists only through a kind of asymmetrical symbiosis. Outside of a physically diverse, materially-rich biome populated with humans, civilization is just a collection of hierarchically organized patterns of power distribution armed with lethal technology and some otherwise innocuous delusional belief systems. Civilization doesn't have a strategy or plan of attack. It doesn't plot a vector of expansion and progress. It merely exploits natural vulnerabilities, piggybacks off human social and psychological proclivities and their easily manipulated fears and anxieties.

And all without forethought or malice.

The relationship between civilization and viruses goes far beyond mere literary device, however. Yes, civilization spreads like a virus, but civilization is the creator of actual viruses as well. When it comes to those deadly and disfiguring viruses that plague the civilized—in the most literal sense—civilization is the mother of all vectors, the virus mother herself. With few exceptions, all of the most virulent diseases of civilization are diseases that have been manufactured, as if on an assembly line, by the very conditions of civilization. Most are a direct result of animal domestication: influenza, small pox, measles, diphtheria, tuberculosis, the bubonic plague, and the common cold. And then there is the SARS family of viruses that have incubated and mutated in bats who themselves live in close proximity to domesticated animals. So, both metaphorically and literally, civilization is a viral lifestyle—a meta-virus.

Maddy got sick in late April, shortly after the governor issued his first state-wide stay at home order in response to the novel SARS virus that made a dramatic appearance a few months previously and was showing every sign of turning into a pandemic that would make the 1918 flu look like a case of sniffles. By the time Carl convinced her to go to the hospital, she was struggling to breathe. She died six days later.

It was Carl who gave Old Dog the news. Not directly, of course—Maddy never told Carl about Old Dog's "abilities," and he probably wouldn't have believed her if she had. Carl was staying at his daughter's place, and had promised Maddy he would look after Old Dog while she was in the hospital. Old Dog overheard Carl tell his daughter about Maddy's death, and something inside him shattered.

A dog's emotional experience is different from that of humans, but mostly only in very subtle ways having to do with how the emotions are expressed physically. Dogs don't label their feelings, so they are not predisposed to the human problem of misinterpreting their emotional state by misreading the context and assigning the wrong label. For example, a person in a chaotic or fear-inducing environment, say on a blind date watching a scary movie, might mistake the source of their movie-induced arousal, thinking it reflects feelings of attraction for the person they are with. Dogs simply can't do this—or, rather, most dogs can't—and so the source of their emotional reaction is almost always clearly identifiable.

And even though Old Dog was different in that he could apply labels to his emotional states, there is no label that could possibly capture the knife-stabbing intensity of the pain he was feeling in that moment. He immediately slunk out the back door, jumped the fence encircling Carl's daughter's yard, and headed off down the street. He made his way back to Maddy's camper and spent the night out of the rain under the bed of the truck. As he drifted into a fitful sleep feeling the underside of the truck lightly press against him, he was reminded of the times in similar weather all those years ago when he had to wedge himself under the side of the front porch.

When morning came, he struck out into the forest, walking along one of their favorite hiking trails, and then headed east, resuming the general bearing he had when he came to the city almost three years ago.

40

THERE are other places like that, but they have become cliché: the empty space between flame and wick, the fulcrum of breath, the distance between heartbeats, the moment in time just before dreadful insight strikes like a cannonball against soft wood. If only the mind could hold its ground in these places—the twitch of a bird's tail as the wind rocks the branch, a spinal reflex to keep hope from failing.

The pain of loss is experienced by all living things, and humans aren't the only creatures who experience grief. Chimpanzees, gorillas, elephants, and even killer whales have been observed behaving in ways that human eyes clearly recognized as expressions of mourning. Modern civilized humans have distorted the natural expression of loss—like modern civilized humans have distorted almost everything else—by forcing it into a technological template. The slow release, the painful letting-go, the thickly unfolding emotional strata of loss is strategically arrayed along an assembly-line progression of "stages of grief." The Kubler-Ross stage progression from denial to anger to bargaining to depression to acceptance has been soundly rejected by careful scientific scrutiny. Nevertheless, the idea that grief follows a pattern of progression fits with everything else in the civilized technological frame, a frame in which things proceed in steps and stages, a frame that translates everything in life into "process." The glaring fact that nothing can be said definitively about the progression of the grief experienced by any specific individual, other than that it typically goes from bad to better over time (and even then, not necessarily so), is not sufficient to counter the technologizing reflex.

Old Dog was never in denial. He could smell that Maddy was deathly ill, and he had no reason to suspect Carl was being untruthful when he announced Maddy's death to his sister. And, anyway, denial is not a psychological state that dogs have any use for. And he never felt anger. What would be the point? Anger is a motivator, a call to action that is only functional in situations where an angry reaction has the potential to change things. Bargaining is something that requires a mind that has experience with power differentials, something that Old Dog did have some experience with, perhaps. But what good would it do to bargain? Dogs don't have religion; they don't have any need to believe in deities with power that could be bargained with. Depression was definitely part of what he felt. But the sadness was chronic and gave no indication of abating; it was not something that emerged as a separate stage, it was continual and persistent. In Old Dog's case the term acceptance made no sense at all. What would it mean to accept something if there was never any chance of not accepting it? Old Dog was in mourning over Maddy's loss, and he would be so for the rest of his life. It wasn't something he would ever "get over" or be done with. It would be with him for as long as he lived. It would become part of who and what he was. The process of grief—if there is anything in the natural world that is at all comparable with the industrial idea of *process*—was a process of incorporation, a process of integration. The grief he felt would eventually meld into everything else that he was, merge with his being in a way that would be impossible to disentangle from all of the rest.

Old Dog eventually found his way back to the river, and followed the river's course upstream to the east as it wound its way through several of the small rural towns that girdled the city at a short distance like derelict Cold War satellites in low Earth orbit. He quickly established a foraging circuit. He would spend a day or two scavenging at one town, where he would invariably draw the attention of the town's animal control authorities—or some farmer on the outskirts—and then slip over to the next. He wasn't a fast dog. And although he was strong for his size, he wasn't a really big dog. But his understanding of humans and his ability to predict human behavior gave him an edge that neither speed nor strength would have been able to match, and he was always able to escape unscathed. And usually with a full belly.

Between towns were areas of residual, second-growth forest where he would spend a day or two reflecting on how his ancestors, and his present-day wolf and coyote cousins, were able to thrive in the wild. He felt that on some level he still had the requisite genetic knowledge, latent and waiting, as if it could burst forth at any moment. Those ancestral ways were still active, they were right there just below the surface. He was sure that this was true for humans as well. There are still groups of people who live in authentically human ways, and these people are not a different species from the civilized despite their radically different lifestyles. And besides, evolution works on a time frame that far exceeds the duration of civilization. Agriculture-based lifeways have only been around for a few thousand years. And it took quite a while for agriculture to become the human norm—and even then, it was only through force, through violence and genocide and perpetual threat of more violence and genocide.

Civilization is temporary. And the planet will not long sustain civilization's recent global iteration. When it eventually crumbles in on itself, if there are still people around, they will have no choice but to fall back upon their genetic heritage as foragers. They will have no choice but to rewild. The world of the future will be different from the world of the past. But, after the dust of collapse has finally settled, there is no reason to believe that it will be less amenable to an authentic human life of meaning and abundance than it was before civilization came along.

One day, as Old Dog was thinking about the inevitable rewilding of future humans and wondering what that would mean for dogs, he stepped out of the tree line, around a weathered post draped with sagging strands of barbed wire, and into a freshly mown field of hay. There was some commotion in the distance, and the sound of chickens in distress. He moved closer to investigate. Just as he reached the middle of the field, he was almost knocked off his feet by four dogs running excitedly in the opposite direction, the largest of which had the neck of a still flailing chicken clamped in his mouth.

The Abundance of Now

41

"START from a dark place, the darkest place. Scour the ground of existence down to base granite. Borrow Descartes' example, *cogito ergo
sum*. Whittle the rational mind down past its inner xylem, into the pith, to
the central core. Doubt even the solidity of this. Borrow Descartes example,
but not his purpose. The purpose of this mental knife-play is not to establish a foundation for belief, or to carve out a premise from which to anchor
a logical proof of your own existence; the purpose is to lay bare your intimate fellowship with the void.

"Prior to birth was nothing. No nouns. No verbs. No past or future
tense. No beginnings or endings to serve as a frame. *Nothingness* itself was
nonexistent. No opposing principle by which to form nothingness into an
object of contemplation. No contemplative being capable of granting such
principles.

"There is little about this state of previous nonbeing that seems personally threatening to me now," the writer continued. "Why is that? Why am
I able to calmly imagine an infinite expanse of time when I wasn't? There
is something about the present moment that renders my prior nonexistence irrelevant. I find myself in the present moment awash in abundance,
occupying a richly furnished living state of being, in a universe populated
with nouns and verbs and tenses—many of which I have yet to discover
and most of which I will never know. Contemplating the infinite expanse
of emptiness before I was born is little more than an intellectual exercise,
nothing ominous or menacing.

"But despite its intimate familiarity—its intimate but ultimately
unknowable familiarity—things appear quite different to me when I turn

my gaze the other direction. When the universe ends for me, the same eternal absence-of-even-oblivion from which I emerged waits only to wrap me once again in its disintegrating, obliterating embrace. I die, but I can never *be dead*. Death is a feature of the living present moment. Death is a verb. There is no after-death in the first-person. In my mind I can project the universe persisting beyond myself, but this is an illusion of objectivity. After this, there is nothing. Death leads us not just to the end of life, but to a complete annihilation of all that ever was; the universe itself, in its unfathomable boundlessness, never existed. Life doesn't come to an end with death. With death, life never happened to begin with.

"Yet here, right now, in the present moment, it seems as if there is something worthy of my attention."

This moment now the evening sky is dim and the reflection of the writer's face has become visible in the window, a grizzled gray beard beneath shadow-darkened eye sockets, the dog is using his outstretched foot as a chinrest, and thoughts of Spanish wine are inserting themselves between the words his fingers are slapping out on the keyboard.

42

O LD Dog stood frozen in place, surrounded by golden whirling slivers of atomized straw suspended in the wake of the dogs who had
just rushed past him. But he didn't stand frozen long. A sudden geyser of
earth and dust erupted next to him, accompanied by the familiar sound of a
gunshot. And then another. He quickly traced the sound to an angry figure
standing at the far end of the field with a rifle leveled for a third volley, and
then bolted in the opposite direction. As another gunshot sounded behind
him, he dove beneath a low strand of rusted barbed wire, and sprinted
toward the spot along the edge of the field where the other dogs had only
moments before disappeared into the trees.

Once safely out of the open, he slowed down and followed chicken
feathers gently arranging themselves like occasional breadcrumbs along a
slender deer trail carpeted with a leafy ground cover. The feathered trail
took him through thickets of snowbrush and salmon berry and into an
increasingly dense forested area. When he finally caught up with the other
dogs, they were spread out in the cathedral-like understory beneath a
cluster of tall cedars, each of them working on a bloody piece of recently
dismembered chicken, seemingly oblivious to his presence. The largest dog
was still in possession of the majority of the chicken's remains, and when
he glanced up and saw Old Dog, he simply stepped farther off to the side,
farther away from Old Dog and the others.

Old Dog couldn't quite read the situation. They had all seen him. But
there were no signs of aggression directed his way—actually, no signals
at all. Then one of them, clearly the youngest dog of the group, the lack
of age still very much in evidence in gangly legs and over-sized paws,

lumbered Old Dog's direction, and crouched into a forward play position with chicken parts dangling from a blood-covered mouth, as if to offer up a game of tug-of-war. Old Dog had very little experience with other dogs since his own puppy days, and this threw him for a bit of a loop. But his instinctual sense was that he was in no danger, and that the pup actually wanted to play. He obliged the younger dog with a halfhearted attempt and intentionally failed, leaving the pup to prance a victory dance and shake the chicken piece violently side to side while the other three dogs continued to enjoy their recent live-kill trophies.

Old Dog wasn't hungry. But he was still a bit shaken from being shot at and winded from his recent sprint, and his old leg injury was starting to make itself known. So, he flopped down on the thick peaty mat of fragrant decaying cedar piled along the periphery, and rested. In time, each of the other dogs came over and introduced themselves through long sniff exchanges. Each of them, with the exception of the pup, wore a collar, evidence that they all had human caretakers at one point. He imagined that each of them probably had a rich and interesting story behind how they came to be where they are now, much like the people living under the railroad overpass each had their unique tale to tell, much like he himself did.

He was glad for the companionship. He stayed with them and enthusiastically joined in as they went about their foraging rounds. The larger dog was clearly the leader, but it was a loose and only rarely expressed leadership. One of the other dogs, just a bit smaller than Old Dog, seemed to be the one in charge of things most of the time, rousting the others for travel in the morning, and circling back to keep any distracted stragglers moving along as they went from place to place. The live chicken turned out to be a one-off thing. Most of their food came from garbage cans and occasional roadkill.

It didn't take very much time before Old Dog's prior scavenging experience earned him the respect of the others. Not respect, exactly. That's a human term, a term originating in civilized power differentials, especially those that have to do with military authority. Respect within a military power structure is just another word for explicit obedience. Respect outside of a military context usually refers to an internalized state of acquiescence. It wasn't respect in this case, because there was no established dominance structure, and thus no need for either obedience or acquiescence. It was perhaps something closer to admiration, the kind of admiration given to an accomplished artist. Or perhaps a tribal elder. It was respect in the sense of an open recognition of Old Dog's superior experience and knowledge.

Even though each of them moved independently, acting in accordance with his—or her, the pup was female—own individual appraisal of the circumstances at hand, they were a pack, and approached evolving situations as a loosely coordinated unit, each anticipating what the others were likely to do, and then altering their own actions so as to make everyone more successful than they would have been if each had acted alone. Old Dog was not a young dog—he was almost twice as old the next oldest of the group. He was not as strong or as fast as the others either. But because he was so good at reading and responding to the nuances of the human world, he nonetheless became the default leader of the pack, the leader by sheer consensus, with even the larger dog yielding to his judgment.

Their social arrangement was one of mutual cooperation, with each dog offering what they could, to the benefit of both themselves and the group. In the civilized human world, the world in which social arrangements are almost always yoked to a hierarchical flow of power, cooperation, *real* cooperation, is far more difficult to achieve. In most social situations involving mutual action in the civilized world, cooperation is a misnomer, and what is actually occurring—when it's not simple compliance or outright obedience—is something closer to compromise. When two people cooperate, they are each acting toward a mutual goal, and their actions serve the interests of both parties; acting together, they can do more than either of them could do if they were acting separately. With compromise, however, one or both of the parties has had to alter their own goals in some way. Compromise is a way of changing the actual goal in order to accommodate the need for mutual action, whereas cooperation is in some sense the opposite of that: changing your actions in order to more easily achieve a mutually desired goal. This is not a subtle difference, and yet people at the middle and upper levels of institutional authority frequently attempt to conflate the two terms. They implore those in subservient positions to be open to compromise. When a subordinate refuses to compromise, however, they are labeled *uncooperative*, even though it is clear to all parties involved that what they really mean by uncooperative is *noncompliant*. Modern bureaucratically-organized authority structures are social technologies designed to coordinate and direct the activity of individual people toward institutional goals—never mind that the idea that institutions can have goals is literal nonsense. But even worse is the insidious way that, using forced compromise coupled with the normalizing of bureaucratically organized power relations, the "goals" of the institution are made to supersede and ultimately replace the goals of any of the actual flesh-and-blood people involved.

Leadership and power in the feral pack was a fluid and transient thing. Actually, the idea of power doesn't really apply in this context. It was not entirely an egalitarian affair—there was always someone who had the principal influence over what was going on at the time. But it wasn't power that was operating. It was something closer to leadership in its most basic sense, in its follow-the-leader sense: the one who was in the front of the line at the time, or the one who was serving as the most salient model for the others to use as cues for their own behavior. And who was in the front of the pack changed with the changing circumstances. Old Dog ended up in that position more frequently than any of the others, but the pack had nothing in the way of a central controlling authority. There was nothing keeping any of the other dogs around other than their spontaneous desire to participate in what was going on at the time. They were all master scavengers in their own right, and although they were still learning from each other, any of them, with the possible exception of the pup, could go off on their own and expect to be successful enough to satisfy all of their physical needs.

But dogs, like humans, have more than just physical needs. As social animals, affiliation and interaction with others of their kind is a need that is nearly as powerful and compelling as the need to eat. And there are more subtle needs as well, even for dogs. And especially for dogs. In the civilized human world, these are sometimes called *spiritual needs*. Dogs have these sorts of needs as well, but a dog's spiritual needs are not expressed and satisfied in ways that any human would be able to recognize. And, besides, civilized ideas of what constitutes spirituality tend to miss the point entirely.

43

T HE writer leaned back in his chair and swiveled in the direction of
the rain-spattered window beside him, watching as one drop collected
another and then another—an entire ocean finding distant parts of itself
in staccato liquid pulses. Reunited friends from childhood, red-faced
and laughing between the syllables, excited to discover that nothing has
changed. The rekindled passion of old lovers meeting again after fifty years.

He turned back to the computer and began reading aloud from the
screen:

"The present moment becomes past as soon as I step into it. The best
I can do is breathe my way through it, experience it as it occurs in fleeting
points of lucidity that fragment and dissipate almost instantly, blown aside
by loud, vaporous exhalations of the restless rutting beasts that inhabit my
mental menagerie: associative half-recollections and tacit anticipation,
fairytales of the past and mythical prophecies of the future.

"Each instant is a non sequitur, an entirely novel emergence, and yet
each is irredeemably saturated with the past. Heraclitus tells me I cannot
step into the same river twice; the water of my first step has long since
flowed downstream by the time I take a second. And, by extension, the
me that steps into the water is not the same *me* that stepped before, only a
moment ago. The river at my feet carries with it its entire prior course, sediment and debris from upstream, water that has passed all points along its
path. In this way too, when I step into the present moment, I carry with me
not just the residue of my entire life's worth of experiences up to that point,
but the entire history of the universe as well.

"And there is something else. Something impossible. This moment right now, as it opens itself up to me, here, as my fingers work against the keyboard in front of me, is not the same moment that is opening itself to the dog curled up on the floor beside me, or the tree outside my window. These are not just different observational perspectives, different facets of the same temporal movement, different features of the same perpetual incipience; they are autonomous and independent, each belonging to entirely unique experiential epochs.

"And yet they coexist, cohabitate—miraculously interdigitate."

Old Dog always enjoyed listening to the writer test his thoughts out loud. He was a smart man, broadly educated, and his prose had a lyrical quality to it, tending toward the poetic. But *interdigitate*, Old Dog thought, might not be the right word. It was a wonderful word in and of itself, almost visual, evoking the interleaving of the fingers of human hands—digit-lined hands that partition the world in terms of ranges of grasp-ability and manipulation. But the image was too coarse, too bulky. A description of the mutually shared living moment among dog and tree and human requires a term suggesting a far finer level of granularity. *Interpenetrate* might be better, Old Dog thought, but even that word seems to leave off something essential. Or perhaps it adds something that doesn't belong.

The real problem, Old Dog realized, is not with the choice of word. It is with the perspective itself, the human perspective that starts with things first, and then, almost as an afterthought, looks at relationships and interactions among those things. Yet another side effect of a mind that emerged from grasping hands, a mind that turns a world of relationships, a world that emerges and is sustained moment by moment by dynamic interaction, into a world of isolated objects, a world of things.

44

DOGS don't have religion. They don't need it. Neither are they spiritual—at least in the sense that civilized humans use that term. In truth, spirituality is itself largely a civilized creation. Spirituality emerges in the human world only when humans are forced to live in ways that diverge from those prescribed by their evolved human nature. The life of a traditional hunter-gatherer is intimately embedded with the lives of everything else, and from the outside this might appear to be a kind of deep and penetrating spiritual connection. But this is an illusion caused by looking through civilized eyes. Imagine a piece of fruit, say, an orange, that has an arbitrary wedge-shaped section cut out of it. Now imagine another orange that has not been cut. If asked how the two oranges are different, it wouldn't make sense to say the difference is that something has been *added* to the uncut orange. But this is how the civilized see spiritualty, as a separate thing to be added to replace something that is missing. This perspective emerges from living a life in which the whole has been violently torn into pieces, a life that was never meant to be separated into parts. From the inside of an authentic human life, spirituality is simply participation in the ongoing cosmic unfolding of the present moment. Which means that everything is spiritual to the same degree. Which makes the entire idea of spirituality empty. From the point of view of an authentic human life—or the life of any dog—the idea of spirituality is meaningless because there is no way to separate the spiritual from the nonspiritual. Spirituality is inseparably infused throughout.

In addition, the idea that there is a transcendent being or power or principle behind or within or (choose your preposition) experienced reality would find no traction in a dog's mind. The idea of such a thing is not just unnecessary. It is incoherent. If there is such a thing, a universal being or power or principle—and if it is truly universal—then how could it be extracted from everything else in a way that would qualify it as a separate entity? As with spirituality more generally, as soon as you distinguish this being or principle or power from everything else, you have separated it from itself and you are left with nothing at all. You would have better luck separating wetness from water.

In order to see a spiritual realm or a transcendent realm or a godhead lurking within nature, you first have to make the irrational leap to a perspective that somehow lies outside of nature. Religion and spirituality require first that you occupy a mental space that is abstracted from the actual universe itself. This is exactly the kind of mental space that emerges from the viral delusion of human exceptionality, the demonstrably false belief that humans are unique and somehow separate from the rest of the natural world, the delusion that serves as the cornerstone of the civilized worldview.

That's not to say that certain events, or a confluence of unlikely events, can't be appreciated as something unique and intensely meaningful, or even mysterious. Maddy and the writer, complete strangers who never met each other, nonetheless had a nodal connection with each other through Old Dog. No mystery there; just happenstance. And that he should happen to end up with these specific people when he did—that he should end up with them at all—is profoundly meaningful. But it is only a mystery if you take an abstract and disconnected civilized view of the universe. Looked at in terms of counterfactual probabilities (the very idea of probability is based on counterfactual thinking), the odds are staggeringly impossible that a dog as abnormal as Old Dog would find himself in the company of a woman like Maddy, a woman whose own abnormality allowed her to recognize Old Dog for what he was. And, then add to that the impossible odds of Old Dog dodging death to find his way into the presence of the writer, a man who just happened to be exploring many of the same topics and issues that Old Dog, through the meticulous instruction he received from Maddy, had acquired considerable expertise with, and the mind reels. But it reels only if you accept the premise that these events were somehow more unusual than any other event—a premise that is not tenable in a universe composed entirely and continuously of impossibly unlikely events.

There is a writer and philosopher who grew up in Lebanon, the same region of the world that, nine thousand years ago, served as an incubating center of early agriculture. His name is Nassim Nicholas Taleb, and he wrote a book titled *The Black Swan*. Maddy had been reading that very book just days before Old Dog limped into her life. It was also among the first books that she read aloud to Old Dog, specifically because it addressed the very unlikely and unusual nature of Old Dog in the first place. The book's title comes from a classic philosophical riddle about a limitation in observational knowledge of the world. The riddle goes something like this: How many white swans do you have to see before you can say that all swans are white? Just because no one has ever seen a black swan doesn't mean that black swans don't exist. So, even if you have seen millions of white swans and never a black one, you are not justified in claiming with certainty that all swans are indeed white. Since all empirical knowledge of the world is like this to some extent, how is it possible to know anything at all with any real certainty? Whatever you know to be true today could turn out otherwise tomorrow. There could always be a yet-to-be-seen black swan lurking in the bush somewhere.

Interestingly, it turns out that there really are black swans. They live in Australia and were unknown to the European philosophers discussing the "all swans are white" limitation to empirical knowledge. Taleb uses the term *Black Swan* in his book to refer to a certain category of unknowable events. Specifically, Black Swan events are events that are so unlikely and so unexpected that no one would ever predict them beforehand, but after they occur, they are readily understandable, and their occurrence is readily explainable. He then goes on to demonstrate that almost every important event, almost every event in history worthy of being included as historical, and almost every personally relevant event in an individual's life, are Black Swans. Almost every single one. But when life is considered in hindsight, from a mind perpetually trapped inside counterfactual symbolic worlds, the prior unlikelihood of these events—and the fact that they could not have been predicted before hand—slips by unnoticed.

And it is this relationship between hindsight and Black Swan events that leads civilized humans to be tragically overconfident in their ability to predict the future, and to know anything at all about the world. Kierkegaard's famous quip "life can only be understood backwards; but it must be lived forwards" highlights this nicely: events can only ever be understood in hindsight. That, in and of itself, is not a problem. What makes it problematic is that people grant unwarranted value to their ability to make sense of things after the fact. The ability to build a reverse-engineered causal chain, to construct a coherent narrative in the past tense, to cast a tightly woven retrospective net across experience, engenders a false sense of confidence in the ability to apprehend the world as it truly exists.

If Taleb's Black Swans are added to this mix, a person's confidence in their knowledge about the world should fall to the zero point. The most potent events are those which are entirely unpredictable ahead of time. These are events that have an extremely low probability but an extremely high impact, events that are impossible to anticipate or prepare for ahead of time but entirely explainable—understandable—after the fact. People can know nothing at all with certainty, and are unable to predict what important events will happen tomorrow with any accuracy at all, yet even the most unprecedented events seem somehow mundane in retrospect.

This should terrify people. But it doesn't. False confidence gleaned through the lucidity of hindsight prevents them from perceiving the precariousness of the actual situation. Everyone is walking backwards toward the edge of a cliff, toward a canyon carved out of otherwise flat terrain. They see the path that they have traveled receding into the past, with all of its previously unforeseen obstacles clearly visible, all once-hidden dangers obvious and discernable, all unexpected twists and turns clearly marked. And when they step off the edge and crash down to the canyon floor, hindsight will be their guide.

Old Dog woke from his nap, and the world, as usual, appeared before him fully formed down to the smallest detail. While he had slept, the writer had stepped out to run an errand, and now he was awake and alone in a room in a modest house in the suburbs of an even more modest city in a universe that existed in its present form precisely because it was impossible.

45

Months passed, and the pack, which had grown to seven, had become a family. They were living a way of life that was very close to the evolutionary default lurking just behind their artificially rearranged genes. And the fact that they so quickly reverted to the default is evidence of how thin and fragile the patina of domestication actually is, which bodes well for the future of humans, for the chances of successful human rewilding after the gears of the global machine finally grind themselves to dust.

They were feral, which means they were no longer living a domesticated lifestyle, but at the same time—because of their artificially rearranged genes—they were not exactly wild, either. They were not like their wolf and coyote cousins who are able to live entirely off of the fruits of nature. They were still packing the vestiges of domestication, and relied on the fruits of the human world. The pack rarely killed other animals, with the exception of field mice and the occasional slow rabbit or nonattentive bird or ground squirrel. Instead, they feasted on the edible overflow of the food-saturated civilized world. They were living in a shadowy in between place that turned out to provide a rich and abundant niche of its own.

The real difference between wild and feral is not so much in terms of lifestyle or diet or any other concrete feature of circumstance or context. The difference is that *feral* is a product of domestication. You can't be feral unless you were first domesticated. And an animal can never fully shake their domestication. It is still there, always with them, encoded in their physical form and behavioral tendencies. And it will be this way for future humans as well, perhaps. As the gears of the global machine start to disintegrate, civilized humans will be left with no choice but to reinhabit the lifestyles of their ancient ancestors. They will be left with no choice but to rewild. But rewilding, the return to human wildness, will not happen within a single generation. Even if civilization ended tomorrow, no civilized person alive today would ever become a wild human. The best they could hope for is to become feral. The best they could hope for is to be drawn back into the natural world and start to relearn what it means to be part of the living planet. Maybe the very young would have a chance to touch true wildness. But, otherwise, rewilding will likely have to wait for those generations who have the opportunity to grow up completely outside of civilization's psychological blast zone.

Old Dog enjoyed his return to a feral scavenging lifestyle. This time he understood what was happening to him as he fell back upon his latent ancestral instincts. But he still occasionally missed human companionship. He still missed the emotional and physical comforts of living with people. He missed living in the house with the family. He liked people and, despite the intensity and excitement and daily sense of comradery and adventure that his life with the pack offered, he would have preferred the life of a plain old domestic dog—this preference no doubt the sediment of millennia of artificial selection for a life of bondage to humans. He missed Maddy's voice intensely. He missed her touch and her smell. And he still had a lot of unanswered questions about the human world. For every question Maddy's readings had answered, a dozen others appeared hydra-like in its place.

He had grown comfortable in his quasi-leadership position, and had led the pack back to the city, where they were careful to stay on the outskirts, making forays into the city early in the morning to feast and then back out to the forested periphery to lay low and rest until the next early morning campaign. They used the riverbank as their path in and out. It offered protection and easy escape routes and plenty of hiding places. He chose their daily targets carefully, and never took them into the same area of the city twice in a row. One morning they would hit the dumpsters behind a cluster of restaurants. The next they would rummage through the spillage around the back of a grocery store or bakery or butcher shop. Then they would spend a few days scouring the alleys of residential areas, a different part of town each day.

And it was in one of these residential areas that his feral days came to an abrupt and violent end. It was a simple matter of turning left when his instincts told him to turn right. One of the other dogs had already wandered in a direction that for some reason made Old Dog uneasy. He tried to warn him that something wasn't right, but it was too late. Animal control had the area staked out, anticipating the dogs' return after an extremely success-ful—and destructive—run in a neighboring area a couple days earlier.

Two of the dogs were looped, their necks roped at the end of a metal pole before any of the others had a chance to respond. Another was chased and quickly cornered. Old Dog watched in slow-motion horror as the pup, now the largest dog in the pack, was pinned to the ground by her throat, helpless and terrified. Before he could settle on a direction to run, his own head was suddenly pressed sideways against the curb, and he could feel the rope bite into his neck. He didn't struggle. He understood exactly what was happening and knew there was absolutely nothing to be done about it. Resistance would only lead to more pain. It was game over. Everything was over. The city pound was already at capacity, so Old Dog and the four others who were captured were taken to a place north of town, the very last stop for most of the dogs that ended up there, a place with the innocuous name "Valley Animal Shelter."

46

T HE rain slowed, falling lightly against the window in pulses like watery seeds being scattered earthward in arcing waves, liquid kernels pulled from a sack tied to a giant's waist, and tossed to the ground with exaggerated sweeping gestures in order to reach into the corners. And then the rain stopped entirely, almost instantly exchanged for sunshine, muted pink and blue around the edges. The writer continued:

"Metaphors and platitudes equally fail. Time is not a river. It is neither linear nor cyclical. And if it is merely an illusion, it is an illusion conjured by the hands of a tireless master magician. Although we *spend* time, *save* time, *gain* and *lose* time, these expressions are absurd on the very surface. Whether spent, saved, gained, or lost, time itself remains unaffected. Time is relative, we are told, time is different for someone in motion than it is for someone standing still. But it is impossible to both leave and stay, so from a subjective perspective there is no relativity—and let's be clear about this, the subjective perspective is all there has ever been, all there can ever be: despite our expansive conceptual imagination, experience can only occur in the first-person.

"And from within this first-person experience there is an alchemical blending of past and present, an impossible convergence, an even more impossible emotional resonance for something as banal as the dog lying on her side on the carpet in the sun. Uncountable dogs from the past and even harder to count patches of sun-radiated carpet, glanced at and registered, perhaps only briefly, perhaps only unconsciously, all pulled together into the still-life sketch on the floor next to me now—woven together across time, bound by threads that I cannot fathom, and stitched tightly into the penumbra of a passing awareness that I mistakenly take for the present.

"Perhaps not threads. But filaments, densely woven networks of fibers stretching deep beneath the conscious surface. Mental mycelium. I read once where a single mushroom colony can cover several square miles. Time may be like that, and the dog, now, on the floor in the sunlight next to me, is a single eruption, a single fruiting body bursting upon the surface, dusting my mind with its spores."

47

L IFE is not a series of days any more than a river is a collection of
raindrops.

His days with the writer were peaceful, and cast a sharp contrast to
the frenetic commotion and constant excitement of his wilder days with the
feral pack. Not much happened, and what did happen followed a predictable routine: an early morning walk around a quiet neighborhood; tranquil
mid-morning hours on the floor in the writer's study while he worked and
occasionally read aloud from one of his latest projects; if the sun was out,
the writer would have lunch on the back deck and then spend the afternoon
doing yardwork; an early evening dinner followed by a couple hours on
the couch while the writer caught up on some reading; and then an early
bedtime. On weekends there were long conversations across the fence with
the neighbors. And three or four nights a month the writer would have
guests for dinner: his sister and her husband, a former student from when
he taught evening classes at the local junior college, occasionally his daughter and granddaughter when they were in town.

Old Dog would have to go all the way back to the years he spent tied
to the side of the porch to find a time in his life that was as predictable
and relatively uneventful. The predictability and relative uneventfulness of
his present situation was much different of course—the predictability of
confinement has a distinctively acrid flavor to it. As anyone who has worked
a mindless hourly job can attest, even the smallest restriction of freedom
can quickly transform predictable repetition into torturous drudgery. Old
Dog sometimes missed the excitement of his more active days, but only
in spirit. The accumulative wear and tear of age was starting to painfully

express itself, and it was an open question as to whether he would be willing to exchange a lazy morning curled up in a warm patch of sunlight on the floor for a lung-searing game of chase in the yard or a high-energy rabbit pursuit through the forest underbrush. He was content with the way things were now. The writer was a good and worthy caretaker—and he did, after all, save Old Dog's life.

Or what remained of his life. Old Dog was truly old, and approaching the inevitable end of things.

Noncivilized people are acutely aware of the transient nature of life, of the fact that everything changes, grows old, decays, and dies, and nothing lasts forever except the mountains. Even the sun and the moon and the stars go through life and death cycles of movement and change, birth, death, and rebirth. The civilized will tell you that the mountains are also temporary. The civilized view of change and transformation is bent and distorted by the warped lenses that civilization uses to view the natural world, lenses ground to reflect back upon civilization itself rather than provide any kind of clear window on what lies on the other side. And the story the civilized tell about the temporariness of life is one that has been meticulously censored and strategically edited with denial.

Despite the fact that civilization itself is predicated on change, despite the fact that civilization encourages and rewards change, despite the fact that civilization runs on the perpetual physical alteration of the natural world, on the leveraging of nature, on the converting of raw nature to energy and refined materials, despite the fact that civilization functions only by displacing natural spaces and eradicating whole species of potential being, modern civilization nonetheless instills—intentionally instills—fear and hatred for certain kinds of change, specifically the natural changes associated with the progression of human life through time. The changes associated with the natural aging process are made into an evil, an enemy with which to do battle—a battle armed with weapons in the form of medical interventions and pharmaceuticals and a cornucopia of consumer products and disingenuous promises fashioned from corporate marketing boardrooms.

Antagonism toward aging might be just psychological residue from living a civilized life, and reflect the latent, unconscious, gnawing awareness that life in a civilized context lacks the authentic meaning and purpose that would render its temporary nature acceptable. It seems that the civilized, in the Western world in particular, are perpetually waiting for something else, for something better, for the chance to finally *live*. But each life transition leaves them in the same hollow state they were in before—only that much closer to the end.

With each sunrise, Old Dog, like all other living things, was one sunrise closer to death. He was still generally healthy, and could expect a couple more good years. But the end was no longer on the other side of the horizon. It was no longer something that he could think of as hovering in some timeless distant future, and the void frequently lingered just below the surface of his thoughts. As a dog, he was not afraid to die, but he occasionally wondered how many more sunrises he had left.

The lifespan of a typical dog is considerably shorter than the lifespan of a typical human, and common belief has long held that dog years were merely a compressed version of human years. Folk mythology, based on back-of-the-napkin math, has a single human year as the rough equivalent of seven years for a dog. But the math doesn't work out so neatly once you take away the napkin. The difference between a human year and a dog year is not an additive difference. Nor can it easily be captured logarithmically. Time does not run any faster for a dog, but time does have a different quality to it from a dog's point of view as compared to the human experience of time—and the difference is truly *qualitative,* a difference in terms of perspective, awareness, and active engagement in time's passing; it is not a simple matter of a seven-fold compression in quantity. And in terms of biology as well, in terms of maturational processes, in terms of growth stages and the physical aging of the body, it is not possible to provide anything close to a one-to-seven mapping.

Recently, scientists have worked out a somewhat more sophisticated algorithm for calculating a dog's age into its human equivalent, one that takes into consideration the rapid physical development that happens with dogs early on—physically, dogs are teenagers by eight months and middle-aged by the time they are two human years old. But even this algorithm misses the qualitative point, the point that time is a feature of experience, and the experience of time is relative to experience itself—to the *kind* of experience, not to some raw countable quantity. And besides, time is really the wrong word to use here. Time is not a real thing. Time is a human creation, a mythical abstraction, not a feature of the universe itself. What we're really talking about in this case is not time, but *duration.*

Under Maddy's tutelage, Old Dog learned how Western philosophers have wrestled with the idea of time since the beginnings of Western philosophy. Aristotle considered time to be a characteristic of movement. Augustine pointed out that there are two distinct facets to time, a cosmological facet and a psychological, or phenomenological facet. Aristotle's time was cosmological. Cosmological time is reflected in the passing of the seasons, the phases of the moon, and the sun's daily return. There is movement in nature; things change; monuments crumble; people age and die. But time also carries an experienced temporality, a "before and after," a psychological cleavage into past, present, and future. And of these three temporal regions, the present is the most difficult to cope with: an enigmatic combination of absolute stillness and continual flow. Momentary happenings fade immediately into the past even as they occur, yet the present moment remains resolute and unmoved, an unyielding boulder standing in the center of a mountain stream. And somehow all of this leaves an irresistible impression of duration.

There is a difference between time, as it is measured by a clock or a calendar, and duration. Time is a technological artifact. Time came into existence with the invention of history, with the unbending of an ever-repeating cycle of emergence and return, with the idea that seasons and days stack upon each other as collections of footfalls on an arrow-straight path from an unrepeatable past toward a unique future. With the invention of the mechanical clock, time became granular and minutely quantified, and, shortly thereafter, monetized, something to be "saved" or "spent" or "squandered." Or "served."

Duration, however, is a feature of direct experience, a quality of movement and transition and transformation—a quality of emergence and passing that is an inseparable characteristic of first-person experience, something on the same plane as emotion, perhaps: the ongoing passing emergence can be *felt*. Both the distance of a journey and the anticipation of a loved-one's return are gauged by the variable and irrepressible impression of duration; *variable* in that entire days can pass by quickly while a single moment can seem to linger indefinitely—duration contains a psychologically adjustable elasticity; *irrepressible* in that it is impossible to step outside of this sense of passing emergence. In addition, the sense of the *passing* of this passing emergence, the speed at which it appears to pass, is relative to how much has already passed. For an infant, a single day has the proportional significance of several decades for an elderly adult. The days spin faster and faster with each passing year because each new day is a smaller proportion of the experienced whole than was the day before.

The clock-time of civilization and the duration felt through direct experience are incommensurate. One is illusory and mechanical. The other is tangible and organic. One is abstract. The other is grounded in the concrete. Yet, civilized humans are made to treat them as if they were composed of the same essential substance, and to consider clock-time as primary, as representing a more fundamental reality, and to ignore or dismiss the relevance of personally experienced duration. They are expected to sift experienced duration into premeasured standardized slices, stretching the boredom inherent in a repetitive and meaningless wage-slave job thinly across empty hours, for example, while squeezing immensely thick and richly textured moments of significance into circumscribed "events" and "special occasions," tiny nostalgic compartments gouged into the surface of an ongoing conveyor belt of otherwise neutral happenings, colorful graffiti quickly scrawled on the drably painted cars of a passing train.

The Western concept of time began with the invention of history as the linear passing of isolated and nonrecurring events. History is a potent binding agent in the civilized mind. It brings an accumulative element to the natural rhythmicity of the seasons, and forms the underlying substrate of modernity's notions of progress. Some Western historians have speculated that linear time began with the Hebrew tribes and their stories of exodus from Egypt, stories that emphasized sharp distinctions among the ancestral past, the narrative present, and a divinely-covenanted future. Judeo-Christian religious tradition is built upon a world that is unidirectional and finite, a world that began with the intentional act of a manipulative deity and will end in the same way, with impossible-to-conceptualize infinities stretching out both before and afterward.

Infinity can be a problem for finite beings with lives of finite duration. Infinity cannot be neatly fitted into history, into a linear narrative of events with beginnings and endings. This difficulty is only exacerbated by mechanical time's analytic division and segmentation. Seconds, minutes, hours, days, weeks, months, years, centuries, millennia, geologic eras, are all equally and impossibly brief when gauged against the foreverness of forever. Infinity is not so much of an issue, either logically or conceptually, when change is grounded in eternal cyclical recurrence, however. It is hard to imagine something different that existed forever before, and will exist again forever after, everything else. The very notion of a possible "when" dissolves into the all-embracing background of an infinite eternity. But it is easy to think that sunrise and the repetitive deformations of the moon and the yearly return of spring have always been and will always be, existing in a perpetual and tireless repetitive dance of succession and return.

Old Dog slowly disengaged from thoughts of his inevitable passing, and drifted back into the immediate experienced moment and to his sunny spot on the carpet, which, in the interim, had moved off to the right so that over half of his body was now draped in a longitudinal shadow. He stood up, stretched, moved to the side in an awkward crab-like sidle, gave his body a good quick shake—the tags on his collar producing their distinctive rattle—and returned his body once again to the floor, and, for a time, back into the center of the perpetually drifting patch of sunlight.

48

"THERE are myths of Western culture, and they are something more than mere myth, so primal and deeply entrenched that their formative principle operates at the perceptual level, the molecular level of thought, too immediate and transient for the slow, slippery grip of consciousness, grasped only obliquely, only through metaphor.

"At face value, these myth-reflecting metaphors are incommensurable. Consider the most pervasive of these, perhaps: 'life is a journey,' life is a road to be navigated through rites of passage, in route to some hazy final destination—in our mechanical modern world, a path to be plotted and mapped and strategized, with lines of travel and turning points, with benchmarks and interim targets and waystations. Yet, at the same time we are also told that happiness is a kind of quarry, illusive prey to be flushed out and chased, to be followed wherever it leads. Surely, such extemporaneous deviation in the pursuit of happiness would take us irretrievably off course.

"But then there are those who would argue that the two are not mutually exclusive after all, that, as long as we stay on the right path, pain and struggle and persistence will eventually lead us to happiness' hidden lair. Platitudes abound. 'No pain, no gain.' 'Anything worthwhile takes time.' 'Slow and steady wins the race.'

"To abandon myth and metaphor, to see myself in the moment, taking only what holds me within the moment itself as primary, ignoring the story I tell myself about where I'm going, about how I got here, the traveler's tale of missteps and wrong turns, obstacles and barriers, stormy seas and uncharted waters, to take myself for what I am now, as I am now, leaves me disoriented and confused and yet somehow wholly free and unburdened, no longer tethered to illusion.

"The real tragedy of modern life is that it is measured from the top-down and lived from the bottom-up. This is civilization's doing, the hierarchical flow of force from greater to smaller, from central to peripheral, through ever-branching, ever-narrowing conduits of control and specialization.

"Priorities in the civilized world are scaled from an inverted, upside-down perspective. What is considered to be the most important is at the top, and what is dismissed as trivial, the least important, at the bottom. It's a matter of simple proportion—a natural and unavoidable side effect of the pyramidal structuring of civilized systems of power and control. Because power radiates from the top down, those at the very bottom, those at the business end of power, those at the terminus of the flow, those people forming the base stones of the pyramid, those many folks laboring at the point where power empties itself against the physical world, are of less importance as individuals simply because they are so many, simply because their individual ration of power is so small in comparison to the massive portions held by those rarified few at the top. But once you step outside of the civilized frame, this topsy-turvy, inside-out, backwards perspective quickly folds in on itself and collapses against a larger, more pervasive and irrepressible reality, an unequivocally bottom-up reality.

"Perhaps the real tragedy is the belief that life can be measured at all. What metric would you use for the taste of a slightly overripe blackberry on a hot July afternoon? What measurement scale can capture the way a grandmother's empty porcelain cookie jar smells to a seven-year-old boy? It is these things, the simple, the common, the everyday, the mundane, that are of unmeasurable importance.

"Kafka understood this, but he was only able to express it obliquely through allegory. We are no longer human, those of us who inhabit civilized spaces and breathe the toxic effluence of the machine. We are couriers of power, bureaucratic functionaries, servomechanisms. And it's not simply that our daily activity is steeped in meaninglessness until our flesh is rendered of its animal vitality, but the ultimate futility of it all has penetrated the very bones of our thought, into the marrow. We are hollow vessels, cyphers.

"To wake up as a gigantic insect would be a welcome change.

"Emptiness is necessary, essential. It is not incidental. Our emptiness is not a design flaw. It is in fact the very source of the machine's power. The modern world is built upon nature's abhorrence of vacuums. Deprivation. Need. Want. Desire. Emptiness to be filled. Emptiness that begs for the smallest crumb of meaning. Emptiness that pleads for the faintest illusion of purpose. It is emptiness—our emptiness—that draws civilization along its ever-expanding planet-eating trajectory.

"On some level, we know this. On some level, like Kafka, we too understand. Although we long ago learned to hide this knowledge, conceal it behind each new consumable distraction, confusing the palliative of diversion for actual remedy. On some level we know this, and we long for someone or something to save us. We wait desperately for a Sherpa to guide us back to ourselves.

"But where would such a Sherpa take us? Where would we go? Where is there other than here? There is no sturdy mountain peak in the distance, no beckoning snow-covered summit to serve as a point of reference, no visible target, no map coordinates to establish direction.

"Any route you choose to take through the void will lead you to the same nowhere.

"There is no Sherpa to guide us. But, as it turns out, a Sherpa is not necessary. We already have everything we could ever need right here, right now. It is all here, at the liminal edge of the present moment, lying dormant, waiting for us to come back to ourselves: a wild and fearsome human hidden beneath the superficial clutter and debris of a paltry few thousand years of domestication, an authentic and courageous being that still shows itself to us sometimes, reflected in the eyes of a dog."

And with that, the writer had finished his manuscript. He leaned back in his chair and looked over at Old Dog on the floor in the center of the room, his entire body curled into a small patch of sunlight, and smiled.

Epilog

THE dog lies beside me as I write. There are more comfortable and interesting places for him to be right now, yet he prefers to be here, close to me.

It is easy to anthropomorphize, to see his behavior from a human perspective. It is in fact impossible for me to take a perspective other than a human one. Any ideas I might have about what a dog's experience might be like are built entirely from my own human experiences. Logic dictates that there is some overlap between us, however. Our bodies are molded to a shared terrestrial-vertebrate plan. We share a similarly formed nervous system. The differences between our sensory systems are mostly a matter of degree; I can see more colors, and he has far more expansive acoustic and olfactory receptivity. We are both social mammals. Although he tends much closer to the carnivore end of the spectrum, we are both omnivorous hunter-foragers by design. Nevertheless, despite these regions of overlap, what the experienced world is for a dog might fall entirely outside the scope of human comprehension.

But I suspect it does not. I suspect that humans and dogs, and all creatures with a spine—perhaps all living things—have commonalities of experience that would surprise us. And not just animals. Even the tree outside my window right now breathes, and enjoys a kind of awareness—if we are allowed to broaden the typical meaning of that term. I suspect that the dog's experience of the world is roughly parallel to my own in many ways. The emotion centers of the brain—or what neuroscience has identified as such—are structured the same, with the same parts apparently doing the same or very similar things, and brain scans show similar oxytocin release for the dog being petted and the human doing the petting (although reducing facets of subjective experience to the activity of specific brain areas risks missing the larger point entirely). Dogs likely feel the full range of emotions that humans do. The differences might merely be in the labelling: language gives us a whole palette of ways to reframe our emotional experiences after-the-fact, to supply them with justifications and rationalizations. We make stories out of our emotions, and they become something different in the process. But distill these stories to their primal essence, and you will perhaps find that dogs tell very similar tales.

How much of what the dog experiences would I be able to understand if I could see the world through his eyes? No doubt, there are things that would remain mysterious to me, but if I had one brief moment to see and hear and feel and know what he does—in the ways that he sees and hears and feels and knows—I am sure that I would find that the two of us are not such different creatures after all.

The reason he lies here next to my chair might simply be that it feels good to do so, in exactly the same way that it feels good to me to have him here. We have a mutual desire for nearness. We are, both of us, pack animals after all. Civilized humans have forgotten that basic fact, the fact of their evolutionary design as band-dwelling social primates. We live in cities and "communities" of strangers stretching into the millions, and occupy a planetary human hoard of eight billion. But we are, deep in the ancient ancestral fibers of our being, pack animals meant for a life spent inextricably immersed in small intimate groups—with our sense of self so entwined with others and so completely embedded within the natural world that there is no place for a boundary of separation to be drawn. In the recesses of his species memory, the domesticated dog misses the pack he never had. And the civilized human misses an intimacy with the world that his lifestyle no longer allows.

If he could speak to me, what would he be able to tell me? Or are the things he would want to tell me, the important things and the things that I really need to hear, things that cannot be captured with words? He recognizes his name. But it was not his first name. What does he call himself—or is such a question simply more evidence of silly anthropomorphism? Yes. He knows himself by an unspeakable name, by a thought so primitive and so direct and so inseparable from his immediate ongoing awareness that it would be untranslatable, using one word or a million, in any possible language. And, I suppose, once you peel back the linguistic overlay, deep in my psychological center that is also how I know myself.

If I could write a story about his life experiences, if I tried to present a narrative account of who this dog is from his own perspective, in a way that touches on something authentic, something genuine, how would I go about it? What would I say? Where would I start?

He appeared to be just an ordinary dog . . . .

www.ingramcontent.com/pod-product-compliance
Lightning Source LLC
Chambersburg PA
CBHW072353030726
47505CB00014B/1804